THE
INSTRUMENTS
OF
FAITH

Asura Press books by Paul B. Spence

The Awakening Series
    The Remnant
    The Fallen
    The Madness Engine
    The Sleeping and the Dead
    The Dark Plaza

The Endless Realms
    Project Brimstone
    Riders on the Storm

The Hand of Providence
    I Won't Cry for Yesterday
    The Instruments of Faith

THE INSTRUMENTS OF FAITH

Paul B. Spence

Asura Press

THE INSTRUMENTS OF FAITH

An Asura Press Book

PRINTING HISTORY
Paperback Edition / 2023

ISBN: 978-1-929928-15-6

www.paulbspence.com
author@paulbspence.com

In memory of those we lost.

CHAPTER ONE

Sometimes a poltergeist is a *really* noisy spirit.

The common assumption these days is that poltergeist activity is strongly connected to troubled teens with latent psychism. That's true most of the time, and that kind of poltergeist is easy to help: just get the kid some psychiatric counseling. The other, rarer kind is harder to get rid of.

I heard a telltale knocking in the walls. As I dodged out of the way of a flying chair, I couldn't help but wonder if psychiatric counseling could help *this* ghost. Maybe it had been a troubled teen before it died.

I call it an *it* because poltergeists aren't like other ghosts. They aren't the souls of people stuck between life and death. Poltergeists are more like residuals; they lack an ego. It's usually just an expression of a specific emotion, particularly rage or terror. True poltergeists are *exceptionally* rare. They occur in a place and then fade over time. It takes a triggering event to reactivate them. That event is usually the release of a powerful emotion of a type similar to the poltergeist's motivation.

The energy has to come from somewhere.

At least this one tended to make noise just before it threw something. Quite considerate, actually. I ducked as a chair went sailing past again. The chair crashed into the corner and lay still. A faint smell of sage lingered in the room. Odd. The couple who owned the place hadn't seemed the type. Maybe they were just trying anything they could think of to clear out the spirits or whatever.

Something else nagged at me, something...

My cell phone rang, and the chair rattled across the floor toward me.

I retreated out of the room and answered my phone. "Hello?" I said breathlessly.

"Michelle?" It was Lawrence. "I want to talk to you about that stuff you had me working on. I have something for you."

"That's great, Lawrence." The hall door started slamming shut and opening again, repeatedly. It was quite loud. "Now isn't the best time."

"It sounds as if you've got a lot on your hands right now, but listen, I really need to talk to you about all this. Soon."

"Okay. How about we meet tomorrow? You can come over to my place around lunchtime. We can talk then." I had to shout to be heard.

"Sounds good. I'll meet you at your place at noon."

"'Bye!" As I hung up, I heard the wood in the doorframe crack.

That spirit was really pissed off.

I ducked out of the hall and into the study just as wood splinters went hurtling by. It was getting unhealthy to stay here. I quickly made my way out of the house.

The noises stopped almost immediately.

It was cold outside; the weather had turned nasty over the weekend. Maria was standing in the driveway, talking to the terrified couple who owned the house. I jogged down to join them. My legs still hurt a little from my injuries back in October, but they were improving daily.

Maria is tall, only a few inches shorter than my five-foot-ten. Like me, she works for the Criminological Research Institute in Dayton, Ohio. Unlike me, she's good with people. She handles public relations for the CRI. I've worked with her a few other times; things usually go more smoothly with her helping.

This sort of job isn't my usual gig. I'm a specialist in occult crimes, not psychic phenomena. I had no idea why I was here, much less what I was going to do to help these people. If it were up to me, I'd demolish the place and tell them to move somewhere else.

You may have figured out that I'm not very good at reassuring people.

The man was speaking. "Ms. Delgotti, do you have any idea when we can go back into the house?" He was wringing his hands.

I didn't like the couple, although there was nothing I could specifically point to as a reason. They were both too smooth and polished or something. They reminded me of well-oiled machines, the kind that grind people up in factories and never even slow down. They had dead eyes.

Maria looked a question at me.

I shrugged.

"Mr. Forester," Maria said, "it can take some time to analyze the specific types of phenomena occurring here. Ms. Fredericks is one of our best specialists." She turned to me. "How long will it take to isolate the specifics of what's happening?"

"I've made superficial contact with the entity," I said. That was a bit of an overstatement, but it wouldn't hurt to throw out some vague nonsense, to make them feel better. "I think it's definitely a true poltergeist. This type of thing is difficult to deal with. It will take some time. I'll need to figure out what's causing it."

"How much time?" Mrs. Forester wailed. "I can't keep living out of a motel!"

I tried to reassure her with a smile, but that's like a shark reassuring a herring. It doesn't work for me. Besides, I didn't feel very bad for them. "I should be able to deal with it within a week, two at the most."

"Two weeks!" exclaimed Mr. Forester. "Thanksgiving is just four days away! We have family coming in from out of town. My father is visiting! You must get whatever it is out of there so we can get back to our life! How much do I need to pay? I'll pay it!" He looked desperate, and he kept running his hands through his thin hair. He was faking, but I didn't know why, or what he was lying about.

My dislike for him intensified.

"Mr. Forester, it's not a matter of cost. That thing in there doesn't give a damn about your money. If you bring your family into that house for Thanksgiving, the energy released might be enough to keep it active for years," I said. "You'll need to consider other options."

Some people seem to think all they have to do is wave their checkbook at a problem, and it will disappear. I hate people like that, and when confronted by them, I tend to dig in my heels.

"It has to be out by Thanksgiving," he insisted.

"Look, a true poltergeist gets its energy from strong emotions. This one must have been triggered by you two arguing." Even as I said that, I didn't believe it. I couldn't believe that these two had ever had an emotion strong enough to trigger anything. The house was dead, flat, empty. Nothing was there at all. Not even passion.

I should have figured it out right then.

"We never fight about anything!" Mrs. Forester exclaimed. I wondered if she was trying to call my attention to their fight.

"Ma'am, you know the saying, *if walls could talk?*"

"Michelle," Maria said warningly.

But there was no stopping me; I was on a roll. "To someone like me, the walls *do* talk. I suggest you both seek marriage counseling, because you," I said, pointing at Mrs. Forester, "not wanting to have sex while you're pregnant is not an excuse for you," I continued, pointing at Mr. Forester, "to be sleeping with your secretary. Ring any bells yet?"

"You have no right to be saying such goddamn lies! I've never–"

"Shut up," I said, giving him a quelling look. He snapped his mouth shut and paled. Something wasn't right. He'd said all the right words, but I hadn't felt any anger from him. He wasn't angry. He looked turned on, which made me feel more than a little ill.

Maria quickly took over. "Mr. and Mrs. Forester, I'm sure that whatever your marital problems are, they can be easily solved. We are here to make your house safe to live in. If Ms. Fredericks says your emotional outbursts have triggered the phenomena, then that's the cause. Stay away from the house for the next few days. That should allow it to wind down enough for you to enjoy Thanksgiving."

CHAPTER TWO

I couldn't believe what I was hearing.

I walked away to get control of my feelings. Maria was setting these people up for a nasty fall. I knew the poltergeist wouldn't just wind down. Not any time soon, anyway. I hoped she had the Foresters both sign waivers before they left.

I was looking at the house when Maria walked over to me.

I could hear the Foresters' car pulling away. Mr. Forester had a Jaguar; it fit him. Everything about him was predator-like. About them both, really.

"I'm sorry, Michelle."

"I'm sorry, too," I said. "You had no right to tell them they could go back into their house. That poltergeist will still be going strong in four days. They're going to have some real problems."

"They don't really believe in the poltergeist right now," she said. "After it scares them this Thursday, they'll pay twice as much as they already have. It's just business."

"It may be murder." I held her brown eyes with my blue ones. "That poltergeist is powerful. It's also very unsettled. There are knives in the kitchen, Maria. It could start throwing them as easily as anything else."

She paled and looked toward the house. "Why didn't you say something?" she demanded.

"I did. I said it would be a week or two before it was safe to move back in."

"What are we going to do?"

"We? *We* didn't cause this mess. You did. Figure something out on your own. I'm going home." I started walking toward my Jeep Cherokee.

She grabbed my arm, and I had to keep myself from breaking hers out of reflex. "You can't just walk away from here. Okay, I made a mistake. I'm sorry. We need to do something about this."

"Maria," I said calmly, "remove your hand from my arm before I remove your arm."

She snatched her hand away. She'd heard stories about me, I'm sure.

I stayed facing away from her.

"I'm sorry." She sounded close to tears. "I don't know what else to say. You know I don't know anything about this stuff. I'm just here to keep people happy – you know that."

I wasn't buying it. She was acting.

"They will *not* be safe, and it is *your* fault," I said.

"Isn't there any way to make it safe for them?"

"Sure. Blow up the house. Then they won't be around to get killed when that poltergeist gets *really* motivated." I took my cell phone out of my jacket pocket and dialed the number for CRI.

"What are you doing?"

I ignored her.

My call was answered on the second ring. "Criminological Research Institute. Jamie speaking," said the secretary. "How may I help you?"

"Jamie, this is Michelle Fredericks. Let me talk to Tony."

Maria stood completely still, staring at me.

"I'm sorry, Ms. Fredericks. Mr. Servanti is in a meeting right now. May I take a message?" She had a perky, cheerful voice that grated on my nerves.

"No, you can interrupt his dinner and tell him that I'm holding on the line," I said, irritated. "He'll want to talk to me."

"Yes, ma'am. Hold, please." Pleasant strings music played while I waited. About two minutes later, Tony answered the line. I was pacing by then.

"Michelle? What's going on?" He had a deep, gruff voice. "Is everything okay?"

"Not really, Tony. I'm at the Forester place. Looks like it's going to take a week or two to clean it up."

"So what's the problem? They're paying for the job, not by the hour. Why, did you want Thanksgiving off? I didn't think you were religious."

"Maria told the Foresters they could reenter for Thanksgiving, after I told them and her it would take two weeks."

I had to hold the phone away from my ear for a moment. Tony can be quite loud when he's cursing. Then, "Let me talk to her," he said.

I handed the phone to Maria.

While she was talking to Tony, I walked around the house. I didn't feel like listening to Maria's excuses a second time. She was getting an earful, I was sure. Tony doesn't second-guess his field agents, and no one else is supposed to, either. I'm supposed to have a free hand to do whatever needs to be done.

Just to be clear, I'm a criminal anthropologist, specializing in occult crime. I just happen to have an additional skillset that lets me deal with other… things. The CRI gets many high-paying clients who need the highest level of discretion possible, mostly police departments and the FBI. Sometimes, though, Tony takes on a different kind of client, private individuals with problems that can't be solved conventionally.

The layout of the house bugged me, but I couldn't quite figure out why.

That couple: they just didn't add up. No one keeps that kind of control over their emotions. They didn't even seem to *have* emotions, but then, why did they act as if they did? Were they playing some kind of game?

Maria found me in the side yard and handed me my phone. She looked as if she'd been crying. I couldn't find it in my heart to feel sorry for her.

"Michelle?" It was Tony, still on the line.

"Yeah, I'm here, Tony."

"I'm sorry about that. We need you on this case. I'm waiving the fees, not charging those people. I'm also pulling Maria out. I'll pay you triple your usual consulting fee if you can get something done by Thanksgiving. Just make the house safe for them. My chestnuts are roasting in the fire here."

He was so eloquent.

"I'll see what I can do. No promises." Triple pay would be quite nice; I wouldn't have to take a case for most of the next year. Maybe I could figure something out.

"I understand. Do what you can, and keep me informed." He disconnected.

I put my phone in my pocket, crossed my arms, and waited for Maria to speak.

"I'm sorry, Michelle. Here are the keys to the Foresters' house. Do what you can." Her voice was cold. She acted as if I'd done something wrong, although she was the one at fault. She stomped away toward her car. I didn't say anything to her; I didn't trust my mouth not to say things that might be unforgivable. I might have to work with her again someday.

I walked around the house again and thought about what I could do in four days. It was actually a nice house: very modern in design, an open ranch-style with lots of bay windows and a finished basement. It had maybe an acre of lawn surrounded by a privacy fence. I could hear an occasional clank from inside. I wouldn't mind having a house like this myself someday. Sans poltergeist, of course.

The house was on the north side of Cincinnati, in the Sharonville area, a quiet part of town. Hell, I'd be able to make a respectable down payment just with what Tony was paying me. If I could get rid of the entity within four days, anyway. I wondered how much a house like this went for; I'd check it out on the internet later. I was getting tired of living in my mom's old house in Latonia. That was a really good house, but I wanted to be closer to shopping and a good movie theatre.

As I came back around to the front of the Foresters' house, I thought I saw something near my Jeep, but nothing was there when I got closer. Sometimes my eyes play tricks on me. It was starting to get late in the afternoon, and the wind had picked up. I shivered inside my light jacket. I was going to have to dig my heavier stuff out of the closet or buy a new coat.

I grinned to myself. Any excuse to shop.

I went back into the house to check on my poltergeist. The knocking started in the foyer as soon as I stepped through the front door. It was almost as if the poltergeist sensed me and was trying to get my attention. That was crazy, though. Poltergeists aren't sentient. I stepped back out and locked the door before it could throw anything at me. I don't like being hit unless I have to be. Well, honestly, I don't like being hit at all.

I made sure all the doors were locked, and then I walked back down the drive.

I thought about going home.

I'd worry about the spirit later.

CHAPTER THREE

The wind was picking up again as I got in my Jeep. The weather was cold enough that I'd have to be careful and watch for ice on the expressway. At least in Cincinnati, they know how to deal with ice, so there was plenty of salt on the road.

I love northern winters. I can't help it. I like the snow and the icicles hanging from trees. Cincinnati is right on the edge of the Snow Belt; it turns cold at the end of October and stays that way until late March. This year, we'd gotten snow on Halloween. I loved it, but I'm sure it made all the trick-or-treaters unhappy. I didn't care. There are never many kids out in my neighborhood anyway.

Weeks had gone by since the mess with Julia ended. My broken bones were healed except for a bit of dull aching. I did still have some pain when I bent over, from my cracked ribs. The cold weather wasn't good for that. I hoped I wasn't developing arthritis. That would be just my luck.

My nightmares weren't as bad as they'd been before... Well, before Julia. I still have nightmares about the project sometimes. Just when I began to think I'd remembered everything that happened in my teen years, I'd have another bad dream and wake up to remember a little bit more. I was just trying to put it all behind me and get on with my life.

I needed to decide what I was going to do this Thursday.

My good friends Mark and Jen had invited me over for Thanksgiving dinner. How could I refuse? Why would I *want* to? Jen was sure to cook something amazing.

Michael still called me every few days and let me know how his case was going. This fugitive hunt was much more laid-back than his last one, fortunately. Whomever he was hunting, she wasn't another Julia.

He told me he was playing nice and working with the local field office more. He didn't think he could make it back to Cincinnati for Thanksgiving, but he hoped he'd be able to fly back for Christmas. If everything went well with his fugitive, that is.

I was still confused about how I felt about him. Michael could be so annoying. I was definitely attracted to him. We also had a deep connection that I'd never felt with anyone else. I guess *love* is as good a word as any. I just hated to think I loved him, when it might not work out between us. The local US Marshals' office had forbidden him to see me. Not that he really cared what they thought. I wasn't even sure they could issue those kinds of orders.

I turned south onto the expressway. Traffic was heavy, and I was tense. Luckily, there were no white vans around; I still got a bit twitchy whenever I saw one. It took me forty-five minutes to drive ten miles. I hate traffic. I kept myself as calm as possible with some good music. I know I must look silly, driving down the expressway singing, but I don't care. It's better than losing my temper and shooting people.

You think I'd joking, don't you?

I checked my mail when I got home.

I had more paperwork to fill out. My lawyer sent me a new stack every week, it seemed. He was still working to get a settlement from the trucking company whose truck had run me over.

I didn't blame the truck driver. It wasn't his fault my tire had been shot out, but he *had* been following me too closely. He'd also been going ten miles an hour over the speed limit. That was damning evidence in a civil case. My lawyer expected the company to settle out of court before the end of the month.

Samson greeted me at the door with piteous meows. I had started giving him a treat of wet cat food every few days, and he had rewarded me by begging for it constantly. I'd vowed that anytime he harassed me, I wasn't going to give him any wet food. The first thing I did once in the door was open a new can for him, of course.

I needed to think about my own dinner. I wasn't in the mood for a sandwich, my usual fare. I wanted a pizza but was avoiding it. I'd lost a lot of weight while I was in the hospital, most of it muscle, and I'd eaten a lot to make up for it. I gained the weight back, but not in a form I wanted. I was now on a careful diet, and hating it. I made a salad and then worked out in the spare bedroom I'd recently converted to an exercise room.

I'd added a weighted practice sword to my hard-style tai chi routine. I needed to push myself harder. I was getting stronger every day. I think I was a bit stronger than I had been, but I still had a little extra around the middle. I spent an hour doing martial arts and then an hour on an exercise bike. That was getting to be a real workout. I'd set the resistance higher every time I got on the bike; it was now at the maximum. My heart was hammering when I finished. I stretched and did a little more tai chi to cool down. Then I took a long bath.

I answered my cell phone on the third ring. I'd been dozing in the water.

"Hello," said Michael.

"Hey, you," I replied softly.

"How are you doing?" I could hear him settling back into a bed. He must in his hotel room.

"I'm doing well." I moved a little bit so he could hear the water.

"Is that water? Did you go swimming?"

"Nope." I couldn't resist teasing him a little.

"Hmm." I could hear him swallow. "Bath, then?" His voice cracked a little at the end.

"I like baths better. You don't have to wear a suit."

He was breathing harder. I smiled to myself.

"I might have to quit this job and fly back early."

"That might not be a bad idea. I'm sure I could think of something for you to do."

"You," he said, "are a terrible tease."

"I think I'm a very good tease, thank you."

He laughed. Then the other line beeped. I decided to ignore it.

"Any luck on your case?" I asked. "Is there any chance of you being back sooner?"

The other line beeped again. "Not really. I have a lead, some cable hacker, but it hasn't paid out yet."

"Hmm. You need to get busy and catch your fugitive. I've been on a diet. I need a good meal." He knew I wasn't talking about food.

The damn line beeped again.

"You may as well answer that," he said with a sigh. "I should go anyway."

"You take care of yourself."

"You take care of yourself, too, 'Bye." He hung up.

Damn.

"Who the hell is this?" I asked as I answered the other line.

"Michelle?"

I sighed. "What do you want, Lawrence?"

"I just want to confirm that we're still on for tomorrow," he said. "I know how you forget stuff."

"You're coming over around noon, right? Do I need to come pick you up?" I suddenly remembered that he didn't drive.

"No, I'll take a cab. Just be home."

"I will be."

"Okay, I'll see you then."

CHAPTER FOUR

I turned off my phone and set it on the toilet. I wasn't in the mood for a bath anymore. I drained the water and took a quick shower. Michael and I seemed unable to get any breaks. We could never even talk for long.

I dressed in pajamas and went into the living room to look over my case files. I couldn't get my mind off that damn poltergeist. It just didn't seem right. The Foresters had moved into the house last year after having it specially built. No one had lived there previously – I hadn't remembered that while at the house. So where had the poltergeist come from? It had to be tied to the house somehow, but I couldn't figure it out.

Something wasn't adding up.

I could think of only two options.

The first option was that an entity had been on the property before the house was built. I could go to the library and see if I could find out about any violence at the house's location. Maybe there'd been a house on the land before the Foresters' home was built. Maybe someone had been murdered and buried there at some point.

The second option was less likely, but it still needed to be checked out. Maybe something had happened in the house to create the poltergeist. I wasn't sure what it could be or even how I could find out.

Maybe a troubled teen had visited for a while? Something worse than that? I didn't trust the couple; Mr. Forester definitely seemed the type to pick up a young hitchhiker and rape them.

Would his wife have known?

To be certain, I'd have to go back to the house and check each room for traces. Hopefully, the poltergeist would leave me alone while I was doing that. Maybe I could make a charm against it or something.

That wasn't really my specialty. I might have to call and ask Mark about it. I looked at the clock: after ten PM. It couldn't wait. I'd make it a quick call and hope I didn't wake Jen.

"Hello, Michelle." I hated when he did that; I was sure they didn't have caller ID. He still had a landline, for god's sake.

"Hey, Mark. Sorry to call so late."

"No problem. You know I sit up late every night, and I know you don't call this late unless you need help with something. What's up?"

I explained the case to him. I told him about my suppositions on the origin of the poltergeist. He was particularly interested in the argument I'd picked up on while in the house. He thought the second option was the more likely.

"So you think the entity was inadvertently created by one of the Foresters?"

"I'm not sure," Mark said, "but it sounds more likely to me than a residual from an older house. As far as I know, that can't happen. If it was a residual, it would be at whatever landfill the wreckage from the house ended up in. If they'd burned it, there wouldn't be any residual at all."

"I'll go back tomorrow and check out the house then. Maybe I can find the problem."

"Be careful, Michelle."

"I'm always careful," I said, indignant.

He just snorted.

Yeah, I couldn't even *think* that seriously.

"Mark, I'll be careful. I have the keys to the house, and I'm always armed nowadays."

"Not much good against a poltergeist," he said. "Stay out of the kitchen."

"I'd planned on avoiding it," I replied. "I have no desire to be on the receiving end of thrown knives again."

Yes, I've had knives thrown at me. No, it wasn't by a poltergeist.

Mark chuckled, damn him.

I decided to ask him anyway. "Do you know of any way to make a charm to get a poltergeist to leave you alone?"

"No, I've never even heard of one."

"Damn. Oh, well. I had hoped." I said. "I guess I should let you go."

"Take care."

"You, too. Good night." I clicked off the phone and sat back on the couch.

Lawrence would be over around noon tomorrow. If I went back to the Foresters' house in the morning, I couldn't guarantee I'd be back by then, so I'd go in the afternoon. I could take Lawrence back home while I was at it. I had no need or desire for an extended houseguest again. Not Lawrence, anyway. I'd gotten used to being alone, and I liked my privacy.

I gave up on the poltergeist for the night. There were too many variables. I'd just have to go and look tomorrow.

I scooped up my cat and went to bed.

CHAPTER FIVE

Lawrence was late.

It was a little after one in the afternoon, and Lawrence hadn't showed up yet. He hadn't called, either. I tried to call his cell phone but could only get his voice-mail. I was pacing the house, driving Samson nuts, when Lawrence finally knocked on the door.

He looked a bit disheveled. I could see a cab pulling away from the curb. He carried a soft-sided briefcase clutched in his arms. I invited him in.

"Sorry," he said, stepping into the house. "I had to change cabs a couple of times. I thought I was being followed."

"Do you think that's likely?"

He shrugged.

I didn't see any cars on the street. I shut and locked the door and took a good look at Lawrence. His eyes were red, and he hadn't shaved in a day or two. His hair was a bit lank and sticking up on his head. The total affect was almost frightening. Lawrence is normally so... *clean*. Today, even his clothes looked tired.

"Lawrence," I said, "are you okay?"

"I could use a drink."

"Okay." I led him into the living room. "Coke? Mountain Dew? Or something stronger?"

"Something stronger, if you have it. I'm not picky." He sat on the couch, still clutching his briefcase.

I left him and went into the kitchen. I don't keep any hard liquor around, but I usually have some wine in the fridge. I poured a glass of white wine and took it back to him. He drank a little and made a face, then drank some more. I guess the vintage was not up to his usual standard.

If he says anything to me about it, I thought, *I will slap him.*

He seemed to calm a little. He even placed his briefcase on the table in front of him. I was itching to ask what had him so upset, but I knew that would only delay the explanation. He needed to tell it at his own pace.

"I've decoded a big piece of your file from Julia's notebook computers," he said.

"Okay." I hadn't talked to him since Lucy's funeral. That had been rough. Marge had gotten drunk and accused me of being responsible for Lucy's death. That had been at the reception hall just after the burial. I was glad Lawrence had been there. I'd been at a loss for words. I hadn't killed Lucy, but I was glad she was dead. How do you defend your actions to a grief-stricken lover?

Lawrence had just been glad to know that everything was over. I hadn't given him all the details; it hadn't seemed to be the right place for it. I had a feeling now that my avoidance of the issue had come back and bitten me on the ass.

"Je-*sus*, Michelle, how much of this did you know about and not tell me?" He was upset: his Eastern Kentucky accent was starting to show.

"Since I don't know what's in those files, I can't answer that. I never had a chance to really explain everything to you. You were always busy, or it wasn't the right time. Tell me what you found out. I'll fill in the missing pieces."

"Right. This is some screwed-up shit, Michelle."

I just nodded. If he was talking about the military-funded project I'd been a part of as a teenager, then *screwed-up shit* was quite an understatement. The project had changed us -- those of us who survived, anyway.

He rubbed his face. "I don't know where to begin. I really don't."

"Okay. I'll start, then." I told him what I could remember of the Providence Project. He was surprised to learn Michael had been part of that, too. I told him about everything that had happened with Lucy and Julia. I had to stop a few times; it still hurt to think about some of it. For me, the revelation about Lucy had been the worst. I'd been close to someone that crazy for so long, and I hadn't seen it. That was scary.

Lawrence was quiet until I finished.

"Goddamn, Michelle." He drank the rest of his glass of wine in a rush. "So you think Julia's still alive?"

"I'm not certain. I think so, though." I shrugged.

"And this doesn't bother you?" he asked, staring at me. He had met Julia once, and she'd scared him half to death, because Lawrence wasn't stupid.

"No. Not really. I think that if she survived, she'll leave me alone."

"I guess I really don't have anything new for you, then." He looked vaguely unhappy.

"No big deal. You'll continue to work on the other files?"

"Yeah, I can do that." He still looked like something was bothering him.

"What's up, Lawrence? I know you aren't this worked up over what was in that file. What has you upset?"

"You know that favor you said you would owe me?"

"Yes…" Now I felt suspicious.

"Does that still stand?"

"Of course. I told you I'd owe you one for working on this stuff. Just because I found most of this information someplace else doesn't mean yours is worthless. You may have found some details I didn't get."

"Okay, then. I'd like to call it in." He sounded worried. He *felt* worried.

"What do you need me to do?" I hoped it would be something simple and morally unambiguous, like killing someone.

It turned out to be much worse.

"I need you to act as my girlfriend when I go see my parents for Thanksgiving this year."

"Oh, fuck me!" I stood up.

"Well, if that's what it takes…"

He didn't need to look so disgusted when he said it.

"Damn it, Lawrence, I thought you'd want me to do something professional for you. I can't run off to your parents' place and pretend to be your girlfriend! What the hell is the matter with you? Hell, I'm fifteen years older than you! Why would you even ask?"

"My dad's dying."

What was I supposed to say to that? "How?" It was all I could manage.

"He has cancer, black lung disease. The doctors don't expect him to make it to Christmas. I should have gone back sooner…" He wrung his hands. "You know about my sexual preferences. Most of my family could never accept that. My mother knows. She begged me to come home this holiday, to see Dad. She also asked me to act normal, to let him think he had a normal son, before he–" Lawrence stopped and turned away.

"I don't know what to say. I'm sorry about your dad. Oh, *hell*. I'll do it. I didn't have any real plans for this Thanksgiving anyway," I lied.

He nodded. His eyes were puffy. "Thank you. Last month, I'd been thinking about what I was going to do. I thought about asking Jen or even hiring an actress to play the part. I didn't like either option. Jen couldn't handle my family, and an actress might mess up. When you showed up and asked for my help, I thought it was the answer to my prayers." He smiled.

I reached over and messed up his hair -- not that it took much in his state.

He gave me an indignant look and then laughed.

"Okay, kid, I'll do it," I said. "I have a feeling you're going to owe *me* after this one."

"You haven't called me *kid* since college. Thank you. This means a lot to me."

"I know. Don't worry about it. I'll knock their socks off."

"It might be best if you didn't hit anyone," he said seriously.

"Lawrence, I was kidding!"

"*Michelle*, so was I!" He laughed.

CHAPTER SIX

We talked late into the day, and I still needed to get back out to the Foresters' house. Lawrence said he wanted to go along with me, if that was okay. He'd never seen a poltergeist, and he was curious about it. I explained the situation at the house as I drove. He already knew most of the basics about poltergeists in general; we'd had some odd talks together back in college.

"All the activity has been limited to the bedroom, den, and front areas of the house. I don't know why." I shrugged.

"So nothing happens outside the house?"

"Nope. It usually doesn't start right away, either. It seems like it waits to make sure someone is actually in the house before starting up. It gets aggressive and dangerous really fast." I was thinking about the chairs and kitchen knives.

"I haven't studied this stuff like you and Mark, but that doesn't sound right to me," said Lawrence.

"I talked to Mark last night, and he said the same thing. It's currently defying all the standard models. It acts like both a teenager-type poltergeist and a real haunting, but the house is empty."

"I hate to even think this, but are you sure the house is empty?" He looked grim. "I mean, I've heard of some weird shit, you know?"

"I know, and no, I'm not sure. That's why I'm going back out there today. I need more information. The owners don't know I'll be there today, either. They're staying at a hotel."

Lawrence just nodded and looked out the window.

It would actually make sense if there was a kid in the house somewhere.

It was late in the afternoon when I pulled into the Foresters' driveway. The house was dark. The windows looked like eyes filled with malice, staring at us as we got out of the car. I shivered. I was starting to get a very bad feeling about going into that house again. I'd left my gun at home, but I keep a spare Glock 9mm pistol in the console of my Jeep. I pocketed the gun and locked the doors.

Lawrence raised his eyebrow at the gun but didn't say anything.

I checked the grounds and the front of the house.

While I was doing that, Lawrence walked around the back. I waited with growing tension for him to return. I couldn't identify the problem, but I knew it was related to the house and what I would find there.

Once Lawrence was back, I unlocked the front door. Everything was quiet inside.

I looked a question at Lawrence.

"I'd like to look around a bit while you're doing your thing," he said.

"That's fine. Just wait until after I've gone through each room. I'd like to get the traces as clearly as possible," I said. "And stay out the kitchen."

He nodded and moved behind me.

I walked from room to room and checked every single surface. Something was definitely odd about the house. All the psychic traces were recent, as if the old ones had been scrubbed away. I even checked the furniture. Nothing.

There has to be something, I thought angrily. I remembered the scent of sage. It would explain how the traces had been wiped, but not why.

This was so frustrating.

I walked back to the Foresters' bedroom.

The argument I felt there between the Foresters was... weird. I let it replay again though my mind. It was starting to fade. The only way it could be fading already was if there wasn't a lot of emotion invested in the argument; a real argument like that should have left lingering traces and effects on an area for years.

I was starting to get a *bad* feeling about all this. I had met the Foresters, talked to them. They seemed normal enough. They were a bit "white bread," but there was nothing unusual about that. They certainly hadn't seemed to know anything about psychism. I had a feeling, though, that they knew a lot more than they'd told me.

I called Maria.

"What do you want?" she answered. She sounded drunk.

"Do you know why I was assigned this case?" I asked.

"They asked for you, *personally*. Why?"

"Thanks." I hung up.

Now I really had a *really* bad feeling about this house.

I heard knocking somewhere. A distant crash sounded, and then a yelp that seemed more from surprise than from pain. I ran through the house. Lawrence stood just outside the den. Books were flying through the air. A lamp lay on the floor, broken.

"Are you okay?" I asked.

Lawrence was rubbing his head. "I'm fine," he said. "A book clipped me on the back of the head."

"Okay." I looked into the den again. All the books had come from the same shelf. Interesting. I caught one of the books as it flew by. I was rewarded with a flash impression of Mr. Forester carefully placing it on a shelf, and a feeling of satisfaction.

Odd, I thought. Books usually have images of being read.

Lawrence saw the strange look on my face and asked me what it was for. I told his about the image I'd gotten.

"So?" he asked with a shrug.

"The book was placed on the shelf carefully, and not after being read. I don't get an impression of it being recently bought, either. It should have a feeling of happiness at having been found in the store, not just being placed on a shelf. Who feels a lot of emotion when putting a book on a shelf? That's not normal," I said. "I need to try to get closer and check out that bookcase."

All the books fell to the floor, and the knocking stopped.

I looked at Lawrence. Something *wanted* me to look at that shelf. I wasn't sure how I felt about that. I stepped cautiously into the room. Nothing happened. Okay. I approached shelf and checked it thoroughly. After a few minutes, I found a hidden latch. It was locked.

Now was not the time for subtlety. I drew my pistol and shot the lock. My ears rang. I had forgotten how loud a gun actually is. I reached out and pushed. The case swung aside; it was a hidden door. Another door lay just past it, and a light switch on the wall begged to be touched. I flipped the light on and pushed against the second door. It swung open easily.

A young boy, maybe thirteen, was curled into a tight fetal position in the middle of a cage. He was dirty and naked. The room was padded and looked as if it had been soundproofed. There were whips and other instruments of torture along one wall. All I could do was stand there and stare at the boy in horror.

I guess there wasn't a true poltergeist, after all.

CHAPTER SEVEN

The police took my statement, giving me only a bit of side-eye.

They'd already dispatched a car to arrest the Foresters. The boy had been partially lucid when the police arrived; he'd been able to tell them it was the Foresters who had... well, *hurt him*, before the ambulance took him to the hospital.

I think I was still in shock.

I'd called 9-1-1 without even realizing it. I was glad I had, though. If I'd seen either of the Foresters, I would have killed them.

Lawrence and I sat and waited at the house while police checked out the torture chamber and looked around in the other rooms. Now I understood what had bothered me from the outside of the house. The missing space of the extra room was obvious now that I knew where to look.

An officer came and told me when the Foresters had been taken into custody.

"The arresting officers told me the Foresters didn't seem alarmed when our men got there," he said. "Or even surprised. You never can tell about people. You think you got them figured out, and *bam*, they turn out to be psychopaths."

"Thank you for letting us know you got them. I'll sleep better tonight."

"No problem, Dr. Fredericks. We've got your statements. You are both free to go."

Lawrence went back home with me to keep me company. I didn't need to be alone right then. We didn't say anything during the long drive. What could be said about what we'd found? The Foresters were animals. No rational being could do that to a child. The Foresters were too young to have been a part of the project I'd been in, but they were certainly the right type for that kind of job.

I wondered if Ohio had the death penalty. I hoped so. Those bastards needed to die. They'd probably get off on some technicality, though. If someone didn't get them in prison first. Even hardened criminals don't like child molesters. It made me feel a little better, thinking they wouldn't make it out of prison alive.

I thought I saw a man or something on my porch as I pulled into the driveway, but it was just an odd shadow cast by a flickering streetlamp. My eyes always play tricks on me when my mind has had too much for it to handle. Once in the garage, I put my pistol back in my glove box.

I wanted to go take a long, hot bath, but I had things to do.

First, I called my lawyer. I thought he might need to know what had happened, just in case the Foresters tried to blame it on me or something. He didn't think that was likely. The boy had been strangely rational when they were loading him into the ambulance -- I knew all about that kind of shock.

I'd been through a lot at his age, too. Maybe that was what bothered me so much. I knew what it felt like to be where he'd been. I'd spent my time in a cage.

Never again.

After I got off the phone with my lawyer, I called Tony, my sort-of boss. His wife answered the phone, and I had to explain carefully who I was and why I was calling, before she would let me talk to him. She must not trust him very much. Couldn't blame her; the man was a dog.

"Michelle? Why are you calling me at home?" He sounded irate, but then, he often did when I called him after hours.

"We have a problem, Tony," I said calmly.

"You can't get the poltergeist out of the house?"

I laughed without humor. "That's not the problem. I got the poltergeist out, all right."

"Then what's the problem, woman?"

"The *problem*, Tony, is that the poltergeist was caused by a thirteen-year-old boy whom the Foresters had locked in a secret torture chamber in their house," I said in a rush.

Tony groaned. "Oh, shit. Was the boy…?" He couldn't finish.

"He's alive. He seemed sane, at least for now. I don't know what hospital they took him to. I'm sure the police would tell you, once you explained to them who you are."

"I'll send Maria over tonight. I'll be down in the morning. Will you be available?"

"No, I'm going out of town to visit family." I met Lawrence's eyes. He smiled.

"Okay, Michelle. Thank you for this," said Tony. "I know it must've been rough, finding him like that."

You have no idea, I thought. "Thanks, Tony. Just make sure that kid gets good medical care. Use some of the money you were going to pay me, if you have to."

"Don't worry about that. We'll cover the expenses. You try to relax over the weekend. Call me when you get back. We'll need to talk about this."

"Will do. Good night, Tony."

I hung up before he could say anything else.

Lawrence and I sat up talking late into the night.

I wasn't sure what to pack, so I put a little bit of everything in my suitcase. I still had the feeling I might be overdressed most of the time. While I packed, Lawrence filled me in on what it had been like to grow up in the hills of Eastern Kentucky.

It sounded okay to me. Better than most of *my* life. I wondered what he was leaving out. He had many fond memories from his youth. Still, if it was so great, what made him leave, and why was he so loath to go back?

CHAPTER EIGHT

I passed through the Gates of Hell.

Actually, I had just turned east onto the Mountain Parkway.

Lexington, the last bastion of civilization – for Kentucky – was receding in my mirrors. Lexington sits right in the middle of Kentucky, in the central region. Central Kentucky is a strange place, stranger than the rest of the state in some ways.

That takes some doing.

There's a sense of spiritual lethargy that strikes people who live there. Mark has always called it the Central Kentucky Ennui. Nobody ever wants to *do* anything there... except root for the Wildcats, of course. I was never into basketball, so I didn't even have that.

I fiddled with the radio but couldn't get anything decent.

"So where, exactly, are we going, Lawrence?" I asked.

"Sou Wimson," he said, obviously distracted by his thoughts.

"*Where?*"

"Sou Wimson."

I pulled off to the side of the road and pulled out a map. "Okay. I looked at this map before we started, and there isn't a *Sou Wimson* anywhere on it. How little *is* this place?"

He furrowed him brow and pointed to a spot on the map. "It's right there."

I looked at the map. Then I looked at Lawrence. I looked back at the map again. "Lawrence, that says *South Williamson*."

The expression on his face was priceless. I decided right then that even if everything went wrong this weekend, that look would vindicate my being there. I'd waited years for this kind of payback.

"Michelle...," he said quietly.

"Yes, Lawrence?" I was trying hard not to smile.

"Kill me if I start to talk like my family, okay?"

"Sure thing, Lawrence. Anything for a friend." I dropped the map into the console and pulled back onto the road.

It's actually quite beautiful along the Mountain Parkway, which goes past Red River Gorge and Natural Bridge. We pulled off at the Slade exit to visit the rest area, where we encountered the usual assortment of cars, campers visiting the parks, and people traveling home for the holidays. I tried not to flinch at the two white vans in the parking lot.

After relieving myself of the result of drinking a thirty-two-ounce soda in Lexington, I stood out in the lobby and looked at the missing-person posters. Something was bothering me. I had a nagging feeling of having all the information to solve a problem but not knowing the question yet.

Lawrence came out of the restroom and stood beside me. "A lot of sick people in the world," he said.

I started to nod and then suddenly knew what was bothering me. I got out my cell phone. Lawrence raised an eyebrow but didn't say anything. He knows my moods.

I typed in the extension number when prompted.

"Detective Herrmann speaking."

"Hi, John. It's Michelle Fredericks."

"Hey, Michelle, what's up?" He sounded bored.

"I want to talk to you about the Forester case," I replied.

"I'm not on that case. I couldn't talk about it anyway. I understand you pretty much caught them red-handed, though. Something bothering you about it?"

"It all bothers me, John. I don't like seeing that happen to kids." I paced a bit.

"Yeah, I know what you mean."

"Listen, something else *is* bothering me, though."

"Okay, I'm listening."

I took a deep breath. "The marks on that boy looked familiar."

"In what way?"

"Like the Little Miami River cases."

"Son of a bitch!" I could hear him shuffling papers. He was probably looking for the report.

"I just made the connection."

"I'll check it out. Thank you. If this turns out to be connected, we may have finally caught those sick bastards."

"Yeah."

"Thanks."

"Later."

Lawrence looked a question at me.

"I've been working on a case for quite a while. Every so often, a body washes up in the river. Some of the bodies were young boys who'd been beaten and killed."

Lawrence looked pale. "So you think the people the other day might have been…?" He trailed off.

"Yeah. I hope it is them. It fits."

"Like I said, a *lot* of sick people out there."

We walked back to the car. It was starting to rain.

"Do you want me to drive for a while?" asked Lawrence.

"I'm fine. Thanks, though."

We rode in silence.

We passed a sign, an electronic marquee, for the Mountain Arts Center.

"Lawrence, does that sign really say *Kentucky Opry?*" I asked, horrified.

"Hmm? Oh, yeah. They have concerts there. Turn right up here, toward Pikeville." He still seemed distracted.

"What's wrong? Worried about your father?"

"Yes and no. We've known he was dying for quite some time now. No, I'm more worried about the rest of the family, actually."

"What's wrong with them?"

"They exist."

"Lawrence!"

"Well, what can I say? My mother is a born martyr. My older sisters are unspeakably nasty." He sighed. "I really hate them, you know."

"*Unspeakably?*" I said, raising an eyebrow.

He grinned. "Yeah. They're eldritch horrors from beyond space and time."

"You've been reading too much Lovecraft, Lawrence."

He just grinned.

CHAPTER NINE

I couldn't stop thinking about it.

"Seriously, what's wrong with your sisters?" I asked.

"Older sisters. You'll see." He smiled mischievously. "They're going to *love* you."

"I hope you mean that figuratively."

He laughed. "I'm fairly sure I'm the only queer in the family"

I just shook my head.

"Actually," he said, "my younger sister is great. I worry about her, but for different reasons. I wish she would move out of Pike County. She needs more perspective. Maybe you could help."

I glanced over at him. "What do you mean?"

"I have a feeling she's going to develop a case of hero worship for you."

"Lawrence...," I began.

"Seriously," he said, "why wouldn't she? You're good looking, smart, and independent. She looks up to me, anyway. She's going to see your nice car, nice clothes, and how happy you are, and want that for herself."

"I'll do what I can." I wasn't certain what I could do, or for that matter, how happy I was. But the subject was making me uncomfortable.

I had to slow down because of the rain and fog. Most of the other motorists slowed, as well. Soon it was just the large trucks that rushed past us at reckless speeds, drenching the windshield with rain.

"So how close are we?" I asked.

"About another hour or so."

"That long?"

"Pike County *is* the largest county in Kentucky. It's about the size of four normal counties."

"Really?"

"Yep. Pikeville is the largest town in the county, too. That isn't much to brag about, though."

As it got darker, so did my mood. At least the rain had eased up. An aura of dull despair pervaded everything; it was a bit overwhelming. I had Lawrence get my extra rings out of the glove box and pass them over. He didn't comment on the pistol in there. He'd seen it before, of course.

Eventually we got closer to Pikeville.

"Turn right up here," said Lawrence.

"The sign says Williamson is to the left. Having second thoughts?" I asked.

"No, I want to get a few things at Walmart. They never have any decent food at the house."

Well, a woman can hope, right? I pulled past a row of closed restaurants and into the parking lot with many cars, most of them beat-up junk held together by Bondo.

"What's with all the cars?" I asked.

"Night before Thanksgiving," said Lawrence. "And it's the only place that stays open this late, besides bars."

I found a parking space near the end of the lot.

"Do you need me to go in with you?" I asked. I was thinking about calling Michael.

"If you don't mind," he said wistfully, "I could use the backup. You know how crazy last-minute shoppers are."

I just sighed and picked up my coat from of the back of the Jeep. I probably wouldn't get cell reception here in the mountains anyway. We got out.

"Do you need your...?" He gestured toward the glove box.

"No, I've got my Smith under my outer shirt."

He blinked, then stepped away and shut the door.

I locked the Jeep, and we walked toward the light.

"If we're walking toward the light, why does it feel like hell waits ahead?" I asked.

"This isn't hell. That's half an hour away," answered Lawrence.

It didn't seem so bad when we got through the doors. Just another Walmart. I got a damp cart and followed Lawrence into the produce section.

"Oh, my god," he whispered suddenly, sounding terrified.

"What's wrong?" I slipped my hand under my jacket to my discreetly holstered pistol.

"That man," Lawrence whispered hoarsely.

I leaned close. "What about him?"

"He has a *mullet*. I'm going to be *ill*."

"Lawrence!" I brought my hand up to my face and wiped it disgustedly. "I actually thought something was wrong."

He looked at me, his eyes wide. "You don't think seeing a mullet is cause for horror?"

I frowned. "Lawrence, I don't really care what his hair looks like. I'd never be interested in him anyway. He looks like a Shar Pei."

"There is that," said Lawrence, and then shuddered.

"So what are we supposed to be getting in here?"

"Decent food."

"Lawrence, this is Walmart. I didn't think you'd even been in one before."

"I try to hide my roots."

"Is it really that bad? Home, I mean. I thought you liked it."

He sighed. "Not really. My older sisters are bitches, as I said. My little sister is cool. My mother is okay if you ignore her. Dad..." He looked away. "Dad was always good to me." He shrugged. "I'm his only son. I think he expected me to follow him into the coal mines. I worked there for two months and couldn't stand it anymore. I knew if I didn't get out then, I never would."

I looked at him closely. "So nothing bad ever happened? I mean…" I trailed off at his look.

"No. My family was good to me, growing up. I know other families were fucked up, but ours was always really loving. I think my sisters just hate me because I date better men than they do."

I laughed.

"Or maybe just because I got out of here. Seriously, Michelle, the dread I feel has nothing to do with how I was treated growing up. I'm just nervous. That's all."

"Okay. I just wanted to be sure. I've heard horror stories. I've been through a lot of bad things myself."

"I know." He placed his hand on my arm. "Thanks for coming with me. It means a lot. I'm going to need your stability this weekend."

Me. Stable. *Right.* "I would have come even if I didn't owe you a big favor."

"Thanks." He looked a bit puffy-eyed.

CHAPTER TEN

The noise of Walmart abruptly crashed down on me.

"So," I said, "what kind of goodies are we getting?"

"Well, we'll need something to eat and drink for the entire weekend."

"Should we get enough for everyone?" I asked. "How many people will be there?"

"I'm not sure who'll be there, but we can just get food for us, and maybe Jean. No one else would eat it, anyway."

"What do you mean?"

"They have plenty of food there, just not anything we would eat. Unless you like fried generic-bologna sandwiches, that is."

"Fried bologna? That's…"

"Disgusting? It tastes a bit like a hotdog, actually."

"You like it?"

"Hell, no. That's why I'm getting real food. I'll let *them* introduce you to the really nasty stuff, like tripe."

"I can hardly wait."

We loaded the cart with soft drinks and junk food. Somewhere under the mounds of carbohydrates was some real food, at least microwavable dinners. Checkout was hell, with long lines and leering men. I did my best to ignore both.

Outside, I let my anger vent a little.

Lawrence just shook his head. "You okay?"

"Yeah. I just don't like putting up with people's bullshit."

"Hell, you could tie those guys up in knots."

I grinned. "That's true. It would be fun, too." I imagined myself breaking bones and smashing faces. It made me feel better.

A wave of darkness rolled over me when we got close to the Jeep.

"Michelle? Are you okay?" Lawrence was holding me up.

I got my feet steady under me and looked around. I thought I saw a familiar shadowy shape moving away. It looked like the form I'd seen the other day.

"I'm okay. Something just…" I trailed off. Maybe I wasn't okay. If that was the beginning of a new round of psychic attacks, I was going to be in big trouble.

"Michelle?" Lawrence asked with concern in his voice.

"I'm okay," I repeated. "Let's get these groceries into the car and get to moving."

"Okay."

We drove for what seemed longer than half an hour. His parents didn't actually live *in* South Williamson, just near it. I was glad I'd brought the Jeep instead of a rental car. Lawrence's parents' driveway was steep. They had a somewhat battered-looking, double-wide trailer. A small, newer-looking shed stood nearby. There were three cars in the driveway, so I pulled over, close to the hillside.

"Nervous?" I asked. Lawrence looked as if he was going to be ill.

"Dread," he said quietly.

"Come on, let's get this over with."

He sighed. "Okay. Leave the stuff for now. I'm not sure where we're staying."

We both got out of the Jeep. An old dog sleeping was under the porch. It didn't challenge us as we walked up.

"What's the dog's name, Lawrence?"

"Snowy. He lives down the road."

"Oh, so he's not your parents' dog?"

"No."

The dog wagged his tail and presented his belly for rubs when I petted him.

We stood at the door.

Lawrence was having a lot of trouble bringing himself to knock. I had a bad feeling about standing out in the darkness. I had a strong suspicion that something was watching me. Watching and waiting. After Lawrence's second attempt to bring himself to knock, I did it for him. I couldn't tell if the look he gave me was one of relief or of irritation.

Then the door opened.

A worn-out looking woman opened the door. At first, her expression was blank, but then she seemed to recognize Lawrence. Her expression ran the gamut from shocked and surprised to irritated. Something else lay under it all – envy, maybe?

"Lawrence?" She didn't sound happy. "What're you doing here?" She had less accent than I'd expected.

"Hey, Sissy. Why do you think I'm here? Let us in."

She didn't budge. "Not until you explain yourself. You can't just show up here unannounced, expecting everyone to fawn over you."

Another woman called from inside, "Is that m'boy?" Lawrence flinched. "Sissy, let him in. What are ya thinkin'?"

As the woman at the door turned away, she said over her shoulder, "Take your shoes off." Then she stomped away.

No one said anything as we stood by the door, removing our shoes. The living room was plain and bare. Some old furniture stood along the walls. A fairly new television sat on a stand near the bar that separated the living room from the kitchen. There were three women in the room: the one who'd answered the door, a younger woman who appeared about Lawrence's age, and a woman who looked too old to be Lawrence's mother but must be.

"Come give me some sugar," said the older woman.

Lawrence walked over and gave the woman a hug and a kiss on the cheek. Sissy scowled at him as he went by, but the younger woman looked happy to see him. She smiled and gripped his arm as he hugged his mother.

"Lawrence, who's your friend?" asked the younger woman.

"Oh." He straightened up, wiping his eyes. "This is my friend Michelle." He turned to me. "Michelle, this is my mother. My sister Sissy, you met, and my little sister Jeannette."

His older sister and mother said hi from where they were, but Jeannette got up and, after a quick hug for Lawrence, came over and gave me a surprise hug. "Call me Jean," she said, and walked into the kitchen. "Can I get you anything, Michelle?" She said my name shyly.

"I'm fine, thank you. We stopped on the way in." I gave her a smile. She seemed genuinely friendly. So this was Lawrence's younger sister. I could see why he wanted to get her out of here. She looked like a wilted flower. She needed space to grow, and some light.

"How's Dad?" I heard Lawrence ask.

"He's asleep, and don't even think about waking him," Sissy said. I could tell she and I were going to have words before this weekend was over.

"I wasn't planning on it, Sissy." Lawrence sounded as irritated as I felt. He looked at his mother. "Is there room here for us?"

"Of course, if neither of you mind sleeping on the couches."

"We could drag in the spare mattress from under the bed in the other room," Jean said from the kitchen.

"The couches will be fine, Mom," Lawrence said. He sounded tired.

"I guess I'll go get the bags," I said.

"I'll help you," Jean offered quickly.

CHAPTER ELEVEN

Lawrence started to move to help us. "We can get it, Lawrence," I said.

I bent down and put my shoes back on; I was glad I hadn't worn my boots. Jean slipped into a fairly stylish pair of backless shoes. I had a feeling I might have an ally in her. We walked back down to the car.

"Oh, a Jeep Grand Cherokee. Nice," Jean said quietly.

"Thanks. How did you know it isn't Lawrence's?"

"He's told me he doesn't drive. Either way, it's a nice car."

I unlocked the doors, walked around to the back, and opened the hatch. "Do you keep in touch with him?" I'd gotten the impression that he didn't talk to his family much.

"Not as much as I'd like to. He keeps trying to talk me into moving to Cincinnati, but I don't know. It seems so scary. I've never even been to a city larger than Pikeville."

I tried not to flinch. *Pikeville. Large city.* "Yeah, Cincinnati can be a bit scary at first. It's not as bad as New York, though. That can be a scary place." I pulled out the two lighter suitcases for her; she was kind of thin and frail looking.

"You used to live in New York?" Her eyes glittered oddly in the darkness. *Envy?* Her emotions were too complex to get a quick read on.

"For a few years after college. I'm from Kentucky, though." That seemed important to say, for some reason. I had that watched feeling again. It was making my shoulders twitch.

"Why'd you move back?" she asked.

"It was too much city for me. I live in Latonia now."

She looked blank.

"It's on the Kentucky side of the river, across from Cinci." I hefted out the two large bags and closed the hatch.

We walked up and placed the bags on the porch.

"It might be easier," Jean said, "if we just leave everything on the porch until we get it all out of your car." Her glace though the storm door into the trailer was full of veiled messages.

"Okay." I headed back to the Jeep.

"So, you work?" she asked.

I blinked at her. "Yes, I'm a –" Caution asserted itself. "A consultant. For the police, mostly. Kind of a detective."

"Really? Cool. Do you have a badge and stuff?"

I grinned. "No. I work for an agency in Dayton, Ohio. I usually work in the Cincinnati area, though. I mostly work with the police departments and the FBI."

I opened the side door and handed Jean the groceries. I picked up the soft drinks and water myself. "That's it," I said as I closed the door with my knee. We walked back up to the porch.

"You might want to lock it again," said Jean.

I nodded and set down the drinks, then used the remote to lock the doors. I'd forgotten that my other gun was in the glove box. We carried groceries inside. Sissy was gone somewhere deeper inside the trailer. Lawrence was talking quietly to his mother on the couch. She didn't look happy.

Jean looked as loath as I felt to walk back in there. "Do you play rummy?" she asked.

I smiled. "I haven't played in years, but I used to play with my grandparents when I was little. You'll have to remind me how."

She smiled and got a worn deck of cards off the top of the refrigerator. It didn't take her long to locate paper and a pencil. I tried to figure out how old she was; she had to be close to Lawrence's age.

We'd been playing cards quietly for about half an hour when Lawrence entered the room and sat down. He didn't say anything, but he looked upset. Jean reached over and held his hands. I could tell they were close, despite the years they'd been separated.

"Are you going to be okay?" I asked.

Lawrence nodded. "I'm okay. I just..." He glanced over his shoulder toward his mother. "I just need time to adjust. She knows exactly which buttons to push, that's all."

Jean nodded. I had a feeling she knew all about having her buttons pushed. I suddenly felt a wave of sympathy for her. I vowed to try as hard as I could to get her to move to the Cincinnati area.

Their mother stood up and came into the kitchen. "I'm going to bed, young'uns. Michelle, it's nice to have met you, dear. Make yourself at home. Jeanie, don't stay up too late. G'night." She walked back through the trailer.

Lawrence was quiet until he heard the door close. Then he looked over at Jean. "Don't stay up too late," he mimicked.

Jean gave him a wry grin.

"Where did your other sister go?" I asked.

"She went home," said Jean.

"But..." I was confused. "We were outside. We would have seen her leave, right?"

Jean nodded down the hallway. "There's another door over there. Sissy lives next door. She walked over."

"Oh, good. I was worried for a minute."

Jean laughed. "Some detective you are." She stood up and began making coffee.

Lawrence glanced over at me and said quietly, "Detective?"

I just shrugged. What the hell was I supposed to have told her?

CHAPTER TWELVE

Thanksgiving Day didn't start well.

We sat up late the night before, playing cards and talking. Lawrence and I had changed into pajamas in the one bathroom. The water stank, a smell that combined sewage and rotten eggs, the result of mining effluvium in the local water supply. I couldn't use that to brush my teeth, much less wash up. I used some of the bottled water and hoped it would last.

I'd been asleep maybe four hours when someone slammed the door. The whole trailer shook.

"Rise and shine you, lazy people!" The man's voice grated on my nerves. *Surely Lawrence's father is too sick to bellow,* I thought.

"Henry! Hush! You're going to wake up Law! Get on in there!" The woman's voice was not much quieter.

The male voice belonged to an average-height man who was quite a bit *over* average in the weight department. His beer belly hung out from under the edge of his Harley t-shirt and over his wide belt buckle. He wasn't wearing a coat.

The woman must have been Lawrence's other older sister; she had the family look. The man – I use the term loosely – was her husband. Jean had warned me about him the previous night while Lawrence was getting ready for bed. He had fingers that tended to stray. Jean said she'd had many run-ins with him. I vowed that he'd better keep those fingers to himself, or he'd find them broken.

Jean came in, fully dressed, and sat down on the edge of the couch. I pushed myself up groggily. I'd been hoping to ignore the annoying people and get a few more hours of sleep, but they were talking loudly in the kitchen. Lawrence sat up with a groan.

The door to the trailer slammed again. Sissy came stomping through the room, glaring at everyone.

I scooped up my bag and made a beeline for the bathroom. This day was not going to end well, I could tell. After I changed clothes and pulled my hair back, I returned to the living room. Lawrence passed me in the hall. He had the look of a man ready to kill. I wondered what I'd missed.

Henry was bitching when I walked back in. "All I said was that that woman of his had a nice trophy rack but didn't seem to have enough trunk space. That ain't no cause for a ruckus, just the truth."

No wonder Lawrence looked ready to kill. It took all my reserves not to reply. I just placed my bag back beside the couch.

Jean walked past with a mug of black coffee, a fixed look on her face. "I'll be right back. Got to take this to Daddy," she whispered.

With my back to the kitchen, I slipped my pistol into my bag from under my pillow. No sense in tempting fate. I itched and wanted to take a shower, but the thought of washing in that water made me ill.

Jean and Lawrence came back into the room together.

"Michelle," he said loudly, "this is my sister Mabel and her husband Henry."

I forced myself to smile. "Hello," I said through gritted teeth. At least neither of them offered to shake my hand. I'm not sure I could have stomached that.

Lawrence's mother came through and into the kitchen. She looked as if she was getting ready to cook breakfast... or something like it, anyway. Jean sighed and went into the kitchen help. I sat on the couch and checked my voicemail. I had a message from Michael. It was good to hear his voice. I needed him right then, more than ever. I'd gotten used to talking to him every few days. I saved the message to listen to again later, even though it was just a simple, *I miss you. Call me when you can.*

The smell coming from the kitchen was so bad that I decided I wasn't hungry.

"Lawrence," I whispered, "what are they cooking?"

He leaned close to me. "Banner sausage and fried bread."

"What is banner sausage?" I wasn't sure I wanted to know.

"Mostly beef tripe," he said. "That's —"

"I know what it is," I said hurriedly. I felt ill. How could they eat that?

Jean called in from the kitchen. "Michelle? Can I get you anything?"

"She can get up and get her own breakfast, Jeanie," Sissy scolded.

"Michelle?" Jean repeated, not cowed by her sister.

I smiled. "I could use a Coke, please. I didn't want to get in the way in the kitchen."

She got one out of the fridge and brought it out to me. "Are you sure you don't want anything else?" She glanced at the kitchen and wrinkled her nose. "I could fry you an egg or something."

"Thank you. I never eat much in the morning." I took a quick sip of soda.

"Jeanie, come get your daddy's breakfast and take it to him."

Jean sighed, went back into the kitchen, and got the plate of food. As she walked past, she stopped near Lawrence. "I'll tell Daddy you're here. He'll be glad." Her voice held an odd quaver. She walked down the hall and went into the room next to the bath.

Lawrence stood up and got himself some Pop-Tarts and a soda. "Are you sure you don't want a Pop-Tart or something, Michelle?" he asked.

I ignored Henry's mocking whisper and declined. I really wasn't hungry. I'd been thinking about the fact that they'd be using the tap water to cook dinner later.

Lawrence came back in and sat next to me on the couch.

"Are they always like this?" I asked.

"No, they're usually worse. This is the first time I've brought a girl home with me. I don't think they know what to think of that." He grinned.

Jean carried the dirty dishes back the kitchen, then came and sat next to Lawrence on the couch. "Daddy asked for you," she said.

Lawrence took a deep breath and walked slowly down the hall. He gave a *wish me luck* look, and then knocked on the door. After a moment, he went through.

"So, Michelle, how much is he paying you?" Sissy said loudly.

I looked up. They were all staring at me. "Paying me?"

"Yeah," said Henry. "You make more as an escort than turning tricks, right?" He guffawed.

I felt myself turning red. I also felt my anger rising. "Excuse me?" I said, standing. "I don't think I heard you right. Just what are you saying?"

"I ain't saying nothing," Henry said hurriedly.

Sissy was not deterred so easily. "I'm saying you're not his woman. That's obvious, so how much is he paying you? If you aren't a whore, then what are you?"

Jean gasped and turned pale.

"Lawrence and I are friends. I don't remember *him* saying I was his woman. I met him in college. I'm here because he asked me to come with him." I was trying hard not to lose my temper. I didn't think Lawrence would forgive me if I killed his family.

"Bullshit," Sissy spat. "What do you do for a living, then? How do you get those fancy clothes and car?"

I was wearing Levi jeans and a simple button-up shirt, nothing expensive.

Jean spoke up before I could. "*She* works for a living. You might try it sometime."

Sissy turned pale, then bright red. Jean had told me the night before that her sister was working the system and going down to Pikeville for her "crazy check" from the government every month so she didn't have to work.

Jean worked part-time at the cookie factory in Zebulon. Most of *her* money went to her mother as rent for the small room she'd grown up in. Lawrence told me last night that he sent his mother money every month, too. I wondered where it all went. I guessed it was to pay their father's medical bills.

"I'm a detective," I said.

"Sure you are, sugar." That was from Mabel.

I walked into the kitchen. They stopped chuckling when I got closer. I glared at each of them. "I've seen a lot of sorry people in my line of work, but never a lot sorrier than you bunch of cowards."

"Now, see here, you." Henry stood and grabbed my arm.

"I'll give you three seconds to let go of me before I forget that I'm a guest here and break you." I flexed my bicep under his hand so he could feel my muscles. "One...," I said.

He let go.

CHAPTER THIRTEEN

"What's going on here?" demanded Lawrence. He was standing at the bar, looking into the kitchen.

"Nothing," I said. I walked past him, back into the living room.

"Something was going on. Why were you holding her arm, Henry?"

I'd never seen Lawrence look so angry before. I saw something hard in him that I hadn't realized was there. I liked it.

Jean was standing next to me. "They called her a whore," she said suddenly.

Lawrence went pale. "Are you okay?"

I nodded. I didn't trust my voice.

He glared at the others. His mother had gotten up and was quietly washing the dishes. "So, Henry, you called her a whore while I was out of the room. You want to do it with me standing here?"

Henry shook his head.

Lawrence wouldn't let it drop. "Maybe you'd like to step outside and explain it to me there."

"I don't think so," mumbled Henry.

"Then you'll apologize." Lawrence didn't say that as a question.

"I'm sorry, ma'am. We was just foolin'." He didn't sound sincere.

Lawrence leaned close to him and said something. Henry's hands clenched on the table, but he didn't do or say anything else. Lawrence went back down the hall and into his father's room again.

"Would you like to go for a walk with me, Michelle?" Jean asked quietly.

I took a long, slow breath to calm myself. "Sure. Let me get my coat." I slipped my pistol into the inside pocket and put my shoes on. I wondered if I should leave my purse. I decided to take it with me out to the Jeep.

Jean held the door for me, and then we walked to my Jeep. Jean was a few inches shorter than me, and her hair was slightly lighter than Lawrence's natural brown. It had a touch of cinnamon in it, as well. Her eyes matched the fall sky visible between the tall hillsides around us. I realized suddenly that she was pretty. She really needed to get away from this area. She was too smart and sensitive to be stuck here her whole life. It would be a waste.

When I looked over at her again, there were tears on her face. I put my arms around her, and she clung to me and cried. With Lawrence gone, she must have been very lonely. After a few minutes of heart-wrenching sobs, she quieted, and I let her go.

"I'm sorry," she began.

"Shush," I said. "Everyone has to do that sometimes, or they pop."

She laughed. "I just don't really know you, that's all."

"Well, you can't cry on a person's shoulder if they aren't a friend. So how about it?" I held out my hand. I liked her. She had a refreshing honesty, just like Lawrence. I had no idea how they managed, with the family I'd seen. Their father must have been a great man.

She shook my hand solemnly and then grinned, wiping away the tears on her cheeks. "I can see why Lawrence likes you," she said.

I smiled. "Lawrence thinks a lot of you, too, you know."

She nodded.

"Have you thought about moving away from here?" We walked down the drive.

"All the time."

"Why don't you?" I turned to face her.

"I don't know." She was looking into the woods past my shoulder.

The watched feeling crawled up my back once more. I turned and glanced over my shoulder, but I didn't see anything. I moved so the feeling would be more to the front of me.

"I guess I just don't know what I'd do. Lawrence's lifestyle isn't for me. I can't embrace the city the way he has."

I got the feeling she knew all about his lifestyle. They probably didn't have many secrets from each other. "I'm sure Lawrence would get you a place."

"I'm not looking for a handout!" she said angrily.

It startled me, but then I thought about the rest of her family. "I'm sorry. I didn't mean it like that."

We stood in silence.

"Look," I said abruptly, "I have an extra room at my house." I raised my hand to stop her objections. "You could pay me rent until you got your own place. I'm sure you could get grants and loans to get into college if you wanted. If not, I'm sure Lawrence or I could help you find a job up there. Between us, we have a lot of friends."

She smiled and then sighed. "I don't think anyone has offered to help me like this before. Except Lawrence, of course." Then her eyes got big, and she stepped back.

I instinctively turned to see what was behind me, but there was nothing there. I turned back to Jean, but she was staring at me.

"You're not... I mean, Lawrence is... You know what I'm trying to say."

It took me a minute, but then I laughed. It was funny. "No," I said. "I'm not gay, not even a little bit." Okay, a *little* lie, but I had no interest in *her* that way. She was practically family.

She laughed. "I'm sorry. It's just..." She trailed off, laughing.

I shook my head, laughing, too. It helped a bit with the stress from earlier.

"So...," Jean said. "Are you seeing someone?"

"His name is Michael. He's tall – taller than me – with dark red hair and amazing green eyes." I missed him terribly. It hurt just to talk about him.

"Does he work?"

"I think you're obsessed with people working. Yes, he works. He's a deputy federal marshal. Unfortunately, he's out of town a lot."

"Does he know you're here with Lawrence?"

"Yes, he knows."

"And he let you come anyway?"

I laughed. "He didn't *let* me do anything. I called him and told him what I was doing. He didn't seem to mind. Why?"

Jean shrugged. "I don't know. I just figured he wouldn't want you pretending to be someone else's girl."

"I'm just here as a friend, remember? It didn't bother him. He knows I'm not interested in Lawrence that way, even if Lawrence were interested in me. I've known Lawrence for years. Nothing has ever even come close to happening. I care about Lawrence very much. Hell, I love him as a dear friend."

"This Michael sounds like an interesting guy. How did you meet him?"

Hmm. How to answer that? "We met during a case a month or so ago. We'd met earlier, when we were teens, but didn't realize it."

"That is so cool." Jean kicked at a clump of grass. "I don't think I'll ever find anyone."

I laughed. "How old are you, Jean?"

"Twenty-eight," she replied.

"I'm forty-five."

She looked shocked. "No way!"

I love getting that reaction. "Come on, I'll prove it."

CHAPTER FOURTEEN

We walked back to the Jeep, and I took my purse out. I let Jean look at my driver's license. While we were standing there, I became aware of a change in the aura of the area. An expectancy had been added to the tension, mixed with dread. Something was wrong, and I couldn't quite figure out what. I wished I could talk to Mark about it. He'd be very interested in the watched feeling, I was sure.

"How do you pronounce your first name?" asked Jean.

"Hmm?" I'd forgotten my license had my full name on it. "Rhiannon," I said.

"That's a pretty name. Why do you go by Michelle? Not that there's anything wrong with it."

I shrugged. "I just like Michelle better."

"Fair enough."

The screen door to the trailer banged.

We turned to look. It was Lawrence. He walked over and draped an arm across Jean's shoulders. She leaned into him.

"What are you two doing out here? They run you out?" He jerked his head toward the trailer.

"No, we were just walking and talking," I said. I took my license back and put it in my purse.

"Michelle is trying to talk me into moving to Latonia, with her. I told her that was far too close to you," said Jean.

"What?" Lawrence looked hurt for a moment and then laughed. "You've been around Michelle too much. You're picking up her sense of so-called humor. So what did you tell her?" he asked me.

"I told her she could rent a room from me. Latonia isn't as large and confusing as Cincinnati."

"And...?" Lawrence looked down at his sister.

"And I told her I'd think about it," said Jean.

Lawrence sighed. "Well, that's better than the replies I usually get. Did you tell her about your work?"

"A detective?" Jean said hesitantly.

I sighed. I was going to have to come clean. "Yes and no. Technically, I'm a specialist in occult crimes. To be honest though, I have... abilities. They let me sense things that help the police."

Jean's eyes got wide. "You mean a *psychic* detective? Like those people on TV?"

"I'm not sure about what's on TV, but yes, basically a psychic detective." I hoped that wouldn't bother her. I didn't want her to be scared away.

"That is so cool."

I grinned. We stood and talked about my job for a while. I told her about my most recent case. I'm sure she'd heard stories every bit as bad from around Eastern Kentucky, but she shuddered when I told her about the bodies in the river. I *didn't* tell her about the project or the events of last month; that wasn't safe to discuss.

Our conversation was cut short by a pickup truck pulling into the driveway.

Lawrence groaned.

"What's wrong?" I asked.

"Our uncle," said Jean.

"Let's go inside," Lawrence said quickly. He led the way around the back of the trailer, and we went in through the side door.

"Jeanie! Come help cook!" their mother immediately called.

Lawrence gripped Jean's arm for a moment before she started

toward the kitchen. Then she turned suddenly. "I'll go back with you," she said. Then she ran to the kitchen.

I found myself suddenly embraced.

"Thank you, Michelle," said Lawrence. "You have no idea how long I've trying to get her to leave this place."

I smiled. "I told you I'd help."

Lawrence glanced at the bedroom door near where we stood. "Would you like to meet my father?" he asked.

How to answer that? Not honestly. "Sure, if he's okay with that."

Lawrence knocked on the door and then stuck his head into the room. I heard a faint, gravelly voice reply. Then Lawrence took my hand and led me in.

Lawrence's father, Law – Lawrence Senior, I realized suddenly – was lying in a fairly modern hospital bed. He wore an oxygen mask and had an IV drip. The fluid was an odd color in the dim light; I assumed it was some kind of medication. His fingertips had a bluish tinge, and each breath looked as if it took all his concentration, yet he held on. He was tough. My heart went out to him.

"Come here, son," he whispered.

Lawrence went to stand by him and held his hand.

I moved closer.

"Daddy, this is my friend I told you about, Michelle," Lawrence said softly.

"Sorry I can't greet you better. Come closer. Let me look at you."

I moved up next to Lawrence.

Law managed a faint smile. "You're a good-looking woman. Where did my boy find you?"

I wasn't sure what he meant by that. "I met him in school, college, sir. We've been friends for years." I held his eyes with mine. I knew how important this was for Lawrence, but I couldn't bring myself to lie to this man.

He nodded slightly. "You must be a good friend to have come *here* with him." He started coughing. It was a wet, unpleasant sound.

"Daddy?" Lawrence said, worried.

Law waved him away weakly.

"Are you okay, sir?" I asked lamely.

"I'm dying, girl. It ain't ever pretty."

I looked away. I didn't know how to reply to that. He couldn't have long.

"Lawrence, is she really your friend? Don't lie to me, boy."

"Yes, sir. I've known her since college. I told you about her then."

I glanced quickly at Lawrence. I hadn't realized that he might have mentioned me to his family before.

Law coughed again. Talking this much couldn't be good for him. "It's just friends, though, right? Nothing else?" He had an odd note in his voice.

Lawrence looked torn.

Tell him the truth, I thought.

"No, Daddy. We're just friends. Nothing else."

"That's what I thought. You might fool your mother, but not me. I know you don't care for girls, son. You never did."

Lawrence choked back a sob.

"Son, are you happy? With whoever you're with?"

"Yes," Lawrence said quietly.

"Then that's enough."

Lawrence looked up suddenly and into his eyes.

"Damn it, boy! Do you think I care who you sleep with? You're my only son. You've made a good life for yourself. I'm proud of you. Now get out of here and let me sleep a bit. I'm not ready to die just yet."

CHAPTER FIFTEEN

We retreated into the hall.

Lawrence looked as if he was in shock. I was a bit surprised, too. I pushed Lawrence outside, and we sat on the porch. Jean came out a few minutes later.

"Is everything okay?" She looked worried.

Lawrence tried to say something but got choked up.

"Your father's an amazing man, Jean," I said.

"Well, *yeah.* Lawrence is just like him." She patted her brother's back affectionately. "So what's going on?"

"He told Lawrence he knew about his, ah, *lifestyle choice.*"

"Oh, my god!" Her hand flew to her mouth. "What?"

"He –" Lawrence choked again. "He was okay with it. Said he was proud of me." He started sobbing quietly.

Jean sat down and held Lawrence. "He should be."

This was turning into a strange weekend.

I should have known it was only the harbinger of worse to come.

We went back inside with Jean when the family started calling for her.

The living room was getting crowded. Mabel, Henry, and Sissy had moved out of the kitchen to watch television. The room held three more people, as well: an older man and woman, and a man who was maybe thirty.

Lawrence stopped when he saw them. "I'd forgotten that my uncle Tracy had showed up," he whispered to me.

"Your *uncle* Tracy?" I said incredulously. "And they think *your* lifestyle choices are odd?"

He just grinned and motioned me through to the kitchen.

I felt six pairs of eyes on me as we crossed the room. They'd been watching some football game. I draped my coat on a chair and quickly sat at the end of the kitchen table. It was behind the pantry, and not visible to most of the room. I could still see the younger man staring at me. God only knew what his aunt and uncle had been told about me.

Lawrence's mother mostly just fidgeted around. Jean did all of the actual cooking. I noted with relief that she was using bottled water for cooking. "I might actually be able to eat today," I muttered under my breath.

Lawrence sat with his back to the room. He leaned close to talk to me. "My uncle Tracy is Mom's brother. Dad hates him. His wife's name is Mary. They pronounce it *Murray*. Their son's name is Blaine. I'm not sure where their daughter is."

"Do we like Mary and Blaine?" I asked.

He laughed. "Maybe? Mary isn't much of a problem. I don't really know Blaine."

"Your uncle, is that really his name?" I asked. "Tracy?"

"Yes. It's an Eastern Kentucky thing."

"Weird."

"He's a lot like Henry, only not a coward. Watch out for him. He could be trouble."

"Can I break him if he touches me or Jean?"

"Try not to put him in the hospital. Maybe just a cast... Otherwise, he's fair game."

I grinned. This could be fun.

"You may have some trouble understanding him," Jean interjected.

I looked up. Her eyes danced mischievously.

"What do you mean?" I asked.

"You'll see." She turned back to the cooking.

Mabel came in and moved the turkey over to a cleared area of the counter. She then proceeded to tear chunks of meat off and dump them unceremoniously onto a plate. I must have looked shocked.

"I never knew turkey was supposed to be carved until after I moved away from here," Lawrence said to me.

I just shook my head, appalled.

"Can you imagine," Lawrence went on, "Jen and Mark seeing this?"

I shuddered. "Jen would have a stroke, and Mark would retreat from the room to get drunk."

Lawrence nodded.

The turkey didn't look all that well cooked, either; it was sort of pink. I tried not to think about it. I couldn't think why they would treat it like that. It's not hard to cut a turkey. I sighed. It was looking like a vegetarian dinner for me. At least I knew Mark and Jen would save a plate of food for me until I got home. That reminded me that I needed to call them later and check on Samson.

Lawrence and I sat and played cards for another half an hour or so, until dinner was done. Jean told us it was done before she told the others. I was grateful to be able to get food unmolested.

Jean sat on the other side of me at the table.

Henry, Tracy, and Blaine stayed in the living room. Mabel and Mary took food to them. I just tried to ignore them and eat in peace. I mostly ate boxed stuffing, instant mashed potatoes, rolls, and pork and beans. The beans were really good. Jean said she'd added brown sugar, ketchup, and diced onion to regular canned beans.

I ate several servings.

Lawrence's mother had taken a plate in to her husband and stayed there long into the evening. She really seemed to love him; she was just a bit off in the head. I worried about what would happen to her after Law died. Surely Sissy and Mabel would take care of her. They seemed to care about *her*, at least.

I helped Jean with the dishes after dinner.

Henry, Mabel, and Tracy came and sat at the table as we were finishing up. They had the cards out.

"You play poker?" Mabel asked me.

I was surprised that they asked me. Then I saw the wary look on Jean's face. "Not really. Thanks anyway."

"Come on, it's just for pennies," Henry said. "Lawrence, you in?"

I looked at Lawrence, but he just shrugged and sat down again.

"I'll have to get my purse," I said. I walked through the living room and put my shoes on. It was starting to get dark outside, and cold. I ran out to the Jeep and got my purse. I remembered to lock the door again, and I was quite cold by the time I made it back inside.

Jean was sitting across from Lawrence with a small pile of pennies in front of her. She didn't look happy. I managed to scrounge almost a dollar's-worth of pennies from the bottom of my purse. I really needed to clean it out.

"Seven card stud," Henry said. "You know how to play?"

I shrugged.

CHAPTER SIXTEEN

Jean quickly explained the rules to me. It was basic poker. I could do that.

Blaine came in and starting talking to his dad while we played. It took me a minute to realize that I could only understand every fifth word or so of what he said. I wondered if he'd been drinking, or if he talked that way all the time.

It was something like, "*Hmymn numb umnumb trum* fish," and so on.

I used my abilities to clean out Mabel, Henry, and Tracy. They were easy to read, even without me touching them. It was fun baiting them and watching them grow redder and redder.

"Cheatin' bitch!" Tracy bellowed. Then he shoved the table into me, hard. I was vaguely aware of pennies scattering across the floor. Tracy had knocked the wind out of me. Henry shoved Lawrence out of the way as Tracy rounded the table toward me.

Then my reflexes took over.

I caught Tracy's thrown punch and flipped him. I was aiming to throw him into the living room, but his feet caught on the ceiling, and he landed on the counter with a crash. Mabel caught me with a resounding slap across the face. I sort of lost track of things for a few moments after that. Next thing I knew, Lawrence was holding my arm down and calling my name. I shook him off and looked around. Henry, Tracy, and Blaine were out cold on the floor. Mabel was huddled in the corner, crying.

Sissy was saying she was going to call the police. Jean was trying to reason with her.

"Go ahead," I said, wiping blood from my nose. "I'm sure the boys in blue will get a big kick out of how a woman like me kicked the crap out of three grown men. How long do you think it would take to get around town?"

Lawrence grinned and handed me a paper towel.

I got my nose under control and walked outside. Lawrence followed me. A few minutes later, Jean came out, carrying my purse and coat. We sat on the back porch and listened to everyone arguing inside. Finally, we heard their trucks pull out of the driveway.

Lawrence's mother was sitting at the table when we went back in. "Lawrence, we need to talk."

Jean grabbed my arm. "Come in here." She led me into the other room. *This must be hers,* I thought. The room was tiny. It contained a twin bed and a battered dresser. The top of the dresser was covered with stacks of science fiction and fantasy books. It also held a couple of pictures in frames: Jean and Lawrence and a man who must be their father. He didn't look the way he did now. He looked full of life, and happy.

"I don't have much," she said as she shut the door.

I sat on the edge of the bed. "You'll really come back with us?" I asked.

She nodded and then sat on the floor with a sigh. "I don't think I'd ever let myself see how crazy my family is. Lawrence always tried to tell me, but I didn't want to hear it."

"I know what that's like," I said.

Jean sighed loudly again. "I can't believe I'm going to quit my job and finally get away from here. I have a little money saved up. I'll be able to pay you a little for rent until I can get a new job."

"How much do you pay your mother?"

"I give her five hundred a month right now."

"What?" I stared at her.

"I know it isn't much, but…" She trailed off. "What?"

"That's a *lot* of money for a little room."

"It is?" She looked surprised.

"Yes. When I said you could pay me rent, I meant about a hundred a month, at most," I said. "And only that to make you feel okay about it. My guest room is about four times this size."

"Oh, then I have enough to pay you for a while."

I shook my head. They'd really been using this poor girl. "Let me guess: the rent was Sissy's idea, right?"

Jean nodded. "You really mean it. I can go back with you two when you leave?"

"Yes. There's room for you in the Jeep. We might have to rent a U-Haul trailer for the furniture."

"It isn't mine. I'll buy some later."

"Okay. I wasn't sure where we were going to put it, anyway."

"Where did you learn how to fight like that?" Jean asked.

I just shrugged.

Luckily, Lawrence knocked on the door, and then came in and sat next to Jean. He looked up at me. "Mom wants us out of here in the morning."

I nodded. I'd figured as much.

Jean stood up suddenly and came back a minute later with the cordless phone. "I was supposed to work tonight," she said. Then she called work and told them she quit.

Lawrence stared at me while she was on the phone. "Is she really going back with us?"

I smiled and nodded.

He jumped and gave Jean a bear hug, dancing a bit.

We sat up for hours talking while Jean packed. She decided to wait until morning to tell her parents. The evening had ended on a positive note. I was just happy to be leaving.

I awoke suddenly in the middle of the night.

The feeling of waiting had changed to one of exultation. It was not a good feeling. Something was wrong in the hills around me: something very, *very* wrong. I burrowed deeper into the smelly couch and pulled the covers over my head. I gripped my pistol under the pillow and let out a silent prayer to any god who cared to listen.

I fell asleep sometime later.

My dreams that night were not pleasant.

CHAPTER SEVENTEEN

My cell phone woke me the next morning.

The phone was right next to my head. I groaned and answered it. Lawrence blinked at me tiredly from the other couch.

"Hello?" I croaked.

"Dr. Fredericks?" said a woman's voice.

This had better be important... "Who is this?" I sat up on the couch. It was 7:46 AM.

"Michelle?" A man's voice, this time. One I recognized.

"Damn it, Tony, it's the day after Thanksgiving, and it's *too damn early* to call me." I was getting fired up now.

"Michelle, I wouldn't have called you if it wasn't important, and it's the same day and time for me as for you. Trust me, I'd rather be shopping with my wife. I need your help."

I sighed. "What now? Another poltergeist?"

"No, murder," he said.

"Shit. Occult? Never mind. You wouldn't have called me otherwise. Where?" I asked.

"Pikeville. That should be near you, from what you said."

"Not far." I was interested, in spite of myself. "I guess that explains why you called me. Who's the sponsor?"

"FBI.".

"No shit?" I hadn't worked for them in a while.

"They asked for you by name."

Huh? I thought. "Why?"

"They said an Agent Henderson from Homeland Security had referred them to you," said Tony.

I felt ill. Could it be connected? I hoped not. "Okay, when do you need me to start?"

"Now, if you can."

"Okay. Usual terms and conditions?" I asked. It was just a formality, though.

"Of course. Let me give you the number."

"Okay." I wrote down the name and number of my local FBI contact, and disconnected. I sighed and sat up. I was trying to think of all I'd have to do. I needed to get into Pikeville and find a hotel room. Then I needed to take a long shower; I felt dirty.

Lawrence was sitting up on the other couch. "Is everything okay?" he asked.

I shrugged. "Things just got more complicated, as usual. I've got a new assignment, in Pikeville."

Lawrence scratched his head and blinked a few times. "Okay, so what does that mean?"

Jean came in and sat next to Lawrence. "Is everything okay? I heard the phone."

"I was just telling Lawrence that I have a new assignment that's close to here. We need to figure out what we're doing. I may be in Pikeville for a while, maybe a week or more, for work."

"Oh." Jean looked confused.

"Lawrence, how long can you stay away from your work?" I asked.

He shrugged. "I make my own hours. I could be away from home for a week or more with no ill effects. I can't stay here, though."

"No, I was thinking that we'd go on and head into Pikeville. We can get rooms at a hotel there. I think I saw a couple of hotels down by the Walmart. Then I can get in touch with the FBI and get to work. Jean, you have a driver's license, right?"

She nodded.

"Good. We'll rent you a car in Pikeville. That way, you and Lawrence can come up here and see your father. That way, you can break the news slowly that you're leaving home."

Jean nodded again. "When do we need to leave?"

"As soon as possible."

She got up. "I'll go get ready."

"Lawrence?"

He met my eyes. "I'm cool. I was just thinking that I may not have much longer to see my dad anyway. This could be good for us."

"Yes." I got up and stretched. I felt good, knowing that at least I wasn't going to have to spend another night on a couch. "I'll go get dressed." I grabbed my bag and trotted off to the bath.

Since their mother wasn't up yet, Jean and Lawrence decided to leave her a note. She knew Lawrence and I were leaving. I supposed Jean leaving, too, wouldn't be that much of a shock for her. They would probably be back by that evening to visit anyway.

It didn't take long to load the Jeep. Jean didn't own much. I vowed to take her shopping once all this was over. I was sure she would fall in love with shopping malls.

Almost no traffic slowed my progress. It was strange: The day after Thanksgiving is usually a busy shopping day, but not in Eastern Kentucky. Most of the people there live in abject poverty, or near enough to it.

We did see more traffic once we got close to Pikeville. There were some regular stores in the shopping centers along the road; I hadn't seen them when we came in because of the rain.

The hotel had no trouble giving us three non-smoking rooms right next to each other. Jean seemed somewhat lost. She'd never stayed in a hotel before. Now she had her own room, bigger than the one where she had spent her whole life. I vowed that I'd take her to Vegas and show her a *nice* hotel one day.

We found a car rental place on the other side of town. They needed a credit card for the rental, and they wouldn't take Lawrence's because he didn't have a driver's license. Jean had a license but no credit card. I lost an hour taking care of that. My name was now listed on the car rental, with Jean as the secondary driver.

Once back at the hotel, I quickly showered and dressed in a spare suit I'd had in the car. I was going to have to buy more clothes if the case went on for long. That would be easier than driving home and back.

CHAPTER EIGHTEEN

I called the number I'd been given.

"Special Agent Taylor," a woman answered.

I'd been expecting a man, for some reason. *I've been in Eastern Kentucky too long*, I thought to myself. "This is Dr. Michelle Fredericks."

"Ah, the occult specialist. Good. We're going to need you to look at the site of the crime as soon as you can. How soon can you get to Pikeville?"

"I'm here now," I replied.

"Damn, what did you do, fly?" She sounded impressed.

I laughed. "I was in a town near here, visiting with a friend. Where do I need to go?"

"How well do you know the area?"

"I don't, other than from a map. I'm from around Cincinnati."

"Yeah, you sure don't sound local. I'm about ready to hire an interpreter, myself. Where are you? I'll send one of these local boys over to escort you here." Her accent sounded familiar, maybe from Indiana.

"I'm at the Super 8, next to the Walmart. I think it is on Thomson Drive or something like that," I said.

"Okay, I know the one. I'll send the boys over," she said. "What do you look like?"

I gave her a basic description, and then I disconnected. Next, I walked out in the hall and knocked on Lawrence's door. Jean opened it and let me in. They'd been sitting and talking. I told them what was going on and gave Jean my cell phone number. Then I went down to the lobby to wait.

After a few minutes, I went out and pulled my Jeep up to the door. I decided I wanted to have all my goodies with me if I was going to be taking this case. I also needed to clear my head and focus.

A police car pulled in a few minutes later.

"Dr. Fredericks?" The officer looked young.

I smiled. "Yes. Is it okay if I follow you over?"

"Sure." He got back in his car, and I followed him to the crime scene. It wasn't all that far from the hotel, which was somewhat scary. I followed the officer up a winding road to what looked like a small park. There were many police cars around, marked and unmarked. A whole pack of reporters milled around behind a small barricade. Small flashes from a police photographer came from what appeared to be an overlook.

It seemed a very public place for an occult murder.

We parked, and the officer led me through the tangle of vehicles to a mass of police officers and people in suits.

"Dr. Fredericks?"

I turned to see a small woman in a black suit. Other than having black hair, she looked a lot like Scully from *The X-files*. It was a little disconcerting, and ironic. "Yes," I said.

She held out her well-manicured hand. "Special Agent Taylor."

I shook her hand. She had a stronger grip than I expected. I could also feel pistol calluses.

She grinned at me and said, "You're not what I expected."

I smiled. "How is that?"

"I figured you for one of those California types. You know: lots of shawls and too much gaudy jewelry. You seem much more grounded in reality than most New Age types."

"Ah, the psychic faire crowd," I said. "I got into the occult business after a run-in with a serial killer in college. Went on to get a PhD in criminal anthropology."

"Yes, I'd read about that," she said. "You had trouble with his woman during the stuff last month that Henderson mentioned, didn't you?"

"I'm not sure what Agent Henderson may have mentioned," I said cautiously.

"Just that you worked with the Marshal Service to track a fugitive, and that – how shall I say it? – there were quite a bit of occult goings-on during the whole thing. You helped take down the fugitive, right?"

"I'm not sure I'd say that. She was shot and fell into a river," I said. "Her body was never recovered."

"Were you the shooter?" asked Agent Taylor.

"No, I was busy getting the shit kicked out of me. The deputy marshal chasing her shot her."

Taylor laughed. "Good, I don't need a trigger-happy consultant. These people are worked up enough as it is. They aren't used to this sort of thing around here."

"So what's going on, exactly?"

"Good question. This is the third occult murder in this region, all in the same county."

"Same M.O. for each crime?"

"Not exactly, but close enough to get us involved." Taylor kicked at a clump of grass absent-mindedly.

"So you think it might be a serial killer?"

"That or a killer cult. We've had problems with this region before."

I must have looked blank.

"I'm surprised you didn't hear about it. In 1996, a vampire cult killed a family down in Tennessee, some scientist. They were based out of Pikeville. We also had killings in Florida traced back to a vampire cult in Murray, Kentucky the same year. There were rumors the two cults were connected, but that was never proved. A few years ago, we had another string of killings across Kentucky that seemed ritualistic."

"I see." I thought of Victor and Lucy's little blood cult in Northern

Kentucky. The connection was tenuous, but then, there was Agent Henderson's referral. Lucy had been from somewhere over here in Eastern Kentucky. I wished I knew where, exactly. I sighed.

"We're having the local PD round up all the cultists they know about in the area for questioning. It's a little crude, but maybe we'll get somebody who'll crack and tell us who did this."

"I guess I should have a look at the body," I said.

"Right." Taylor reached into her jacket and pulled out some papers. "These set you up as a civilian attaché to the FBI. It was easy, since you were already in our system. You're armed?"

"Yes," I said. No sense in lying. "9mm semi-auto, silver hollow-points."

"Well, if we have any run-ins with werewolves, you'll be set."

"I find they make surprisingly large holes in most things they hit."

"I don't doubt it."

Agent Taylor led me along a path to the overlook. I wasn't sure where I stood with her. She seemed friendly on one level and hostile on another.

I didn't get it.

CHAPTER NINETEEN

I mulled it over until I got to the body.

Suddenly I could see why everyone was so edgy. The body was that of a young woman – girl, really. She had been split open and pinned down like a butterfly, or a frog in a biology class. For a wound such as that, there wasn't much blood. Her face was contorted in a look of agony and terror. She hadn't died easily.

"Gloves," I said. One of the officers standing nearby handed me a pair of purple rubber gloves, and I squatted down for a closer look.

"What do you think?" Taylor asked.

I used my senses to scan the body, and sighed. This was going to be a difficult case, both because what I saw was frightening and because I wasn't sure what I was seeing. I could see a method, but I didn't understand it. The girl had died in terror, but I couldn't get much more from her. The people who did this to her had been masked.

"Ligature marks on the wrists and ankles. She was bound. From the bruising on the shoulders, she was probably bound to a table. You might check for splinters or fibers on her back. Chaffing around the mouth indicates she was gagged, at least some of the time. These marks..." I brushed the closest one with my fingertips and got a flash of something, but I couldn't quite make it out.

"These marks," I began again. "They were branded into her flesh."

"Any idea why?" asked Taylor.

I took a closer look. "They're zodiac signs," I said. "Look: Aries on the forehead, Gemini on the right bicep, Leo on the right hip, Cancer on the left breast, Scorpio... Scorpio on the groin. Sagittarius on the right thigh, Capricorn on the left knee, Aquarius on the right shin, Pisces on the left foot. Hmm." I looked around the body.

"What?"

"We're missing some of the signs," I said.

"Maybe on the back?" Taylor suggested.

"No, they should all be on the front. I..." I really didn't want to do what I was thinking of doing.

"What?" Taylor said again.

"Why was the body cut open?" I asked.

She shrugged. "Why do these nuts do *anything* the way they do?"

"No, this was done according to a ritual, a purpose. They wouldn't have skipped any of the signs." I sighed and reached toward the open chest.

"What are you doing?"

"Something I don't want to." I pulled open the chest and looked inside. I had to fight down my gag reflex. "There," I said, pointing. "Leo burned onto the heart, Virgo on the stomach, Libra on the large intestine. Where is Taurus?" I nudged cool flesh around. "Ah," I said, "here it is, burned into the back of the opened throat."

I sat back quickly and pulled my gloves off. I felt sick.

"Okay, so some nut-job kills this girl and burns all these into her." Taylor stood and shook her head. "How'd they kill her?"

She didn't understand. Not yet.

I stood up. I was a little lightheaded. "No," I said. "This took more than one person. Those marks were all burned into her at the same time, while she was still alive."

Taylor gave me an odd look. "How do you know that?"

"I can tell from the bruising around the burns, as well as from what I know of this kind of ritual magic. The cultists need the victim to be alive. She died from shock and damage to the heart, not from being cut open."

"She was *alive* during all that?"

"She was. Probably conscious, from the bruises on her wrists and ankles," I said. "She wasn't killed here."

"Yeah," said Taylor. "Not enough blood around here for that kind of wound." She shook her head. "So what kind of cult are we dealing with? Satanic?"

"I don't know yet. I only knew to look inside the body because some of the signs were missing. It could be anything right now. Those symbols have been used for thousands of years. It could be any kind of crazy cult. You might check to see if there's any DNA in... She might have been raped at some point."

"Sick bastards."

I nodded. "This looks like a binding of some kind. I don't think we're looking for Satanists."

"So..., what, then?"

"I'm not sure. I wouldn't mind sitting in on the interrogations of the suspects."

Taylor raised an eyebrow. "Interrogations? We call it *questioning*. What are you, ex-military?"

I gave her a humorless smile. "I'm not at liberty to say."

CHAPTER TWENTY

Special Agent Taylor and I drank bad coffee at the main Pikeville police station while we waited for the officers to bring in the suspects. It was a modern-looking facility, squat and sterile, with a certain uniform gloom about the place. The majority of local police problems were drug-related; domestic abuse, child abuse, and animal cruelty made up the rest of the arrests, according to the internet on my phone.

"I have to admit," Taylor began, "you're a big question mark in all of this. I read your basic profile earlier in the week. I tried to pull your full FBI file and was told I didn't have the clearance to even be asking for it. I don't like that. You want to tell me why your file would be classified?"

"Honestly? No." I took another sip of burnt coffee. "I *can* tell you that I didn't know it was classified until you said so."

"But it doesn't surprise you that you have an FBI file, or that it's classified."

"No," I said. "It doesn't surprise me."

Taylor sighed.

"My guess would be that it has to do with my case last month," I said, lying.

"What about it?"

"The fugitive was ex-CIA. I assume they classified my file because of that."

Taylor didn't look convinced.

A police sergeant worked his way over to us. "The first of the suspects have been processed, ladies. I can take you to the rooms."

We stood up and followed him.

The room we were led to reminded me of the many crime movies I'd seen. It held a table with a single, uncomfortable-looking metal chair on one side and standard office chairs on the other. One-way glass was set in one wall, where cameras would record the whole thing.

We sat and waited for the police to bring the first suspect in. I had a feeling this was going to be a long day. At least my chair was comfortable.

Two officers brought in a tall, young man who was protesting loudly. His hair was shaved into a Mohawk, and he had a lot of visible piercings and tattoos. I wrote him off immediately. He was too obvious. The police had grabbed him because he looked different.

The officers let go of him and walked around to stand behind us.

"I want a lawyer," the man said sulkily.

"Mr. ..." Taylor looked down at her sheet, although I sure she'd already memorized the scanty information there. "Mr. Vance. We'd just like to ask you a few questions. That's all. Please, sit down."

"Who the hell are you?" he asked, belligerent now.

She smiled. "Special Agent Taylor, Federal Bureau of Investigation. Sit!" Her voice lost its friendliness and took on a hard edge.

He sat.

"Mr. Vance. Were you or were you not part of a vampire cult in this area during the year of 1996?" Taylor asked.

"I didn't have nothing to do with them people that got killed down in Tennessee," said Vance.

"I didn't ask you that, Mr. Vance."

"Yes, but I was just there to roleplay. I never hurt anybody." His eyes darted around the room; he was nervous. "Besides, that was a long time ago. Hell, I hardly even remember it."

"Where were you last night?"

"What?" That had taken him by surprise.

"Last night, Mr. Vance."

"I was at work. I work at the Walmart, night stock."

Taylor sighed.

"Can I see your hands, Mr. Vance?" I had an idea.

"What?" He looked confused.

"Your hands, Mr. Vance. Hold them out," Taylor said sternly.

"Okay." He moved his hands slowly across the table. He probably thought we were setting him up.

I reached out and grabbed both his hands. I caught flashes of many disgusting things, but he hadn't killed anyone. I let him go.

He jerked his hands back. "What the hell was that?" he asked, holding his head.

Taylor turned to the officers. "Get him out of here."

As soon as they were out, she turned on me. "What the hell are you doing?"

"He wasn't involved," I said. My hands felt dirty.

"What? I'm just supposed to let your intuition guide me? Shit!" She stood up and paced.

"Look, Taylor," I said, "that guy was dirty, yeah. But he didn't have anything to do with the killing last night, or know anything about anyone doing it."

She looked at me oddly. "You got all that by touching his hands?"

"I can get a lot from body language," I lied. "Want proof? When you shook my hand this morning, you were thinking about your sister. She looks a lot like the girl who was killed."

Taylor stood rigid for a moment, then walked over and sat down. "Shit. I should have known you were for real when the damn Gestapo stuck their nose into this case. What are you, psychic or something?"

"Something." I grinned. *Gestapo* was a good way to refer to Agent Henderson, more accurate than she could know. "Look, if it makes you feel any better, I only met Agent Henderson last month. I was working for the Marshal Service on the case. Henderson did his best to impede the investigation. He almost got me killed. I was frankly surprised when

I was told he'd recommended me."

"You're a strange one, that's for sure." Taylor sighed. "Okay, I guess we should get on with this. Are you going to do your thing with each of the suspects?"

I nodded. "It works best if I can touch the target."

"Of course it does," she muttered.

It was a long day. By the end, I knew more about the seedy underside of Pike County than I had ever wanted to, but we didn't find anyone connected to the crime. I'm not sure Special Agent Taylor was convinced of their innocence, but she didn't have enough to hold anyone overnight, anyway.

CHAPTER TWENTY-ONE

The rain was starting again as I drove back to the hotel. I had a pile of manila folders with me, filled with information about the other two murders. One body had been found near Grundy, Virginia, and the other near Chattaroy, West Virginia. Pikeville was right between the two. Both of the other murder victims had also been young women. They'd been butchered and branded, more or less in the same fashion as the Pikeville victim. All of them had lived in Pike County.

Something didn't add up somewhere, though. I thought of the feeling I'd gotten in the area when I first arrived, and then in the middle of the night. It took many people to produce such a wave of emotion. Special Agent Taylor was convinced it was the work of a lone serial killer, but she was entertaining the notion of a Satanic cult. I knew it was no cult – not Satanic, anyway – but I couldn't prove it.

I wondered if there were other occult slayings that the police had missed the signs on or were covering up for some reason. Moreover, what purpose would it serve to brand the victims? Why torment them like that? If it was some kind of binding, where was the animating spirit? I was getting nowhere fast.

As I pulled into the hotel, I noticed the rental car was gone. Damn. That meant Lawrence and Jean had gone back to South Williamson. I'd been hoping for a relaxing dinner with friends. Maybe I'd order a pizza.

The little old lady at the front desk, busy reading some celebrity gossip rag, didn't even look up as I walked past. I took the elevator up to the third floor. The air smelled wrong as I stepped into the corridor: a faint odor of decay.

I shook my head and walked down the hall to my room. I fumbled my keycard in the lock the first time. I was feeling jittery. It was probably just the lack of food and too much bad coffee.

Nevertheless, I bolted the extra lock once I was in my room. Then I carefully went around and set up basic wards on the walls, window, and door. I didn't want any surprises tonight. The murder had me shaken.

I called and ordered a pizza, and then I took a quick shower. I felt much better after the hot water had had its way with me. I got out my notebook computer and made some notes about the killings. It didn't take very long; I didn't have much information to work with.

I sighed. Nothing is ever easy.

The pizza arrived early, and the two-liter of Coke was ice-cold, so I gave the delivery girl a generous tip. My brain felt like hamburger. I couldn't think about anything for a while. I just sat and ate.

I must have dozed off, because a few hours later, I awoke with a start. It was dark outside, and the wind was lashing against the window. I'd had some nightmare about eyes in the darkness, but when I checked my room, it was clear. It made me nervous, though.

I decided to call Mark and see how my cat was doing.

He answered on the first ring. "Hello, Michelle."

"Hello, Mark," I said, annoyed that I hadn't been able to surprise him. "How are you and Jen?"

"Fine. Samson is doing well, too, although he seems to be missing you terribly."

I grinned. I had trouble sleeping without my cat under my chin. "I've been delayed a bit," I said. "I've been recruited by the FBI to help with some occult-related murders in the area."

"Really? How interesting. Anything unusual?"

"Yes and no. Nothing that appears to be related to my other problems, but Agent Henderson referred me to the FBI."

"And how did good Mr. Henderson know you were in the area?" asked Mark.

I hadn't thought of that. "I'm not sure. Probably had me followed."

"Possibly." Mark could be so damn obscure sometimes.

Time to change the subject. "Do you mind taking care of Samson for a week or two, until I can get home?"

"It's no trouble at all. He is a very well-behaved feline."

Yeah, he really talks like that. "Great. Also, I'd like your opinion on something," I said.

"Something related to your case?"

"Yes."

"I thought so. I should start charging consulting fees. Go ahead."

Mark never changed. Never charged, either, for that matter. I think he likes mysteries. "The bodies they've been finding are all marked with the signs of the zodiac."

"Hmm. Marked, you say? Are they tattoos or brands?"

I got a sudden cold chill. "Brands," I said. "Some of them are inside the body cavity."

"Interesting." I heard him take a sip of something, probably Scotch. "That sounds like one of the bindings."

"Bindings? I thought it seemed familiar, but binding *what*?"

"Demons," he replied.

"You mean a ritual sacrifice to bind a demon to this plane?"

"No, I mean a ritual sacrifice to banish one inside the possessed victim."

"Oh. What system is this from? Is it Caballa?"

"No," Mark said irritably. "I'm not sure it has a system, per se. I just remember reading something about it having been done, maybe in sixteenth-century Scotland. I can't remember the specifics. I'll do a little research, though. It irritates me that I can't remember."

We talked of other things for a while after that. Mark promised to call me if he found or remembered anything else. In the meantime, I had a few more clues. Something was wrong with the whole thing, and it was driving me crazy.

My cell phone rang.

"Hello," I said.

"Hey, you."

"Michael!" Gods, it felt good to hear his voice.

"How are you doing?" he asked.

"Okay. I've got a new case."

"Already? You're working overtime."

"Yeah, it's for the FBI. Our friend in Homeland Security referred me to them."

He was silent for a moment. "Damn. Does this have something to do with last month?"

"Not that I know of, but I'm not ruling it out."

"Hmm. So what's the case?"

"Three occult-related murders in Eastern Kentucky, Virginia, and West Virginia. Same MO for each murder. The latest one was here in Pikeville."

"I see," said Michael. "Some bad people over that way. Lots of vampire cult activity."

"That's what Taylor said. I wondered if it could be related to Victor and Lucy."

"Taylor, huh? Someone I should be jealous of?"

"Special Agent Taylor of the FBI, and no, not unless you think I'm attracted to short, brunette women," I said.

"Oh," he said. "Are you?"

"Not particularly," I replied dryly.

"Then I have nothing to worry about. I assume you're staying safe."

"You know me. I've got wards up and my pistol under my pillow."

"Silvertips?"

"Of course," I said. Michael could be a bit overprotective. Not that I minded.

"Sounds like you have things under control. I wish I could say the same." He sounded really tired.

"Michael, what's wrong?"

"I've..." He hesitated for a moment. "I've had problems."

"With your fugitive?"

"No, not exactly. Problems with the locals, actually. There are a lot neo-Nazis up here. I had to put one of the animals down yesterday. I've had two attempts on my life since then."

"Damn, where are you? Are you safe?" I asked, suddenly worried. "Are you okay?"

"I'm fine. I got winged this morning, but nothing serious. I'm holed up in a police station right now. I've got the fugitive in custody. Something is bugging me, though."

"What?"

"I'm not sure they wanted to kill me."

"Were they trying to kidnap your fugitive?"

"Maybe."

"Michael, what aren't you telling me?"

"They may have been after me," he said.

"Why?"

"I don't know. One of them called me *der Metzger*."

"What does that mean?"

"Well, *der* just means *the*, basically. *Metzger* can be either a name or a title."

"What title?"

"*Butcher*."

We talked for about an hour, altogether. I missed Michael. He had to go to New York and then down to Washington, DC. He was hoping to be back by Christmas, though. After we disconnected, I lay back in bed and thought about everything we'd discussed. Our relationship was so strange. We never said *I love you* or anything like that. We hadn't even...

I stopped myself.

I needed to get some sleep.

I had to meet Special Agent Taylor for breakfast.

The windows rattled all through the night, long after the wind stopped blowing.

CHAPTER TWENTY-TWO

I got up early and carefully cleaned the lint and dirt from my suit. I dreaded having to go back home just to get clothes, but I'd probably have to. I hadn't brought work clothes with me, nor had I seen any places to buy suits.

On the other hand, I thought, *why do I care?*

I could probably get away with jeans at least some of the time. Maybe I could find some nice suits somewhere in town. Pikeville was the medical hub for Eastern Kentucky; surely there would be *some* place here to buy decent clothes. Until then, I had a couple of different shirts that looked nice enough with the one jacket I had with me.

I called Lawrence's room after I'd finished getting ready. I had some time to talk before breakfast with Taylor. Lawrence told me to come on over, so I did. Jean looked as if she'd been up most of the night crying, and Lawrence didn't look much better.

"Are you guys okay?" I asked.

"Yeah," Lawrence said. "Everything is okay. Mom just took things a little personally last night when Jean told her she was leaving."

"Ah." I sat on the edge of the desk.

Jean wiped her eyes. "You look nice," she said.

I smiled. "Thank you. I have to meet with the FBI again this morning over breakfast. What are you two going to do today?"

Lawrence shrugged.

"I don't know," said Jean. "We're not going back up there."

"Would you like to meet me for lunch? Then you could show me around Pikeville."

That got a small smile from Jean. "Is that okay with you, Lawrence?"

"It sounds good to me. I'd like to get out this room, but like you, I have no intention of going visiting again right now." He looked me over. "You do look spiffy, don't you?"

I rolled my eyes at him. *Spiffy, indeed!* I thought.

I looked at my watch. "I've got to be going. How does two o'clock sound for lunch?"

They both nodded.

"There's a Burger King across the parking lot. They have decent breakfast. Get some food in you, okay?"

"I'll go get us something," said Lawrence.

"See you later." I stood and left the room.

The smell was gone from the hall, but the elevator took forever to get to me. When I got into it, it smelled like cigarette smoke. Someone had smoked here despite the *No Smoking* sign, and I had to suffer for it.

The same little old woman was sitting at the desk. I stood and watched her for a moment to make sure she was real, but she was turning pages of her magazine, so I walked on out. Maybe she was the only person who worked here. I hoped she didn't have to clean the rooms, too.

The parking lot was full of cars. I guess many people were traveling through the area for the holiday. The just-visible Walmart parking lot was packed, as usual. I got in my Jeep and made it to the restaurant just in time. I didn't want to be late; it wouldn't look good.

Taylor walked over to me as I parked. She looked as if she hadn't gotten much sleep last night. I got out and shook her hand. She made small talk as we walked inside and found a table.

"So, Dr. Fredericks, did you have any insights last night into our problem?"

I cleared my throat. "Well, as I said, the branding may be part of a binding ritual." I paused as the waitress brought our drinks. "I have a friend looking up the specifics."

"A binding ritual?" Taylor took a long drink of her coffee. "Shit. Do you really believe in all this crap? I mean, empathy, I can sort of see, and telepathy and stuff, but demons? You probably believe in vampires, too."

I smiled. "I take it you're not religious."

"Me? Hell, no." She snorted and grinned. "I ask too many damn questions."

"I ask questions, too. That's why I believe in what I do. Not that I believe in vampires. Not real ones, anyway."

Taylor just shook her head.

"The important thing in all this isn't what you or I believe," I said. "The question is, what do the *cultists* believe? Someone killed those girls for a reason."

"Okay, enough. So what can you tell me about this case?"

"All right. The ritual, for those who believe in such things, is used to bind a demon inside a host it has already possessed. It's a rather extreme way to rid the world of a demon. Even a Catholic exorcism would be gentler. At least the host usually survives those."

"So let's assume that's what is being done. Why would a Satanic cult want to destroy a demon?"

"It doesn't really destroy it, just banish it. Nevertheless, I see what you mean. The answer is that they wouldn't. This is more likely the act of a rogue Christian sect. There are many odd little churches in this part of the country. Some of them would consider a girl possessed if she said she didn't want to marry the person they wanted her to, or wore makeup."

"Oh, hell." Taylor rubbed her eyes. "Shit. So now we have to worry about freaky Fundamentalists, too?"

"Don't we always?"

The waitress came and took our orders. I ordered light, since I would be eating again in a few hours with Lawrence and Jean.

"You don't have to eat like a bird," said Taylor. "The FBI is buying this morning."

I smiled. "I'm meeting some friends for lunch in a few hours. I don't want to be too full then to eat."

"The same friends who are looking up this ritual of yours?"

"No." I didn't elaborate.

We didn't get much settled over breakfast. The food was terrible; I was glad I'd only ordered a little bit. I walked Taylor back to her car talking.

"By the way, I was wondering about any other occult-related or strange deaths in the area. Do you think you could look into it?"

Taylor smiled and took a thick file folder out of her car. "I thought you might ask for this. I stopped and got it on the way over this morning."

"Thanks. This will help." I glanced through the folder. "There may be a connection to the recent murders that the local police have missed."

"I doubt it. Call me anytime, if you need to. I'll be in touch with you tomorrow at some point. I'll see you Monday morning at the police station, unless something else comes up."

"Right. Talk to you tomorrow." I walked back to my Jeep.

CHAPTER TWENTY-THREE

That damned *watched* feeling was back again. I looked around, but other than a few flitting shadows that might not have been substantial, I didn't see anything. I put the folder in the Jeep's console and drove back to the hotel. There were quite few little stores to the right, and some of them looked as if they could be specialty clothing stores. I might be in luck.

There were fewer cars in the lot at the hotel when I got back, and no one was behind the desk. I knocked on Lawrence's door when I got upstairs. Jean answered, dressed in jeans and a blouse. She looked a lot better than she had earlier; breakfast and a shower had done wonders for her.

"You're back early," she said.

"Special Agent Taylor and I didn't have as much to say to each other as we thought," I said. "Where's Lawrence?"

"He walked down the hall to get ice."

Lawrence came in then with a pail of ice. "Hey, Michelle." He placed the pail on the desk and shoved a couple of sodas into it. He looked better, too.

"Do you guys still want to go out running around?" I asked.

Jean and Lawrence both nodded. "I don't think we'll be ready to eat for a couple of hours, though," said Lawrence.

"No problem. I'll go change into blue jeans, and we can get on the road."

"See ya in a minute," he said.

I walked next door and quickly changed clothes. I noticed that the lack of regular meals for the past few days had started to have an effect: I'd trimmed down some. I grinned to myself as I finished getting dressed.

Jean and Lawrence came right out when I knocked on the door.

"Ready to go?" I asked.

Jean smiled shyly.

We walked down the hall together and took the elevator to the lobby. The little old lady still wasn't at the desk, but a man was waiting for her there. He looked impatient. We walked outside.

"Do you want to drive, or shall I?" I asked Jean.

"You can," she said, blushing.

We climbed into the Jeep. Lawrence sat in the back so Jean could sit up front. She still looked embarrassed. I guess she wasn't used to people asking her what she wanted. I pulled out of the parking lot and headed for the stores I'd seen earlier.

The clouds were low in the sky today, brushing the tops of the hills around us. *I've got to remember to think of them as mountains*, I thought. Once you've seen the mountains out West, the ones in the East seem like mere hills, mostly just because the foothills rise high against the mountains' flanks in the East.

We spent most of the afternoon shopping and hanging out. I got two suits and few blouses in nice colors. Lawrence and I even managed to talk Jean into getting some new clothes. We had a late lunch at a little Mexican restaurant that I swear was the best I've ever eaten at.

We drove around Pikeville after that, just looking around, although there wasn't a lot to see. It was starting to rain again by the time we returned to the hotel. A police car was parked by the door when we arrived, and two officers were looking around the lobby and into the area just off from it. They asked if we'd seen the woman from the desk.

"Not since early this morning," I said. "Is she missing?"

"We're not sure, ma'am." They looked concerned.

I thought about the odd smell upstairs, but I'd seen the woman alive after that. I turned to Jean and Lawrence. "Why don't you guys go on up? I'm going to help the police look for the missing woman."

They nodded and headed for the elevators.

"Officer?" I said. When the one turned back to me, I continued. "I'm here in town working with the FBI on the overlook case. Maybe I can help."

"I'd have to see some credentials, ma'am," he said apologetically.

I smiled and dug out my papers; I carried them everywhere anyway.

He and his partner glanced over the papers and handed them back. He looked a bit relieved. "We could certainly use the help. I know the lady that works here; she goes to my church. I hope she's okay. We're at a loss on where else to look."

I was starting to get a bad feeling again, a sense of foreboding. I walked around the desk and looked at the computer terminal, which displayed a room. The person whose room it was, was overdue for checkout, on the third floor. I felt butterflies in my stomach.

"Officers?" I called. "There's a room displayed on the monitor here. It's upstairs."

They came around and looked at the display.

The first officer shrugged. "Worth taking a look. We don't have any other leads."

We took the elevator up. Then we turned right, away from the elevator. I was thankful: our rooms were to the left. Down at the end of the hall, the smell was stronger.

"Do you smell that?" asked the younger officer.

The other just nodded. He looked grim, and knocked on the door. No one answered.

"Now what?"

They both looked at me.

"Shouldn't we try to get in?" I asked.

"I think we would need a warrant for that," said the one I had talked to earlier.

"I'm thinking it looks like probable cause. That smell…" It was the smell of death and decay.

"What do you want me to do, shoot the lock off?" he asked. I could tell he wanted to check out the room but didn't know what to do.

"I'll be back in a minute," I said.

I could feel their eyes on me as I trotted down the hall to the elevator.

I'd watched people at hotels make keycards many times. *How hard could it be?* I thought. It only took me a minute to figure it out, and I was on my way back upstairs.

The officers were still standing there, looking frustrated. I held up the key as I walked up.

"Where did you get that?" the older officer asked.

"The room was still up on the terminal. I just selected the *make key* option and swiped a blank card through the reader." I handed him the key.

The officers looked at each other and shrugged, then unlocked the door.

The smell was much stronger then. As the older officer pushed open the door, I heard him groan. I stepped closer and had to look away.

We'd found the old lady, and a lot more.

CHAPTER TWENTY-FOUR

Back out in the hall, the younger officer had gotten sick.

I felt the same way myself, and I've seen a lot of this stuff. The air was clearer in the hall, even with the smell of vomit. After a moment, the older officer regained his composure.

"John," he said. "Johnny!"

The younger man looked up.

"Go downstairs and call this in. We're going to need a forensics team out here. We also need more officers. We're going to have to question everyone in this hotel."

The young officer nodded and ran down the hall to the elevator. Now that he knew what to do, he was able to regain his composure.

"You said you're working for the FBI?" the older officer said to me.

"Yes. I'm Dr. Michelle Fredericks. I'm working with Special Agent Taylor."

"Officer Jenkins," he said, offering his hand. "You might want to call your Special Agent Taylor. I wouldn't mind handing this over to someone else, not at all." He shook his head.

I got out my cell phone. *So much for a peaceful weekend*, I thought. Within the hour, the hotel was a zoo.

The halls were packed with police officers: city, county, and state. I found a few minutes to talk to Lawrence and Jean before Special Agent

Taylor arrived. Jean was scared. Hell, I think I was, too. A killing like that, just down the hall from us, was a little too close.

Taylor and I worked our way up through the police to the room. The smell was overwhelming now. Dried blood covered every surface in the room. The little old lady was just inside the door. It looked as if she had died of a coronary. Her face was frozen in a look of horror.

The two other bodies in the room had been dead for at least three days. That made me feel a bit better; the murders had happened before I got to the hotel. I hated to think that someone might have been murdered right down the hall from me, and I didn't even notice it. The bodies seemed to be those of a woman and a man, but it was hard to tell. They'd been flayed alive. Their ages were indeterminable at the moment.

There were the stubs of candles all around the room, and a pentagram burned into the carpet. The walls and furniture bore deep, odd gouges. Strangely, there were no actual footprints in the blood. There were, however, some suggestive tracks.

"So what do you think?" asked Taylor.

"I think I should have brought some Vicks," I said.

Taylor frowned.

Right. To business. "The flaying and dismemberment are suggestive. The pentagram obviously indicates something occult was going on. Those are usually used to protect a summoner during a ritual."

"A summoner? Demons again?"

"Not necessarily. A protective circle is common for any practitioner."

"Didn't seem to do them much good," she said.

"Hmm. I'm not convinced yet that it's connected."

Taylor turned and stared at me for a moment.

I shrugged. All I had were gut feelings. "I think this was staged," I said finally.

"What do you mean?"

"Just a feeling," I said. "We'll need an autopsy to determine the cause of death."

"I think exsanguination would be the obvious cause," said Taylor, gesturing to the blood on everything.

"Maybe," I said. I stopped the forensic tech, who was starting to leave. "What do you think of the pattern of blood splatters on the wall?"

"Huh?" He looked around again, and then shrugged. "Looks like blood splashed on the walls." Then he turned and walked out.

"What about it?" asked Taylor. "Oh, wait." She looked around again. "It looks like blood *splashed* on the walls! Not arterial spray."

"Exactly. This is another body dump. These two must have been killed elsewhere and then left here for us to find."

"Shit."

"Their skin isn't in the room, either," I said.

"Let me go talk to the coroner." Taylor moved back out to the hall.

Why would someone go to so much trouble?

I took a closer look at the pentagram. I couldn't tell how it was burned into the carpet. It was burned all the way down to the poured concrete, yet the carpet to the sides was undamaged. Also, now that I was looking closer, the carpet on the inside of the pentagram was a different color. The hair on the back of my neck stood up. *Maybe something was supposed to have been summoned into the pentagram,* I thought.

I carefully felt along the edge of it. The carpet was crushed down along the front edge, near the door. Someone had crossed the boundary. What had they let out? What had been let in?

"What is it?" Taylor asked quietly.

She'd startled me. I met her eyes. I was scared. "Do you know who's been in this room?" I asked.

She scratched her head. "You and I, a few police officers, the forensics team, the coroner, and the photographer, maybe a few others. Why?" Taylor was beginning to look worried.

"I need to see them," I said. "Now." I stood up. A cold knot of dread coiled in my gut. I hoped I was wrong.

Something in my look must have scared Taylor. She didn't ask any more questions. She went out in the hall and began calling to everyone out there. She ordered everyone who'd been in the room to stand over to one side.

I checked the room once more, but nothing was lurking in it. Whatever had been in the circle, it was gone now. What I was afraid of was that it had gone into one of the people in front of me.

"Okay, Fredericks," said Taylor. "They're off to the side."

I walked out into the hall. I knew at once that someone was missing. "Is this everyone?" I asked.

Taylor shrugged. "As far as I know." She scowled at the collected people.

"Officer Jenkins," I called.

He stepped forward. "Yes, ma'am?"

"Do you know where your partner is?"

"John?" He looked around. "No, he should be here. He was, a minute ago. Been taking it kind of hard. Maybe he took off to the restroom."

I felt sick, too, with dread. "Did he go into the room after we left it?"

Officer Jenkins looked down and scuffed his feet. "Yeah, he wasn't morbid or anything, but he said he needed to see what was in there, after he... you know."

"Did he go in alone?" I asked.

"Yes. What's this about?"

I ignored him and turned to Taylor. "We need to find him. *Now.*"

Jenkins grabbed my arm. "He didn't do nothing wrong!"

I jerked my arm out of his grasp, surprising him. "No? He left a federal crime scene without leave, didn't he?" I didn't know if that was allowed or not, but I was betting Jenkins wouldn't know, either. "Maybe tampered with evidence?"

Jenkins just nodded.

CHAPTER TWENTY-FIVE

Taylor took control of the situation again.

"Okay, people, I want him found," she said loudly. "Now! Search the building. Chief?" She turned to a tall man who'd been standing back and watching. "If he's not in the building, I'll want a SWAT team assembled and ready to go after him."

"I'm sorry, ma'am, we don't have a SWAT team yet," he said apologetically. "The council has authorized me to form one but hasn't allocated funds yet."

"Shit. Get me out of this place," Taylor muttered. Then, "Okay, I want a team of experienced officers assembled in the parking lot in body armor in ten minutes."

She turned back to me. "What are we looking at here, Fredericks?"

"That officer may be a danger to himself and others right now. He may not be thinking clearly. He could act on suppressed impulses that he normally wouldn't: envy, greed, lust, rage, anything. We need to find him."

Taylor's eyes narrowed. "Why do you think that?"

"He crossed the edge of the pentagram in there. I think he let something out."

"So... *what?* You think he's possessed or something? Give me a break. I'll play this one out for you, Fredericks, but if you make me look like a fool on this, you're done. Do you understand me?" She stared into my eyes.

I met her glare, unflinching. "If you don't believe me, why the armed response?"

"I'd like to ask this guy why he fled my crime scene. That's suspicious. I also want to see if you're full of shit or not."

"It would be better for everyone if I were full of shit, but you know I'm not. We need to find him *now*. Before he does something terrible."

"Let's go." She turned and headed for the elevator.

"Officer Jenkins." He jerked around to stare at me. "I'd like you to come along."

He nodded and followed me over to Taylor.

We got onto the elevator together.

"Why ask me along?" he asked.

I met his eyes. "I trust you to do the right thing when you have to. I don't know these other men who are going. He was your partner. You should be with us, just in case." I was going on intuition. "Does he have a family?"

Jenkins nodded and stared ahead at the doors. "Yeah. Been having trouble with his wife. New kid in the house."

"Does he resent them?" I asked.

Jenkins sighed. "He's a good man, but young. Yeah, he bitches about them sometimes."

"We need to get there."

Taylor was looking at me curiously. She stopped me when we reached the doors to the outside and waited till were alone. "Who the hell *are* you?" she asked.

"Just who I said I am. Why?"

"The only person I ever met that kept me guessing as much as you was an ex-CIA officer I met in boot camp," she said. She shook her head. "There is more to you than you've told me, Fredericks."

I just nodded.

There were seven officers standing outside in the rain. Jenkins got his body armor from the trunk of his squad car and put it on. No one helped him. *Friendly department*, I thought. Maybe they'd already decided his partner was guilty of what they'd seen in the hotel.

Taylor motioned for me to follow her. She popped the trunk to her car. "Here." She handed me a set of level-three body armor.

I took it and laid it on the edge of the open trunk. Then I took off my coat and shoulder holster and got into the body armor. I hadn't been in ballistic armor as an adult, but my fingers remembered how all the straps worked. Then I slipped my adjusted shoulder holster back over the whole thing.

I looked up to see Taylor's eyes on me; I'd gotten dressed quickly. I gave her a smirk and walked over to my Jeep. I took the Glock 9mm out of the glove box and put it in my jacket pocket.

Back at Taylor's car, I got out my cell phone and called Lawrence. I briefly informed him that I was going out for a bit with the police, and that he and Jean needed to stay in their rooms with their doors locked and not leave for any reason.

Taylor just shook her head and gestured for me to get into the car. Then she walked over and talked to the assembled officers. She came back and got into the car, wiping the rain from her face.

"At least he lives close," she said. "Keyser Heights, just down the road." She turned on the car and followed the cruisers as they pulled out of the hotel and made for the main road. "You and I are going to have a little heart-to-heart after this, understood?"

I just nodded.

The sense of urgency was getting stronger.

I was afraid we were already too late.

CHAPTER TWENTY-SIX

Keyser Heights was only a couple of miles away. I'd passed it earlier, coming back from town. It was directly across from an old, decaying footbridge over the river that gave me cold chills when I saw it. Something bad had happened there.

We turned right at the top of the hill. Officer John's house was the second on the left.

When I saw the dead dog in the yard, I knew we were too late.

All the lights were on in the house, but the blinds were down. We wouldn't be able to see anything inside unless we got close. While Taylor organized the officers for the raid, I checked the dog. Its neck had been broken. I reached down and unhooked its chain. It must have known that something was wrong with its master and broken its own neck trying to stop him.

Taylor had Officer Jenkins going to the door, with the two of us right behind. Two officers would be behind us, and the other four would go in the back door. She checked to make sure everything was in order and then nodded to Jenkins.

I drew my Glock and held it down to the side.

Jenkins knocked on the door and called out to John. "Come on, Johnny!" he shouted. "Open up! It's me, Tom!"

We stood blinking in the rain. One of the officers appeared around the side of the house and shook his head. The door must be locked. Taylor gestured for him to go back and wait.

Then the door opened.

John's face twisted into a sneer as he saw us. He was covered with blood and still in uniform. I started to call a warning, and then Jenkins let out a coughing cry and crumpled to the porch. John slammed the door shut.

"Shit!" cried Taylor. A butcher knife stood out of Jenkins' chest. "Get that bastard!"

She kicked open the door to the house, and we charged in.

Like the hotel room, blood dripped from the walls. A young woman lay on the floor with her throat ravaged. Her throat hadn't been slit; it had been shredded. A few feeble squirts still pulsed from the ripped arteries. She was alive, but not for long. I heard a gunshot, and the lamp next to me exploded. John had his pistol out, and he was taking aim.

Everything happened at once.

John fired again, and the officers behind me came in shooting. I dove to the side, knocking Taylor off her feet. A bullet hit the wall where her head had been. I rolled to my knees and brought the gun up. I looked around to find John. He was yelling something and shooting at the other officers. One was down in the doorway. John had been hit at least six times in the chest. It didn't seem to be slowing him, even though I could see gouts of blood pump from the wounds.

The dark, malignant shape of the thing riding him was becoming visible. I took careful aim and shot John twice in the head. He stumbled forward, his mouth working, and then fell to the carpet, twitching.

No matter how resistant to pain, you can't animate a body with no brain.

It was then that the other officers burst in from the back of the house. I wondered what had kept them. They should have come in at the same time we had.

I helped Taylor to her feet.

An officer was already on the radio, calling for an ambulance. Jenkins was dead, his glazed eyes staring out over the hills. The knife had gone right through his bulletproof vest, between the ceramic plates. The officer who'd been shot was okay; he'd taken a round in the leg and three in his chest, but his body armor had protected him from the chest shots.

"Don't touch him!" I said suddenly.

Two officers had been about to check John's body. I walked over and tried to sense the entity that had been there when we arrived, but it was gone. I sighed. I'd hoped it wasn't the kind that could jump bodies. Everyone here seemed clean of it, at least.

An entity like that – a demon, if you will – can only influence. It doesn't take control, like in the movies, but it can suggest things, whisper into your mind. It can push people to do things they wouldn't normally do. Kind of like being drunk, actually: your inhibitions are lowered. In this case, they were lowered enough to let the man kill his family.

Now, I want to point out that I've never met someone who was actually possessed. I understand that to be a little different, and more terrifying. I think the person being ridden would have to accept the demon willingly into their mind. Not that I understand why anyone would do that.

Taylor and I checked out the rest of the house together. John had had enough time to kill his entire family before we got here. He'd stabbed and sliced them to death.

"I can't believe it," said one of the officers.

I turned and looked at him.

He shook his head. "John was a good father. What made him do this? Even the baby..." He trailed off, stricken.

I felt the same way.

We were in that house for hours. It was a nightmare. No one understood how a good cop could just snap and kill his entire family. I met Taylor's eyes and saw worry there. I think she was starting to believe me.

I hoped so.

I was going to need an ally.

I knew this was just the beginning.

CHAPTER TWENTY-SEVEN

Taylor drove me back to the hotel. All the police cars were gone. So were most of the people who'd been staying at the hotel.

She pulled into the space next to my Jeep and parked. "Okay," she said, "let's talk."

I felt vulnerable sitting outside in the dark. "Would you like to come inside? This might take a while, and it could get cramped out here."

Taylor sighed. "All right, let's go. No funny business."

I led her up to my room. A scared-looking man was sitting at the front desk, and we had to reassure him before getting on the elevator. The hallway upstairs smelled of smoke, decay, and some horrible, cheap air freshener. I stopped by Lawrence and Jean's rooms and let them know I was okay. I told them I'd talk to them later.

Once in my room, I stripped off the body armor. That stuff got heavy.

"Okay," I said, sitting down on the bed with a sigh, "what do you want to know?"

Taylor had taken off her armor, too. She hung it over the back of the desk chair and then sat against it. "We'll start with the basics," she said. "Who are you?"

I resisted the impulse to tell her, *I'm Batman*; I didn't think she would find it very funny. "I am just who I said I am. My name is

Rhiannon Michelle Fredericks; I work for the CRI out of Dayton, Ohio, as a freelance consultant. I have a PhD in criminal anthropology. I specialize in occult crime."

"Bullshit," said Taylor. "You're CIA or something."

"Then it's *or something*," I replied. "I don't work for the CIA, and, as far as I know, I never have."

She gave me an odd look at that. "As far as you know?"

I shrugged. I really didn't want to get into the subject of my past; it wasn't safe for either of us. Henderson was still playing games, trying to see if I would reveal anything.

"Are you ex-military?" she asked.

I shook my head. "No. Not that I know of."

She stood up and paced. "Damn it, just tell me what's going on!"

"Have you ever heard of black projects?"

Taylor stopped pacing and looked at me. "I assume you're talking about secret, off-the-books government projects. You're saying you're part of something like that?"

"I'm not saying that. I'm saying that whatever made me the way I am, it's something you really don't want to know about."

She sat back down and looked thoughtful.

"When?" she said. "Hypothetically."

"When I was a child, a teen." I didn't know how much was safe to say.

"Some branch of MK-Ultra or something?" Taylor asked, surprising me.

"I don't know. Maybe. Maybe not." I shrugged. "All I can say is, most of the things I do that make you question me, I learned there. I really *can't* talk about it. You'd be at risk."

She nodded. "Hell, I almost wish you'd told me you were CIA."

I just nodded.

"Let me guess," she said with a grin. "If you tell me, you'll have to kill me, right?"

I smiled sadly. "Actually, it's not me you'd have to worry about. However, you would almost certainly end up dead. I'm sure they'd make it look like an accident."

"Right. So... do you go by *Michelle* or *Rhiannon*?" said Taylor, wisely changing the subject.

"Michelle."

"I never got a chance to thank you, Michelle."

"Thank me for what, Agent Taylor?"

"Call me Jessica," she said then, holding out her hand. "I know I told you not to shoot anyone, but I feel like I need to thank you for saving my life earlier."

I shrugged and smiled. "Seemed like a good thing to do at the time."

She laughed. "Well, I'm glad. Feel free to do it anytime."

I stood, suddenly fidgety. "Can I get you anything?" I asked. "I can make some bad hotel coffee for you."

"Ugh. I think I've had enough bad coffee. Thanks, though."

I nodded and sat back down.

"What happened tonight, Michelle?"

"We got monkey-stomped by whoever is behind this. I fucked up."

She blinked a couple of times at my bluntness and then laughed. "Wasn't your fault."

"Seriously," I said. "We got caught by a rather simple trap. I let you down, and two good cops and an entire family paid the price for it."

She scowled. "I don't see how it was your fault. You didn't make that guy go nuts."

"Come on, Jessica. You and I both know what really happened. I could see the thing that was riding him."

She shuddered. "*Riding him?* Okay, assume you're right, and something..." She hesitated. "Possessed him." She bit off the word as if it tasted bad to her. "How, and what now?"

"I think it was a carefully laid trap. That pentacle was burned down with a blowtorch or something. They summoned something into it and left the bodies there to lure someone into breaking the circle."

"Why? I don't get it. It seems like too much work to get the results they did. Couldn't they have just killed a cop and his family if they wanted?"

"I don't think he was the specific target. They could have killed those people, but would it have had the same effect on morale that this did?" I sighed. "Look, I don't have all the answers. Last month, I had a private military company try to kill me by shooting out my tire on the expressway. Then a killer cult kidnapped me and prepared to ritually rape and murder me, before I escaped. Either of those groups could have put a bullet through my head at any time, but they didn't. Why? I don't know. I'm not crazy enough to understand it, I guess."

"Is that what happened last month? Is that what got the attention of Henderson? Damn."

"That was part of it, maybe not even the worst. It's too much to go into right now, and too close to that other subject."

Taylor blew out a blast of air. "Okay. So... about this thing tonight. Was it a demon?"

"Yes, *demon* is as good a word as any. I'm not sure what kind yet, or if it even matters. I usually use the term *entity* when referring to such things. Leaves out the religious connotations."

"Are there many kinds of these... entities?"

"Many. I don't claim to be an expert on them. I don't know if there *are* any experts on such things anymore – outside the Catholic Church, anyway."

"So do we need a priest or something?" asked Taylor.

"No. I can take care of things, if comes to that."

She raised an eyebrow.

"Just what did you think I do for the CRI, anyway?"

"I just figured you, you know, consulted." She shrugged. "You're an occult crime specialist, like you said."

"Oh, I do that most of the time. I also do things for them that are more complex. I sometimes banish spirits and sometimes perform exorcisms."

"This conversation just got really weird."

"*Just?*" I laughed.

"Okay, another point to you. What do you think we need to do now?"

That sobered me up again. "I wish I knew. We need to figure this bitch out so we can cut down on the collateral damage. I hate seeing innocent civilians caught in the crossfire."

She was looking at me weirdly again. "You know, Michelle, most of the time you come across as a normal, highly educated woman. Then, sometimes, you slip into this quasi-militaristic personality. It's creepy. Do I need to worry about *you* being possessed?" I could tell that she was only half joking.

"Sorry," I said. "I had a lot of suppressed memories, from before. When I get tired, I sort of slip into that mindset."

She stood up. "I guess that's my cue to leave. I'd like to go over this some more with you in the morning. I want to know more about what we're dealing with." She yawned suddenly. "Damn, it's been a long day. I need to get some sleep, too."

"Okay, I'll see you in the morning. Do you need help carrying all this down?" I asked, patting the Kevlar vest.

"I'll leave that with you. I have a feeling you might need it again before this is over. I can manage this one myself."

After she left, I called Lawrence. He told me Jean had gone to bed. We talked for a few minutes, but I was so tired that I kept nodding off. We agreed to talk more tomorrow, and I rolled over and fell asleep.

Sometime later in the night, I awoke to sound of the windows rattling again. It was an ominous sound. I got up and changed into flannel pajamas and a t-shirt. It took me awhile to fall back asleep.

I kept seeing that maniacal grin on John's face, just before I shot him.

CHAPTER TWENTY-EIGHT

I woke to the sound of banging on my door.

I walked over and answered it, my heart pounding. Two police officers stood in the hall. I blinked blearily at them.

"Can I help you, officers?" I wondered if something had happened to Taylor.

"Michelle Fredericks?" one officer asked.

"Yes," I said hesitantly. "I'm Dr. Fredericks." Something was wrong here. They had their hands on their guns. I scanned them, but I didn't sense anything but irritation and anger, both directed at me.

"You're wanted for questioning downtown. Come with us, please."

I sighed. I should have known. I'd have to call Taylor. "Just a moment."

I started to shut the door, but he shoved it open. "Please come with us now, ma'am."

I wasn't about to change clothes with these goons watching me.

"I'm stepping into the bathroom to change. I suggest you get out of my way."

I dressed quickly, came out, and grabbed my jacket. I felt naked without my pistol, but I knew they would shoot me if I got close to it. They seemed extremely edgy.

The officers frisked me in the hall and then handcuffed me. They took my cell phone and purse, and marched me down to their waiting squad car. I was starting to feel a bit scared. They seemed far too serious. Bad things could happen to a single woman in a small town.

The trip to the station was quick and uneventful. The officers were angry for some reason, but they were behaving professionally. The atmosphere in the police station was one of sullen despair.

I saw open hostility on most of the faces of the officers working there; I didn't recognize any of them from the previous night. The two arresting officers led me to the interrogation room Taylor and I had used the other day. The chair was every bit as uncomfortable as I'd thought it would be.

They made wait for an hour, and then two officers came in, both in suits. They uncuffed me and sat in the chairs across the table. One plainclothes officer had a scar on his cheek; otherwise, they were pretty much the same in build and appearance.

They just sat there and watched me.

"What's this all about?" I asked.

"We'll ask the questions," the one with the scar answered. The other just glared.

Shit. They'd decided to play hard-nosed.

"What was your relationship with John May?" asked Scar Face.

"My *what*? Who is John May?"

"Officer John May was shot and killed in his home last night. The officer present said you shot him. We want to know why."

"Uh... Because he was shooting at *us*?"

The quiet officer stood up and walked behind me, where I couldn't see him. It made me uncomfortable, as I'm sure it was supposed to. I knew it would be a mistake to turn and look at him. I concentrated on the one in front of me.

"What was the deal? Were you having an affair with him?"

"Was I *what*?" That, too, caught me off-guard.

"Were you *fucking* him? Is that why he killed his family? Did you induct him into some kind of cult or something?"

"This is ridiculous. I'd never even met him before yesterday." I stood up.

"Sit down. We aren't through with you."

"The *fuck* you aren't!" I said. "I'm out of here now. If you know what's good for you, you'll get out of my way." I heard the door open behind me.

"Sit down, bitch!" Pain shot through my back. The bastard behind me had sucker-punched me in the right kidney. I felt my knees go weak. He was a big man, and he'd hit me *hard*. My temper flared then, and I spun, catching him in the jaw with a surprise right hook. It dropped him.

"What the *hell* is going on in here?" shouted Taylor from the doorway.

I felt a wave of relief go through me. I hadn't been sure where this was going. I hadn't expected them to hit me. It was an escalation out of proportion with what I knew about the police.

"Well? I'm waiting?" Taylor walked into the room with police chief. I'm sure he would deny any knowledge of what was happening, but I'd caught a glimpse of him as I was brought in.

The officer on the other side of the table stood at attention. "Uh, ma'am, we were questioning a suspect in the recent occult crimes."

"First of all, this is my *fucking* case, not the *fucking* Pikeville Police Department's. Any more questioning will be done only on *my* direction, or every damn one of you will be brought up on obstruction of justice."

She paused for quick breath, and the chief started to speak.

"Shut the *fuck* up," Taylor said coldly. "This woman is, in effect, a federal agent at the moment. Striking a federal agent carries some stiff penalties. Any of you yokels want to take a swing at me?"

No one said anything.

"Are you okay, Fredericks?" she asked me quietly.

I nodded. "I'll be fine. I'd like my cell phone and purse back, if we're leaving."

The man on the floor was still out cold.

CHAPTER TWENTY-NINE

My hotel room was getting crowded.

When I got back, Jean and Lawrence had insisted on coming in and helping me. Then they left to get breakfast. I hoped they'd bring me some.

Taylor was sitting at the desk. Her face showed a complex series of emotions that I couldn't quite pin down. Overall, I would say said she was angry and worried, but there were other feeling there that I couldn't figure out. "These locals are *fucking* nuts. Excuse my French. Do you want to file charges for what happened?"

"No, they're just scared. I was a convenient target for them to lash out at."

"Yeah, but..." She gestured at my back.

I settled against the piled pillows. I'd picked up a heating pad at Wal-Mart. My back still hurt from where I'd been punched; I was going to have one hell of a bruise.

I grimaced. "I'm not happy about what happened, but I understand it. I'm an outsider. I have knowledge of the occult. That scares them. Around here, anyone here with that kind of knowledge is probably a witch or a Satanist."

Something clicked together inside my head as I said that.

Taylor started to laugh and then stopped when she saw the look on my face. "What?" she asked.

"I'm not sure. I think I just found a piece of the puzzle, but I have to figure out what it is and where it goes."

"You know," she said, "sometimes you're a little scary."

I smiled. "You manage to work up a high intimidation factor, yourself."

She shook her head.

"By the way," I asked, "how did you know what had happened to me?"

"You're going to laugh..." She sighed. "I had a strong *feeling* that I needed to talk to you. I rushed over, but you were gone. The girl who was in here, Jean – she said she saw the police arrest you." She shrugged.

I nodded.

"That was some right hook," Taylor said suddenly.

"I probably shouldn't have hit him, but he caught me off guard with that kidney punch."

"You're a lot stronger than you look. I saw it. That hit took him off his feet."

I met her eyes. "Yes, I'm much stronger than I look."

She sighed and looked away.

The arrival of breakfast saved me from having to say anything else. Jean and Lawrence had brought egg-and-bacon croissants back from Burger King. We sat and ate in silence. I could tell they were all worried for me. I felt a sudden surge of affection for them, and that I'd begun a strong, solid friendship with Jessica.

I grinned. "You guys need to lighten up. I've been hurt a hell of a lot worse than this and bounced back."

Lawrence grinned. "Yeah, you looked like you'd been hit by a truck last month."

"I *was* hit by a truck last month."

"I meant the second time."

I laughed.

"Truck?" Taylor asked.

Lawrence shook his head. "This crazy woman gets her tire shot out on the expressway and then manages to drive her old Jeep under a tractor-trailer."

"I didn't do it purposely!" I shrugged. "They had to cut me out of the wreckage."

"And you were up running around the next day," said Lawrence.

"I wasn't *running* anywhere. I'd broken both legs. I think it was almost a week before I took the casts off. You weren't even there!"

"I know, but Mark told me about it after the van thing. He said you couldn't wait to get out of the hospital."

"True enough."

"Sounds like you live an *interesting* life," said Taylor.

"Yeah," I replied, "just like the Chinese curse."

She laughed.

"I'm okay, really. I'm just tired and sore."

We talked for a little while about other things, but my mind was spinning. I was starting to put the disparate parts of this case together. I was tired and sore, but not hurt all that badly. I'm tough, and I heal quickly. After a while, I think they realized I wanted to some time to think. They all left me to get some rest. Taylor and I agreed that we would meet for dinner. Jean and Lawrence were going back to their parents' home for the rest of the day. They promised to stay safe, and then they left me to sit and brood.

When I'd thought of the local police as superstitious about witches and Satanists, my brain had been jolted. The packet of information on other occult crimes was still in the console of my Jeep, and I didn't feel like going after it, but I had my laptop in the room. I logged onto the local Wi-Fi to surf the internet and started researching.

I couldn't find any information on witch trials in Kentucky, but I still felt I was on the right track. I knew there must have been some. The whole world had been witch crazy around the time Kentucky was settled. Surely, some of the witches had fled to the frontier.

I got up and stretched. I was sore, but not as badly as I'd pretended to be while Taylor was in the room. I didn't want her asking any more questions about me. I still remembered Henderson's warning from that day on the bridge. The less Taylor knew, the safer she would be.

I spent a couple of hours doing tai chi. It felt good to stretch and push my body; I had been neglecting myself recently. Afterward, I felt calm and pain-free. I took a long, hot shower and tried to figure out what to do next.

Unfortunately, I couldn't think of much. I was going to have to wait for the mysterious cultists to make another move. I decided to catch a nap while I could.

Who knew what the night would bring?

CHAPTER THIRTY

My cell phone woke me up later in the afternoon.

I was instantly alert. "Hello," I said.

"Hello, Michelle."

"Hey, Mark. How are you doing?"

"I'm fine, thank you. Yourself?" He was a creature of habit and would never get to the point without basic civilities.

I sighed. "Hanging in there. It's been a rough weekend. Do you have anything for me?" I asked.

"I do, indeed. It is a demonic binding ritual. It was performed in Scotland and Ireland occasionally during the seventeen hundreds. It is a Qlippothic ritual used to bind an entity to the flesh so that it dies with the host. The symbols are those of the Cabbalistic gates."

"The Cabbalistic gates use standard astrological symbols?" I asked. That didn't sound right.

"Of course not. Why would you think that? They use the gate seals."

"Okay, so how does this help me?"

"What do you mean?" he asked.

"Mark, the symbols I saw were those of the zodiac, not magical seals. They were burned pretty clearly. I know the zodiac."

"Then the ritual was done incorrectly."

"Could you be wrong about the ritual?"

"I suppose that is always a possibility," he said stiffly. He could be so touchy when questioned about one of his specialties. I wondered briefly how the engineers he worked with could stand it.

"I'm not saying you're wrong, I'm just saying that this must be a different variant of the ritual. I checked the bodies myself. Trust me, these people seem to know what they're doing." I told him about what had happened yesterday and this morning.

"Interesting. It was careless of you not to check the pentagram for an entity."

I gritted my teeth and waited for him to continue.

"Still," he said, "I'm not sure I would have thought of it under the circumstances, either. People are far too complacent in life nowadays."

"So what are these *cloppy* things?" I asked. I was trying to get a reaction out of him. I knew that the Qlippothic realms were the flip side of the Cabbalistic tree of life; they were synonymous with the Bardo realms of Hindu magic practice.

He sighed. "*Qlippothic*, and I'd be careful, Michelle. Kentucky has a bad reputation for a reason."

"What do you mean?" I asked.

"You really don't want to know. Just trust me on this one."

Fair enough. "Could the ritual be performed with alternate symbols?"

"You know as well as I do, Michelle, that it is the *intent*, the will, which drives magic. If whoever it was believed that the ritual would work with the symbols of the zodiac, then it probably would."

"Probably?"

"The abilities of the practitioner must always be considered. The purpose of ritual is to draw on the established thought forms of thousands of years of magical practice. It would be hard but not impossible to create your own meanings for things."

I nodded to myself. "So we're no closer to knowing why the ritual was performed, right?"

"That is correct. I still believe that it is a binding."

"Okay, so what does this have to do with the Qlippoth?" I asked.

The word was uncomfortable on my tongue.

"The Qlippothic realms are the flip side of Cabbalistic reality for us," said Mark, warming to the subject. "You may say it represents the universal dualism of nature."

"Okay," I said. "So it's kind of like Satanism for Christianity, then?"

"Don't be obtuse. There is absolutely no similarity. I'm not talking about some borrowed myth. I'm talking about basic reality. Religion has no place in it."

Mark is Jewish. I think he may have taken my comment more personally than I meant it. "I'm just trying to understand, Mark. The Qlippoth is evil? Help me here."

He sighed. "Evil is a moral assignment. Think of it more as the forces of chaos and entropy. A little of either can be a good and necessary thing. Too much..." He trailed off.

"I see your point." *I think.* "You think forces of this nature are moving here, now?" I was a little uncomfortable with that idea.

"I think you should consider it a possibility."

I sighed. Mark never liked to give direct answers. "I will. Thank you."

We talked of other things after that. I really did need to get some rest at some point; it had been a long weekend. I ended the phone call and lay back.

I awoke suddenly that evening.

The clock said it was just after seven PM. I tried to figure out what had awakened me. I could hear the sound of a plane passing high overhead, but that wasn't what had awoken me. I got up and looked out the window. The clouds were low in the darkening sky. I suddenly felt claustrophobic. The room, the cliffs, the clouds: everything was pressing in on me.

I turned and almost ran to the light.

Once it was on, I felt foolish.

It was like a child's fear of the dark. Then I saw the deep areas of shadow where the light didn't reach, and was almost overwhelmed. What was wrong with me? Where was this feeling coming from?

I dug through my purse and brought out all of my amulets, talismans, and charms. They didn't seem as if they'd be enough to push back the darkness. I started a basic tai chi warm-up. It seemed to clear my head. I could still feel the fear, but now I knew it wasn't mine.

I walked back to the window. I could feel the fear throbbing in the darkness, from all around me. Something was happening. Forces were moving. I had a sudden burst of insight in which I saw a map of the region overlaid with waves of light and darkness, doing battle.

Then it faded.

Something was going on. This went way beyond a few deaths. There were powerful forces at work this night. Now I just needed to figure out what they were trying to do.

CHAPTER THIRTY-ONE

A knock on the door startled me out of my reverie. I grabbed my pistol from under my pillow. I'd be damned if I was going to let the police get ahold of me again. I unlocked and jerked the door open in one motion.

"I can come back later," said Taylor, eyeing the gun.

"Shit. Sorry. Feeling a bit paranoid. Come on in." I held the door for her.

She came in and sat at her usual perch.

I tossed the pistol on the bed and sat down.

"Did you forget we were meeting for dinner?" she asked.

"Oh, hell. Sorry, I got a little distracted."

"Yeah, I can see that. What's up?"

"I'm not sure. I've had some odd dreams, and even stranger feelings since I woke."

"You really look out of it. Do you feel okay? Is this from being hit?"

"Hmm? No, I'd actually forgotten about that. That was this morning. No, something big is happening tonight. I can feel something happening out there, but I don't know what. I suspect we're going to have more bodies in the morning."

"Yeah, some of them might be police," Taylor said sourly.

"What?"

"They've got two cars watching the hotel."

"That makes sense."

She shook her head. "You are entirely too forgiving."

I shrugged. What did she want me to do? I was just a consultant, not actual FBI.

"Are you still up to dinner, or should we postpone that?"

"I'd love to go to dinner. I'll need to get ready, though."

"Go ahead. I'm in no hurry."

I grabbed some clothes and went into the bath. I looked like shit. I decided to take a quick shower. After I finished and got dressed, I came out to find Taylor looking through the channels on cable.

"I should get a room over here," she said. "The hotel I'm in really sucks."

"Why did you choose that one, then?"

"I didn't. The FBI picked it for me."

"Ah. Do you have any ideas for dinner?"

"I was hoping you could help out there. Any place but that Shoney's or a McDonald's is fine by me. A place to get a good salad would be great, but I may be asking for too much."

I laughed. "Is Special Agent Jessica Taylor dieting?" I asked.

"Always," she said with a sigh. "I have the kind of metabolism that makes me gain weight if I even smell a hamburger."

"Well, I'm not quite that bad, but I'm still trying to shed a few extra pounds from last month's hospital stays."

"You gained weight eating hospital food?" She looked mock-scared.

"No, but I ate everything in sight when I got out."

She laughed. "*That*, I can understand."

"Have you discovered the Mexican place over on the other side of Pikeville?"

"I can't say as I have. Is it any good?" She looked dubious.

"Quite good, actually. I ate there the other day." I picked up my coat and placed my pistol under it.

"Do you mind if I ask you a personal question?" Taylor said once we were on the elevator.

"I can't promise to answer it, but you have very little chance of offending me if you ask."

"What is the deal with you, Lawrence, and Jean?"

It took me a moment to see what she was asking. I blushed. "Friends," I said. "Nothing more. Really." We walked across the lobby. "Lawrence is an old friend from college. He's..." I wasn't sure what I should say. What the hell. "He's gay. Jean is his sister. She used to live in South Williamson. We came up for Thanksgiving. Their dad is dying of black lung." I shrugged. It was hard to explain.

"He's really gay?" she asked. "Figures."

Evidently, she'd found Lawrence attractive. It was the typical curse: all the good ones were taken or gay. Probably both.

We walked over to Taylor's car.

CHAPTER THIRTY-TWO

The restaurant was pleasantly crowded.

There were just enough people inside to make sure our conversation was lost in the background noise. Taylor just shook her head when I ordered my meal, roast beef tips in white cheddar sauce.

"Some diet," she said, ordering a taco salad.

"Getting beaten up by the police is hungry work. Besides," I said, "I worked out for two hours this afternoon."

"Your hotel has a workout room? Fuck. I'm definitely changing hotels."

"No," I said with a laugh, "I do tai chi."

She grimaced. "Ugh. I tried that once, but I never could keep track of all those moves and positions. The judo I learned in basic was hard enough for me."

I laughed. "It's not that hard, once you teach your body what it needs to know. Then you can just relax and let the workout happen. It's very satisfying. I always feel cleaner and full of energy afterward."

"If you say so," said Taylor. "Give me a treadmill any day."

"I hate treadmills."

"So... You look the way you do, and you don't really work out. Where do I sign up for that?"

"I don't think you'd enjoy what they did to me to make me this way. I know I didn't."

Taylor sighed. "This is some weird shit. Did your physical abilities come from that project, or did you always have them?"

"Yes," I said, and then laughed at her look. "I'd say it enhanced what I had naturally. I understand that all of us who survived are tougher and stronger than most people."

She raised an eyebrow. "Survived?"

I took a drink of soda; my mouth was suddenly dry. "A lot of the kids died or went nuts from what they did to us."

"I'm sorry, Michelle. I shouldn't pry."

"No, it's okay. I mean, I hate what was done, but I didn't even remember most of it until last month, you know? I find it hard to believe sometimes. I think talking about it helps some. I've not talked about it much with anyone."

Taylor nodded. "Understandably," she said. "Do you know anyone else who was in the project?"

"Well, Julia, the fugitive we were chasing: she was part of it," I said. "And Michael." I smiled as I said his name. I needed to talk to him soon.

"Was she the one you said ended up in the river?" When I nodded, Taylor went on. "Who shot her? You said it was a marshal? Who's Michael?"

"Michael is the deputy federal marshal who was assigned the case. Julia's brother Victor was also involved, both in the case and in the project. He had some sort of blood cult in Northern Kentucky. Lucy, a friend of Lawrence and me from college, was with Victor in the cult. She tried to kill me."

"Damn, sounds like you had a hell of a time."

"It got weird, that's for sure."

Our food arrived, and we ate in silence for a bit. I was watching Taylor to see how she was processing the information. She didn't seem to have any trouble with it.

"I was worried when you told me Henderson had referred me to you," I said.

She nodded. "Any idea why he did that?"

"I've thought about it. I'm still not sure. It could be that there's a connection of some kind with what happened, or it could just be that he knew I was for real and wanted to help. The man is strange."

"That's for sure," said Taylor.

"You've met him?"

"Yeah. He showed up at the crime scene for the second murder. Gave me your information, said you were *the real deal*, I think is how he put it. I shelved it, at first. But then the third murder happened, and we still had no clues." She shrugged.

"So here we are," I said. "We've got a lot of bodies and no idea who's killing them, why, or even how they're all connected."

Taylor just nodded.

We both declined when the waiter returned to ask if we wanted desert.

I snatched up the check when it came. "I'll get this one."

"Michelle, you don't have to do that."

"You got breakfast the other morning, so I've got this." I gave the waiter my credit card.

Taylor sighed and shook her head. "Do you make good money as a consultant?"

"I guess." I shrugged. "Depends on what you call *good money*, I suppose. I have enough to pay the bills and still buy what I want. I don't get paid like a CEO or anything. What about you?"

Taylor finished her drink. "I like what I do. The money is okay. I hate this Homeland Security crap, but what can you do?"

"I know. Just about everyone I talk to hates it."

The waiter brought back my card and receipt. I gave him a generous tip. The food had been great.

We went outside. The rain had stopped, and the air was colder. Thick fog blanketed the hills; it deadened sounds and made the night seem even darker than normal. I shuddered.

"What's wrong?" asked Taylor.

"I've had this sensation of fear and claustrophobia ever since I woke up earlier. I can't really explain it."

"Is that why you thought we would have more bodies in the morning?" She unlocked the car doors, and we got in.

I felt strangely better once in the car. "Partly," I said. "I can feel something stirring." I shrugged.

She started the car and headed back to the hotel.

"Be careful when you go back to your hotel," I said.

She glanced at me. "I'm always careful. I park right outside my room and have my hand on my gun. Supernatural horrors aside, I'm a decent-looking woman." She grinned. "Not every bad guy is a cultist or a demon."

"Still, be extra careful tonight. Really."

She glanced at me again. "Okay, I will. You have a bad feeling or something?"

"Nothing specific, or I would ask you not to go back at all. No, as I said, I can feel things moving. It's not a good night to be out. Trust your instincts, Jessica."

"I try to," she said with a sigh.

The rental car was back at the hotel. A police car was at the far end, parked.

"Remember what I said." I got out of the car.

"I will. You be careful, too."

"I will. Good night," I said as I shut the door.

She locked it as soon as it was closed and waited for me to get inside before pulling away.

I sighed and took the elevator up.

I still needed to check on Lawrence and Jean before getting some sleep.

CHAPTER THIRTY-THREE

I was finally able to get some sleep that night.

That was a good thing, since the phone rang early. I had just gotten out of the shower.

"Hello?" I said.

"You hit it on the head, Fredericks." It was Taylor.

"Shit." I sat on the edge of the bed. "Tell me."

"We've got two more bodies. These are in Majestic. It's a ways from here. The state police have the site secured until we get there. Want to ride over together?"

"Sure. Are you on your way over?"

"Yep. Have you had breakfast?"

"I'm not sure if I should."

"Hah! Your stomach is probably tougher than mine is. I'll be there in ten."

"Okay, I'd better get ready."

"Okay." She disconnected.

I had to rush. Luckily, I rarely wear much makeup, so I just had to get dressed and dry my hair. I decided my hair was a lost cause and pulled it back in a ponytail. I'd want it out of my face anyway. I wore a new, dark suit. It didn't fit as well as I would like, but it was all right; I wasn't trying for a fashion award.

There were people at the end of the hall, working on the room where the murders had occurred. They had the carpet rolled up and out in the hall. They'd probably have to replace everything in the room. *Maybe I should offer my services to clean out the psychic aura*, I thought as I waited for the elevator.

I chuckled at that as I took the elevator to the lobby.

A police officer stood in the lobby, eating a donut. I ignored him and walked outside just as Taylor pulled in next to my Jeep. I walked over to her car.

"Want me to drive?" I asked.

"Might not be a bad idea, at that. I'm not sure what the roads are like over there."

She pulled a briefcase out of the back seat and locked the doors.

I started the Jeep. Taylor got in a moment later.

I saw the police officer walk to his car as I was pulling out. I carefully suppressed the impulse to run him down.

"Do you know how to get there?" I asked.

"I printed off a map in my room before I left."

"You have a printer with you?"

"Yep, and a fax machine."

I laughed. "I can see that those would could come in handy."

"Go straight up here," she said.

"Toward Williamson?"

"Yes. We'll turn before then, but not for a while, unless you want breakfast first."

"Not really. I've never liked eating in the morning. I usually just have a Coke or a cup of hot tea."

"Sounds healthy," Taylor quipped.

I shrugged and concentrated on driving.

"This is a nice Jeep," she said suddenly.

"Thanks. I just got it last month."

"Your friend said you'd been hit by a truck?"

I nodded. "They had to cut me out of the wreckage. I broke both legs, an arm, and some ribs. I also had a scary time with some glass in the eyes."

"Ugh!" Taylor rubbed her eyes. "Makes my eyes hurt to think about it. You seem to have made a remarkable recovery."

"Yeah, I do that, but I didn't enjoy the experience."

We didn't say anything for a few miles. I was lost in thought. I wondered about Julia and if she was still alive. She'd been on my mind a lot recently.

"Turn right up here," said Taylor.

I slowed for the turn. I noticed a police cruiser hanging back, following.

"We have a friend," I said.

Taylor growled something under her breath.

"So what are we looking at up here, Taylor?"

"The two bodies?"

I nodded.

"I'm not sure. The call came in a couple of hours ago. The state police said they had a double homicide I might be interested in." She shrugged. "I don't know any details."

She told me to turn left.

The sun was clearing the mist out of the mountains, and it looked to be a pretty day. Under other circumstances, this would have been a very pleasant drive.

"Damn, this is way the hell out in BFE!" Taylor complained.

I laughed. "I think everything in this part of the state is out in the middle of nowhere."

"Yeah, at least till that new interstate comes through."

"New interstate? Are they still planning that? I thought they'd cancelled it or something."

"Did they? I don't know. I heard it was still on. You never know. The plan was for Interstate 66 to come across from Virginia, through the width of Kentucky, and all the way over to San Diego, California. It would usher in a new era of interstate drug trafficking," she added cynically.

"I think it might help some people escape from the poverty of this region, too. They'll get to see a bit of the outside world." I was thinking of Jean.

"If they want to leave," said Taylor. "I think a lot of people like the isolation."

"Not me. I grew up near Cincinnati," I said. I hoped Taylor would tell me a little about herself. Our conversations kept straying into uncomfortable subjects.

"Cincinnati is a nice city. A bit conservative, but so is the whole Midwest."

Taylor wasn't giving anything up.

"Turn up here. We should be getting near."

I turned down a narrow road. I decided pretty quickly that it must be the correct one. A state police officer was turning back traffic on the road. I slowed and pulled up next him, rolling down my window.

"Can I help you ladies? The road is closed ahead. You'll have to turn back." He had a frosting of gray at his temples and seemed very sure of himself.

Taylor held out her badge past me. "I'm a federal officer who has been called to the scene. Who's in charge here?"

He looked at the badge carefully. "Just a moment, ma'am." He walked a few steps away and talked into his radio for a moment. "Okay, you're cleared. Sergeant Reynolds is waiting up ahead, about two miles."

I pulled on past him, rolling up the window. It was a lot colder up here.

CHAPTER THIRTY-FOUR

I drove slowly for the two miles to the crime scene. Several police cars and a coroner's van were parked along the shoulder of the road. Another van farther down was probably a forensics team. I parked, and we got out, looking around.

"Special Agent Taylor?" An older police officer was walking toward us. "I'm Sergeant Reynolds. I was told to hold the scene as-is until you got here." He held out his hand.

"Pleased to meet you," Taylor said, shaking his hand. "This is Dr. Michelle Fredericks, a consultant assigned to the case."

"Ma'am." He shook my hand briefly. I noted that he didn't try to crush it, the way some men would have.

"What have we got, sergeant?" Taylor asked.

"Hmm. It might be easier to show you. Let you make your own opinions." He started leading us into the woods.

"Who found the bodies?" I asked.

"Two local hunters found them early this morning."

"Little late for deer season, isn't it?" asked Taylor.

"Bow-hunters," he said. "Their season runs through to January seventeenth. We've got a black powder week coming up in a few days."

"Do you hunt?" I asked. Something about how he talked about it didn't make me think so.

"No, ma'am, but we get a lot of people shot during hunting seasons. It takes a while to figure out if they're all accidents or not. Real pain, if you understand me. Many people in this region depend on hunting as a primary source of food. This is the most impoverished part of our state."

I nodded; that made sense.

"Any positive IDs on the victims?" Taylor asked.

"Not yet." Reynolds pursed his lips. "We'll need forensics for that."

"Ah." Taylor didn't say anything else.

"Here we are, just the other side of these trees." He looked as if he wanted to say something else, maybe to warn us. Then he shrugged and pushed through the trees.

Two police officers stood guard over the crime scene. They had their backs to the bodies and appeared a little pale and greenish. They were young, probably rookie cops getting the treatment. We pushed past them for a better look at what was going on.

My first impression was that there were more than two victims. Then I realized that I was looking at two bodies that had been skinned. The skins had been stuffed with straw and stood up like obscene scarecrows.

"Do your thing, Fredericks," said Taylor.

The sergeant looked at me oddly.

I checked around the crime for any mystical landmines. "All clear," I said.

"What a mess," Taylor said. "What do you think?"

"It reminds me of the victims from at the hotel. These victims were older, though. Both are women this time. I'm not sure if that's relevant. From their hair, I would say that they're both over fifty, maybe older. We'll need to see the teeth for more accuracy on the age."

I felt a mental tug to the left and kicked at some bloody leaves.

"We've got clothes over here," I said.

"Right. Ask the forensics team to come up, please, sergeant."

"Yes, ma'am."

"I don't see anything that looks like a purse or a wallet. The clothes seem to be hand-made, maybe even handwoven."

"Really?" Taylor carefully walked over and took a look. "You're right. I wonder what the hell that means."

"Do you mind if I check something?" I asked, picking up a small stick.

"Go ahead. I doubt we'll find much anyway."

I poked through the clothes. "Taylor, look at these," I said. I had uncovered several small charms and fetishes. They were made of feather and bone, with small bits of stone tied into them.

"What are those?" Taylor asked. "Do I want to know?"

I held my hand close and could feel power from them. "They're psychic artifacts. Probably meant for protection and warding against evil."

"Didn't seem to do *them* much good."

"Such things aren't useful against a physical attack." I was trying to figure out the construction without touching them. "There's an almost Native American element to the construction of some of these. It's certainly an influence."

"Ah, shit. I guess we'll need a Tribal consultation."

Sergeant Reynolds came back, leading the forensics team. After a short discussion on how to proceed, they started moving around the crime scene, taking pictures and making notes into recorders.

Reynolds didn't think there were any Indigenous people nearby.

"So, Fredericks, what's with the scarecrows?" asked Taylor.

"I don't know." I shook my head and looked around some more.

"I was doing some thinking, Fredericks. Let me know what you think of this." Taylor leaned again a tree. "It seems to me that we have two different kinds of murderers and two different types of victims, not including what Officer May did."

I nodded. I'd been thinking the same thing.

"I've been trying to put it all together with one type of killer," she said. "I think we have two different cults to be looking for here."

"At least two," I said. I wasn't sure why I said that, but I trusted my intuition. "We have one set of bodies that's marked with signs and may represent some type of perverse exorcism. We've got another type that's... what?"

Taylor waited for me to continue.

"I think these two women were hill witches," I said.

"You mean like Wiccans or Satanists or something?"

"No, I mean old-style witches. There are many old traditions in these hills. Mothers pass them on to their daughters. At least one of these victims was a witch. Probably both. Those charms held real power."

"So what about the other victims?"

"The two from the hotel were probably witches, too."

"One of them was a man," said Taylor.

"That doesn't matter. Men can be witches."

"So why would someone want to kill these hill witches?"

"I can think of lots of reasons, most of them religious, but this doesn't appear to be the case for these."

"How is that?"

"No crosses or anything. Also, the pentagram trap and summoned demon are not common for most Christian cults."

"I'll grant that."

"So we're looking for a cult that worships demons or something."

Taylor sighed. "Okay, what about the branded girls?"

"Definitely a different killer," I said.

"Yes, but who?"

"I still think we may be dealing with a Christian cult for those. We need IDs on the girls, and we'll work from there."

Taylor nodded. "I guess we should go talk to the hunters."

I followed her over to the sergeant. He told us the hunters were down by the police cars.

I tried to get a sense of the area as we walked. A heavy darkness hung over the woods: something new, a kind of anger, maybe. I wasn't sure if it was directed at me. I hoped not.

CHAPTER THIRTY-FIVE

The two hunters were leaning against the hood of a police car. Despite being pale and shaken, they produced the typical male response: I felt their eyes crawl over Taylor and me as we walked up. I smirked. Sexual desire is a typical human response to danger and fear.

"Taylor, FBI. We'd like to ask you some questions." She didn't hold out her hand.

The older man stood up straight. "Ma'am." He nodded.

The younger man continued to slouch and check us out. We were probably a welcome distraction.

Taylor got their names, Larry and David Anderson, and contact information. Larry was the older one. Then they each gave a short description of what they'd been doing that morning. It all sounded normal. I didn't detect any lie in these two. They were just what they seemed.

"Are there any witches living around here?" I asked suddenly.

The young man jerked as if he'd been slapped. The older man, Larry, just stared at me for a minute and then said, "I don't know no one 'round here that would do something like that up there."

"That's not what I asked," I said. Taylor didn't say anything.

He sighed. "There's a couple of old women. Sisters, I think. They live near here." He scowled at the younger man. "Some people 'round here say they're witches, but I think they're just plain old simple hill folk. They didn't do that."

"Can you tell us where they live?" asked Taylor.

I was betting that if he couldn't, the younger man could.

"You don't think that they..." He looked confused and a little angry.

"Mr. Anderson," I said, "did you get a good look at the bodies this morning?"

"No offense, ma'am, but I didn't want to look too close. I don't like seein' people trussed up like deer."

I hadn't thought of that angle. "The two bodies up there belong to older women," I said.

He paled. "Oh, God. You think it might be them old ladies?" He looked as if he was going to be ill.

"We'd need to go to their house to determine that," said Taylor. "Can you tell us how to get there?"

"I ain't ever been there."

David stirred. "I was there, once, a couple of years ago."

We all looked at him.

"I'd heard of them witches and went for a look, that's all. I followed them back from the church one day."

The older man just shook his head.

"Could you tell how to get there?" I asked.

"No, but I could show you."

"Is it far from here?" asked Taylor.

"Nah, we could walk it in 'bout half an hour or less." He spat tobacco juice to the side. "Depends on how fast ya walk."

"Fredericks, could I talk to you for a moment?" Taylor led me a few feet away. "What do you think?"

"I think we should check it out."

"I do, too. I'll get the sergeant to send someone with us. I don't trust the younger one."

"I don't sense anything bad from him, but it wouldn't hurt. He has been eyeing us."

She went off in search of the sergeant.

I walked back over and talked to the two hunters. "Why did you think the old ladies were witches?"

David shrugged. "I don't know. They just looked it, you know? They had this wild look and lived alone together in the hills. People around here said they was witches. I never really thought about it."

"You never think much about anything, boy. That's your problem," said Larry. He was David's uncle.

"You said you followed them back from church?" I asked.

"Yeah, they used to go to my church, up the road."

"If they went to your church, why did you still think they were witches?"

"They was weird. They stopped coming around after a while."

I shook my head. The young man's ignorance was stunning.

Taylor came back a few minutes later with the police sergeant. "He's coming along with us," she said without preamble. "Lead the way."

"Is it okay if we leave our bows and stuff here?" asked Larry.

Sergeant Reynolds nodded. "It'll be fine. Our boys will be here for a while."

David started walking through the woods to the left of the crime scene.

We followed along. It was briskly cold that morning, and although it was clearer, there was a sense of impending snow. I dreaded the thought of inclement weather in the mountains. At least my Jeep has four-wheel drive. Of course, that won't keep you on the road if you drive stupidly, but it does help get you back out of the ditch.

We came to a creek and began to follow it. There didn't seem to be any kind of trail that I could see. I hoped David knew where he was going. The creek meandered through the shelter of some rather steep cliffs. It would be easy to get lost.

"Their hut is about a mile up this here holler," said David.

It took me a few minutes to figure out that he meant a *hollow*.

The trek was long, through brambles and pines. I was glad it wasn't summer. I'd hate to try to walk through here when it was grown over.

I wondered how the old ladies got in and out. Maybe by the creek.

We came around a bend in the hill and saw their home. *Shack* was more accurate. It was a decaying heap of wood and stone and looked as if they'd put waxed newspaper or something over the windows. I could see the remains of a small herb garden off behind it.

"It must be tough to live up here," said Taylor.

"Some of the people from *my* church," Larry said, "give them food and stuff when they come down from the hills. We've never thought nor cared if they was witches."

David blushed but didn't say anything.

"You two wait here," said Taylor. She walked forward and knocked on the front door. It creaked open a few inches. "Hello? I'm from the FBI. We're just checking to make sure you're okay."

Silence was the only reply.

I could tell no one was home, but I had a sense that we were being watched. "Taylor," I said, "I don't think we're alone out here."

Sergeant Reynolds looked startled. "I had the same feeling," he said.

Taylor just nodded. "Sergeant, if you don't mind, why don't you stay out here and keep an eye on things. I'd like to look around in there and make sure that if the ladies aren't the victims we found, they're okay."

"Sure thing, ma'am." He had his hand on his pistol and looked a little spooked.

"Fredericks, come with me, if you please." Taylor pushed the door open.

I followed.

My eyes took a moment to adjust; the little shack was dark inside. Taylor took a small flashlight out of her pocket and started looking around. Strings of herbs hung from the ceiling along with the dried carcasses of what looked like two rabbits. There were small piles of clothes and knickknacks, the accumulated junk of at least two lifetimes, crammed into the single room. It was obvious the women weren't here. The shack had no place for anyone to hide. Judging from the little charms here and there, I thought it probable that the victims were these women. It was almost unbearably sad.

"Taylor," I said.

She turned and met my eyes. "You don't look so good."

"I need to step outside. I'm sorry. The aura of this place, the sadness…" I trailed off. Bad things had happened here, a long time ago. A lot of pain and suffering. These women hadn't had an easy life.

"Go. I'll be out in a minute."

I left quickly.

The sergeant and the hunters were nowhere in sight.

CHAPTER THIRTY-SIX

"Taylor, we have a problem!" I yelled.

Taylor came out of the shack. "What is it?" She stopped and looked around. "Where the hell did that cop and the hunters go?"

"I'll be damned if I know. They weren't here when I came out." The watched feeling was gone. "I have a bad feeling about this."

"No shit," she said. "Me, too, and I'm not even psychic. Where did they go? I thought I could trust that damned cop, at least." She kicked shut the door to the shack.

I felt the same way she did. "Look, he wouldn't have left if it wasn't important, right?"

"He shouldn't have left at all."

Just then, the sound of gunshots echoed from the surrounding hills.

"Shit! Come on." Taylor drew her pistol and took off in the direction the shots came from.

I glanced around quickly, then drew my pistol and followed her. We moved from tree to tree, keeping each other in sight. I wished I knew the terrain better.

I heard talking up ahead, and we stopped. The voices sounded like the sergeant and Larry.

"Sergeant Reynolds?" Taylor called quietly.

"Is that you, Agent Taylor?" His voice sounded strained.

"The one and only. We're coming in from the direction of the hut. Don't shoot us." Her voice had an edge to it. We walked forward until we could see the men.

The sergeant was on the ground with his back against a tree. He had his gun out. Larry had his belt off and was using it as tourniquet around the Reynolds' leg. Blood covered the ground around him. Reynolds hadn't been shot: the wound looked wrong.

"What the hell happened to you?" asked Taylor.

We both moved closer.

He grimaced. "David saw something in the woods behind the shack that scared him, and he took off running. We took off after him. I figured I could grab him and be back in a minute. Didn't you hear me call out?"

I looked at Taylor; neither of us had heard anything. While he was talking, I double-checked the tourniquet, but it was properly placed. I tore a strip from his pants leg and tied the jagged wound tightly, then slowly released the tourniquet. It didn't bleed too badly.

"We didn't hear anything until the gunshots," said Taylor.

Reynolds sighed. "Mr. Anderson here was in front of me about fifteen feet. We'd lost track of his nephew. Then some psycho jumped me with an axe." He gestured toward his leg. "Took me down with it. Would have taken me out if Anderson hadn't tackled him. He went down over there. When he got up, he'd lost his axe and took off running. I fired a couple of warning shots, but it didn't slow him. So I aimed for his legs. I must have missed, though. He kept on running."

I looked around. The axe was on the ground a few feet away. I walked along the line Reynolds indicated for about thirty feet, where I found spatters of blood leading deeper into the woods. I walked back.

I tore another strip from his pants and tied it over the other bandage. "Looks like the bone is broken," I said, looking at his leg. "We're going to have you taken out of here on a stretcher or something. There's no way you're going to walk it."

"Damn," Reynolds said. He looked pale. "I'll radio it in. I'm not sure if they'll find us all that quickly."

"I remember the way in," I said. He got his radio out, and I gave directions to the police officer on the other end. They'd have to get a rescue team here first, and that was going to take a while; the country was too rough to land a helicopter.

"What's your story?" Taylor asked Larry.

He just shrugged. "I don't know what got into David. I can give a decent description of the guy that jumped the officer here, though."

"Well, that's something." Taylor was pacing.

"For what it's worth," I told Reynolds, "you hit the perp who jumped you. I found a blood trail about thirty feet from here."

"Good, that'll help." He got on the radio and told his men to get a tracking team up here as soon as they could. They told him a rescue team was on the way from Phelps, just a few miles away.

The sergeant passed out a few minutes later. We each took off out coats and covered him up. Shock was the main worry, now that the blood had stopped flowing from the wound. Taylor and I kept each other in sight as we watched for trouble. We didn't want any surprises.

When I first heard the rescue party, I didn't know what it was. "What is that?" I asked.

Taylor shrugged.

"Sounds like four-wheelers," said Larry. "That's probably the rescue party."

Taylor got on the radio and talked them to our location. It didn't take long; I give good directions.

Three men rode up on two large ATVs. One of the vehicles had a stretcher mounted to a rack. The men jumped off and ran over to the sergeant. Other than their odd mode of transport, they looked like any other paramedics I'd seen.

It was surreal.

They wrapped Reynolds' wound tightly with gauze before moving him. The three of them hoisted him over onto the stretcher and moved it carefully over to the lead ATV.

Six police officers came running up as the paramedics were strapping Reynolds down.

"Is he going to be okay?"

The paramedic just shrugged. "Gotta bad wound to the leg. He needs some blood and stitches, maybe a cast. He'll be okay if we can get him out of here soon."

"Go," said Taylor.

They left, and she talked to the officer who'd led the men up here. They were going to wait for the dogs, so as not to disrupt the trail.

We started walking back with Larry.

I glanced at my watch; it wasn't quite ten AM yet.

CHAPTER THIRTY-SEVEN

We made our way back to the cars without incident.

Dave still hadn't returned, so Larry went off with the police to see about organizing a search party. I was worn out, and my new clothes had blood on them. Taylor and I walked to my Jeep. The ambulance was already gone, and a couple of guys were loading the ATVs onto a trailer.

"I handed over immediate control to the state police," said Taylor.

I nodded and unlocked the Jeep.

We both got in, and I started it and cranked up the heat. I was freezing. After a few minutes, I started to thaw and began driving back to Pikeville.

"So what have you learned, Michelle?" asked Taylor. "Do you think the guy with the axe was connected to the murders?"

"I don't know. Connected? Almost certainly. Responsible?" I shrugged.

"You don't think he's our cult killer?"

"No."

"Me, either." Taylor sighed loudly.

"What's the plan?"

"I, for one, could use a good, hot shower and then some food."

"I second that motion."

We parted ways in the parking lot, agreeing to meet in an hour at a little place up the road called the Windmill. Jean had said they had good food there. The rental car was gone, so Jean and Lawrence were probably headed back to South Williamson. I really needed to spend more time with them when I had the chance.

The hotel clerk glared at me when I went through the lobby. I smiled at him, just to scare him, and took the elevator up. The cleaners were still banging away at the room down the hall.

I was glad to get into the sanctuary of my room. I stripped off my clothes and took a long, hot shower. I needed to do some meditation to clear my mind, but I had to meet Taylor for breakfast. I sighed to myself; I needed to eat anyway. I dressed casual.

I arrived at the Windmill before Taylor and went on in. I ordered a Coke and sat back to wait. If the food was as good as it smelled, I was finally going to get something decent to eat.

Taylor pulled in about when I was starting my second drink.

She stomped into the restaurant and came over to my table. She looked pissed off. She dropped into the seat across from me. She was wearing another dark suit, just like the others I'd seen her in. I was going to tease her about it, but something about her mood prompted me not to.

"Those ignorant bastards have gotten a court order to suspend the autopsy on the last girl," she said.

"I thought an autopsy was required by law in a criminal investigation."

"It is. They got some idiot judge to pass a stay on it anyway. I'll have to file an appeal. It'll go in for review. It's stupid."

The waitress came over, and Taylor ordered black coffee. By mutual unspoken agreement, we didn't talk as we looked over the menus. We waited until the waitress brought the coffee, and then we ordered our food. Once the waitress was away, we resumed talking.

"How could they get a judge to pass a stay on that?" I asked.

"I haven't a damn clue. The papers said *religious reasons*."

"And they just happen to have a problem with autopsies."

"You got it. I asked around about what proof was given that their religion was against autopsies. You're going to love what I was told by the DA."

"What?" I was almost afraid to know.

"He said the judge was a *holy roller* and that they were all of the same faith."

"Oh, hell. I didn't realize they had those up here."

"What? Are you kidding? There are more snake-handling cults around here than normal churches, and there's one of *those* on every corner." Taylor sighed and sipped her coffee. "Finally, some decent coffee!"

"I wonder what they're afraid of us finding out."

"I have no idea. We checked out the bodies at the site. We have pictures and such, and autopsies of the first two girls, or we will when the coroner releases them to me."

"Maybe they don't want DNA evidence of the killer found."

"Why would they not want...? That's it, Michelle! Those bastards know who the killer is, and they're trying to protect him. Damn!"

People at a couple of tables looked over at us curiously.

The waitress came out with our food. It tasted every bit as good as it smelled. I had pancakes, eggs, and bacon. Taylor had ordered an omelet and biscuits. Neither of us had much to say for a while.

"Ah, that was good," Taylor said, sitting back. "I was starving."

"Well, look on the bright side, Jessica. We have a lead now."

She nodded. "I was just thinking that." She finished off her coffee. "Okay, to hell with the locals. I want another look at those bodies, and I want the results from the first two autopsies. What do you say?"

"Are they all here?"

"Yes, I had them all brought to Pikeville, to keep things organized."

"Why haven't you gotten the results from the first autopsies by now?" I asked.

"I don't know, but I intend to find out."

CHAPTER THIRTY-EIGHT

We arrived at Pikeville Medical Center around noon.

Taylor had left her car at the Windmill, after breakfast, and ridden with me. I parked in a spot far away from the doors. The lot was full. Medicine is big money in this part of the country. *It's no wonder, with all the coal mines,* I thought angrily.

"You ready for this, Fredericks?" Taylor always used my last name when she was being official.

"As ready as I ever will be. You don't think the families will be around, do you?"

"I doubt it, but you never know."

"Great," I said.

"Come on. Let's get this over with."

Taylor flashed her badge at the information desk, and we were directed downstairs to the morgue. We took the stairs down to avoid people. A single tech was working the desk.

"Hello," Taylor said as we walked up. "I'm Special Agent Taylor, with the FBI. This is my associate, Dr. Fredericks. The FBI had three bodies transferred here for autopsy and holding for a criminal case. I'd like to see the results on those cases and the doctor who performed the autopsies."

The tech was out of his league. He stuttered for a moment and then got on the phone with a supervisor. "The chief coroner will be down in just a moment, ma'am. He'll know more about all this." He looked intimidated.

Taylor flashed him a smile. "Certainly. Thank you." She turned to the sign-in record and started looking through it. I could tell the tech wanted to ask her to stop. That was probably why she did it.

A few minutes later, a harassed-looking middle-management type came striding into the room. Taylor waited for him to walk up to her and then took a half-step forward so his last step would carry him just a little too near to be polite. He rocked back on his heels, unbalanced. She kept him that way.

"I'm this close to hitting you with an obstruction of justice. Do you have any idea how long I've been waiting for those reports?" She didn't shout or raise her voice, but her every word demanded attention. I wanted to applaud.

"Reports? I'm sorry, ma'am, you'll have —"

She cut him off. "I don't have to do anything but my job. I require you to do yours. Are you responsible for this department?"

"Well, yes, but—" he started.

"And as the person responsible for this department, you were given a job by the FBI. Isn't that correct?"

"Yes, but you have to understand—"

"I understand that the first victim was killed a week ago. The second was two days later. The third was two days after that. What have you been doing down here? I expected the reports from the first two last week. I should have had the last one today."

"I'm sorry, but the family requested that there not be an autopsy," he said.

"When? When did they identify the body?"

"They were in here Sunday evening."

"Which family?" I asked.

"All of them," he said.

Taylor and I exchanged glances.

"And why was the autopsy not done by then?" asked Taylor.

"It was Thanksgiving weekend," the coroner said helplessly.

"I don't want excuses. I want answers. Where are the reports for the first two autopsies?"

"They should be in the file." He gestured behind the tech at the desk.

"Why don't I have a copy?" asked Taylor.

"I don't know," he said. "I gave them to the police officer who asked for them this morning."

"Shit." Taylor walked over to the cabinets and jerked on one of the drawers. It was locked. "Open it!"

The coroner fumbled with his keys. I met Taylor's eyes across his back. We'd have to make another visit to the Pikeville police station.

The coroner finally got the correct key in the lock and opened the drawer. Then he sifted through the files for a moment, and turned to the tech.

"Please find me these files, Mike."

The tech jumped out of his chair and started looking through the files. After a few minutes, he looked up, stricken.

"Well?" asked Taylor.

The coroner carefully wet his lips. "They don't seem to be in there, ma'am. Let's go inside and check in the inner office. Maybe our medical examiner left them in there."

We followed him inside. The tech looked relieved not to have been asked to follow.

It was cold back here. The coroner led us through an examination room to a small office and unlocked the door with a key from his ring.

The office was small and neat, with a single, small desk in the center. The desk's top held a few folders. The coroner smiled and rushed over to look at them. It didn't take long for the smile to fade.

"Those aren't the correct files," Taylor said dryly.

He shook his head. "I don't understand it. They should have been in the cabinet in the outer office, I swear to you!"

Taylor sat on the desk and rubbed her temple. "Okay. Call the medical examiner and get him over here."

He looked upset again. "I can't."

"*Why?*" She didn't bother to keep her voice down this time.

"He took an extended leave of absence this morning. He said he had to leave town to visit his family in New Orleans."

Taylor just stared at him.

"Okay," I said, measuring out each word carefully, "what about the police officer who came this morning? What was his name?"

"I don't remember, but I'm sure he signed the register out front."

"Let's go look, shall we?" Taylor looked as if she was about to strangle the man.

We walked back out to where the tech waited. Taylor walked around and looked at the log again.

"You know," she said quietly, "I really don't like it when people lie to me. I'll ask you one more time for the reports."

"What? His name should be right there!" The coroner walked over and flipped through the pages.

I knew he was telling the truth.

"The whole page is missing! There's no one logged in for today." He glared accusingly at the tech.

"What?" The tech pulled the log over and looked at it. "We had six people in here this morning."

I clenched my fists, making the knuckles pop loudly.

Everyone turned to look at me.

I smiled. "Let's be reasonable. Write us descriptions of the people who have been in here. Also write down everything you can remember about the police officer."

"Officers," said the tech.

"What?" The supervisor looked surprised.

"Yes, sir, the other officer had walked into the bathroom when you came down."

I walked over and touched the cabinets. There were many overlapping impressions, from all of the people who had used those cabinets over the years. I tried to sort out the emotions and images. "You both walked back with the police officer to check that the bodies were still there. You left the cabinet unlocked. The other officer came out and took the files while you were gone."

"What? How could you know that?" The coroner looked confused.

"We can go, Taylor. I've got an idea of what the two police officers looked like. Let's try to find them, shall we?"

She grinned and gestured me toward the elevator before turning back the two men. "Breathe a word of our visit, and I'll make sure that you never work again, either of you." Then she followed me out the door.

CHAPTER THIRTY-NINE

We walked across the parking lot to my Jeep.

"So how do you know what the officers look like?" asked Taylor.

"Trade secret," I said, and then laughed at her expression. "I'm psychic, remember?"

"Seriously, Michelle, how do you know?"

I unlocked the Jeep's doors, and we got in. "I am being serious."

"Okay. I believe you. It would be stupid not to, at this point." She shook her head. "You learn something new all the time. Okay, let's get over to the police station before everyone takes leave of more than just their sanity."

I drove us over to the police station downtown.

Large, heavy flakes of snow were beginning to fall. Not much accumulation yet, but I worried about driving on those narrow roads if the snow kept falling.

"I hope the weather doesn't get worse," I said.

"You and me, both," Taylor replied.

The watched feeling was back as we got out of the Jeep.

"That is really getting annoying!" I said.

Taylor stopped walking and looked at me. "What's getting annoying?"

"I've had this feeling that something has been watching me for days now, dogging my footsteps. It seems familiar, but I can't quite figure it out. It's bugging the crap out of me."

"Hmm, I see. Did you mean to say *something* instead of *someone?*" asked Taylor.

"Yes, actually."

"Ah, well." She looked around nervously. "I guess we'd better get inside."

Once in the building, it didn't take us long to find the police chief. He didn't look very happy to see us. I smiled, to reassure him.

"Chief Williams, we'd like to talk to a couple of your officers about some papers that were removed from Pikeville Medical Center illegally today."

"Certainly," he said through gritted teeth. "What are their names?"

"We're not sure. We can give you accurate descriptions, though."

"Agent Taylor—" he began.

"*Special Agent*," Taylor corrected.

He forced a small smile. "*Special* Agent Taylor, have you nothing better to do that harass my men and waste my time? And as for this... woman, she has no place in any investigation, if you want my opinion."

"I don't remember asking your opinion. Dr. Fredericks is a valuable part of this *federal* investigation, and you will give her the courtesy she deserves." Taylor smiled mirthlessly. "Let's cut to the chase. I really don't give a shit what you think about me, her, or the FBI. You'll cooperate, or you'll find yourself out of a job. It's that simple. If I tell you to bend over and kiss your ass, I expect you to slip it some tongue. Do we understand each other?"

He'd turned dark red during her speech. Now he paled. I don't think he was used to anyone daring to speak to him in such a way. He'd probably been picked on in school; he had the look of a bully and a coward. "If you give the descriptions to my clerk up front, he will do everything he can to assist you," Chief Williams hissed through clenched teeth.

"Thank you." Taylor turned to walk out.

"Remember, it's *Special Agent* Taylor and *Dr.* Fredericks," I said before leaving. "Don't get us confused."

We didn't get any real assistance at the police station. They said the descriptions were too vague to be positive about which officers might have been at the hospital. Our inquiries met with so much resistance, it was tempting to think all of the officers were in on some crime. However, I knew it was just the typical small-town mindset. It wasn't even exclusive to police. I kept my eyes open, but didn't see either of the officers in question.

It had been fun baiting the chief, though.

Taylor and I returned to the Windmill for dinner. We agreed to meet again in the morning, to try to outline a plan of attack for the case. I was so tired that I barely made it back to the hotel. I was asleep by the time my head hit the pillow.

CHAPTER FORTY

I was beginning to hate telephones.

"Hello?" I answered groggily.

"Rise and shine, shorty. We have work to do."

"Taylor, you're, like, nine inches shorter than me," I said.

"Ten," she replied gleefully. "Seriously, get up and get ready. We have work to do today. I'll be over there in about ten minutes."

I groaned.

It was actually more like twenty minutes, which gave me time for a brief shower. I let her in when she arrived, and then quickly dried my hair.

She was flipping through the case files when I came out of the bathroom.

"What's the rush today?" I asked. It was just seven AM.

"We have to take a road trip."

"Where?"

"Nashville. Get a suit on, but leave your gun."

"What is the hell is in Nashville?" I asked, taking a dark suit out of the wardrobe.

"The Tennessee Prison for Women. They have a guest I'd like to talk to."

I scratched my head and yawned. "Okay, give me a minute. How long does it take to get to Nashville from here?" I went in the bathroom and changed into the suit I'd selected.

"About eight hours," she said as I stepped out.

"We're driving it?"

"Unless you have a quicker and less expensive method, yes."

I just shook my head and tied my hair back.

"We can take my car. It's waiting just outside."

"No gun?" I really didn't like the idea of leaving it at the hotel.

"You can bring it with you, but not into the prison."

"Well, of course," I said. "Okay, I guess I'm ready. Do I get to sleep on the way?"

"If you can sleep through me singing with the radio to stay awake, you're welcome to try."

I sighed. It had been too much to hope for.

We took the elevator down to the hotel lobby and walked out to the waiting car. No police car was waiting for me in the lot this morning. I wondered what that meant. Had they finally given up on harassing me?

We took the Mountain Parkway to Lexington, and then the Bluegrass Parkway to Elizabethtown. From there, it was a straight shot down I-65 to Nashville. It was a mind- and butt- numbing trip.

True to her word, Taylor sang the whole way. I will neither confirm nor deny that I joined her.

We stopped for a quick lunch in Elizabethtown.

We gained an hour on the way; I would've been elated if I hadn't known we'd be losing it on the way back to Pikeville. I longed to be home in my own bed, with my cat and a good book, or with Michael if he could fly back from Seattle.

The prison was off the Briley Parkway, near the river on the west side of Nashville. It was a forbidding-looking structure with a seventeen-foot-high fence and no less than five coils of concertina wire. I really didn't want to go in there.

I left my gun under the car's seat. Taylor wore hers in but checked it at the security desk. The prison corrections officers also searched us for pencils, pens, keys, etc. They argued a bit over my underwire bra but eventually let me keep it on. If I'd known they were going to make such a fuss, I'd have worn a sports bra. They made me leave all my jewelry at the desk, even my earrings. I had a feeling I was going to miss them.

"You're just in time for dinner," said the burly female prison guard who was showing us around. "We're having sliced beef liver in gravy and onions, a favorite here."

I had to fight down my nausea.

"I don't think we'll be able to stay for dinner, thanks," said Taylor. "I'd like to talk to Thacker as soon as possible."

"Certainly, ma'am." She led us to an open room with small, round tables and uncomfortable-looking chairs, and left us there. The whole prison was stark off-white and drab. I couldn't help but think that I might have ended up in a prison myself, after the project. Julia had been in solitary somewhere even worse.

There were small vending machines along one wall of the visitation room, with signs warning that inmates were not to handle money. I struggled to maintain my composure. I hated being here.

"Are you okay, Fredericks?"

"This place is so full of hate, fear, and despair. It's hard for me to cope with."

"You get vibes off the place as a whole?"

I laughed unsteadily. "I guess *vibes* is as good a word as any. I feel waves of emotions washing over me. I can tell they're from an outside source, but I still feel them like they're my own."

"Damn. Is it like this all the time? How do you sleep?"

"Most of the jewelry I wear is to help block stuff like this. It really helps."

She just shook her head.

A few minutes later, the guards brought a young woman into the room. She was a bit above average height, maybe five-foot-six. Her short light brown hair hung limply. Her hands were cuffed, but she was otherwise unrestrained. She was dressed in a two-piece outfit of light blue, with a white, long-sleeved t-shirt underneath. The guards treated her as if she was a Manson.

Hell, maybe she was.

CHAPTER FORTY-ONE

The inmate sat quietly at the table the guards indicated, but her intense blue eyes scanned the room restlessly. She looked like a caged tiger, ready to pounce. She looked hungry.

I shook my head. I was getting too into her mindset.

"Do you want us to remain here, ma'am?" asked one of the guards.

"I think we can handle Heather if she acts up."

The guards moved to the far side of the room, where they could watch and intervene but not overhear our conversation. I followed Taylor over to the table, and we sat down across from the woman. We sat there for about ten minutes in silence.

Finally, the woman spoke. "Who the hell are you? I hope you're not more goddamn Christian funda-fucking-mentalists here to screw with my brain."

"We're not here to screw with you at all," said Taylor. "But if you screw with us, I'll make you wish you'd never been born."

At that, the woman laughed; it had an odd edge to it. "What you gonna do? Add another few more lifetimes to my sentence?"

She was serving six consecutive life sentences for murder, with no hope for parole.

"I don't know. Maybe I'll have someone I know in the Justice Department accidentally reclassify you as male, have you transferred to

Terre Haute Federal Correctional Complex for men, and see how you like getting all the attention for the next sixty years."

I reminded myself never to piss Taylor off.

Heather paled. "So who are you, and what do want with me?" She sounded much meeker, but I didn't buy it. Her eyes were full of fury.

"We're FBI. You don't need to know more than that. Before I get to *why you*, why don't you tell us in your own words why you're here."

Taylor had refused to tell me anything about the woman, other than that she was serving life sentences for murder. She said she didn't want to prejudice me against her. Tayler needn't have worried; Heather was doing a fine job of that without help.

"I killed six people. What's there to tell?"

"Tell us why and how you did it."

"I moved to Louisville in '96, after all the shit came down back home," said Heather.

"Where did you move from?" I asked.

"Pikeville. *What the fuck do you care?* Anyway, I moved there after the police started snooping around because of those idiots that went on that little sightseeing trip. You ask me, they should have just snuffed the juvies and crossed that border. What the hell good would turning back do?"

"Back to your own story, please," said Taylor.

"Right. Anyway, the cops were conducting a fucking witch-hunt through the city. We all knew each other. Hell, I was even at that little hotel get-together they had. It was Victor's idea to step on that scientist from Oak Ridge."

"Who? Last name, please." *It couldn't be...*

"Owens. You want me to tell this story, or what?"

Taylor darted a look at me, and then said, "Go on."

"I got out of there fast and shacked up with this bitch in Louisville that thought she was into the occult. She had all these little crystals and shit. She never fucking shut about her and her friends and how neo-pagans would win against persecution in the end because they treated everyone fairly. She thought she had power. I taught her different."

Heather's voice started getting huskier at the end. I realized that she was getting excited, talking about what she had done.

"We didn't fuck. I ain't no dyke. I like a good hard one, you know? But she was a lipstick lezzie and was always on my case. I got home from work one day, and she was gone with her little coven to some retreat. I decided it might be fun to follow them and see what they did at these things. Her and her friends were running around the woods, chanting and waving incense. Every damn one of them butt-naked. I walked into the middle of them and asked them what the fuck they thought they was doing. They gave me some crap about summoning up the goddess into each of them, but I knew they was just a bunch of dykes. You know?"

Her eyes glittered, and there was a line of spittle running down her jaw. She never moved, but I could feel her getting tenser as she talked. This woman belonged in a mental ward, not a prison. She was as insane as a person could get. I wondered why no else had seen it.

"I told them I was the fucking *GODDESS*, and they should be worshipping *me*. They fucking laughed at me. They *laughed*. At *me!*"

She was trembling.

"I had me this nice, long filleting knife. I took it out and made them lie on the ground. Then I took some rope and tied them up." She grinned.

"Where did the rope come from?" I asked.

"What, are you stupid? I fucking took it with me. I figured I'd have me good fun with these whores. They was way out in the middle of nowhere, so not like anyone was going to hear them scream."

I wondered how much of this was true. She was so psychotic that her thoughts were narrowly focused. I could just barely perceive some emotion under all the layers. I hated to think that people like her existed, but I knew they did. I couldn't be sure how much of what she said was just sick fantasy, though.

"Finish your story," said Taylor.

"Yeah, where was I? Oh, yeah, the screams. I carved them up real sweet, one by one, and I made Josie watch the whole thing. She tried keeping her eyes closed, but I took care of that. I don't think she appreciated my work. I even shared choice bits of meat with her, but I had to stuff it down her throat. I'd thought she liked me."

She sat trembling for a moment. I wanted to see Taylor's reaction to all this, but I didn't dare take my eyes off Heather.

"Come morning, she wouldn't play anymore. So I made me some dolls and stood them around to watch us, to dance and amuse us, but she wouldn't play anymore."

"Okay, thank you, Heather. I think we've heard enough." Taylor got up from the table.

Heather lunged with her teeth bared, an inhuman scream tearing from her throat. "You're done when I *say* you're done!"

I smacked her hands away and pinned her head to the table while the guards ran up. They grabbed Heather and dragged her, screaming and sobbing, away. I stood and watched them pull her through the door.

I was trembling.

Madness like that can be infectious.

CHAPTER FORTY-TWO

The first guard came back in a few minutes later. "Everyone okay in here?"

Taylor nodded.

"Yes, thank you," I said.

"You sure got her riled up. I've never seen her go that bonkers. Find what you needed?" she asked.

I looked at Taylor.

"I think so," said Taylor. "I really think maybe we did."

We went back through the checkpoint after that and collected our stuff. I was glad to get my jewelry back. I felt calmer as we walked to the car. It was getting dark outside.

"Well," Taylor said, "we have a long trip back in the morning. Are you doing any better?"

"I am, now that I'm out of there."

"FBI put us up in the Super 8. We'll have to share a room."

"That's fine," I said. I was too worn out to care.

Taylor swung us out onto the loop, and I watched the cars go by outside the window. My head was spinning, and I felt nauseated. Taylor was quiet as she drove. I think she was letting me process what Heather had told us. I didn't want to think about it, but I couldn't stop.

I say didn't anything until we were checked in at the motel and settled in the room. We were both hungry, but Taylor didn't think she could eat, and I knew I couldn't. Not after what we'd just heard.

"So she is connected to the murders in Pikeville," I said finally.

Taylor sighed and put down the papers she was reading. "Yes, and there may be more of those murders than we thought. Not everything that happens in those hills gets reported, you know."

"I do."

"What was the business with this Victor Owens character? Have you heard of him?"

"Remember what I told you about last month?" I waited for her nod. "The fugitive's name was Julia Owens; I killed her brother while attempting to defend a federal witness at a safe house. The witness was going to testify about… He was involved in… special projects. Using kids. Illegal government stuff. After everything was over, Henderson admitted to Michael and me that he'd leaked the information to Julia's people."

"Julia's people?"

"Julia was ex-CIA. She had a nasty little private military company to do dirty work for her."

"Her brother's name was Victor, I take it?"

"Yes, and he had a little blood cult that he ran."

"The one that tried to kill you."

"Yes. Lucy took over the cult after Victor died. After I killed him."

"Damn. So all this *is* linked somehow. No wonder Henderson suggested your name."

I growled. "So did this little trip really have a point?" I asked.

Taylor glanced at me. "I wanted to see what you thought of the murders Heather committed. She didn't tell it all. She tried to frame the roommate. She stuck the knife in the roommate's hand, and when she got home, she called the police and reported her roommate missing. It took the police weeks to link the DNA evidence to her. She probably would've gotten out of all charges if she'd been able to keep her mouth closed in court."

"What happened?" I asked.

"The prosecuting attorney asked her if she was a lesbian. She went berserk and attacked him with a pen. Almost killed the man. She also screamed a lot of stuff that helped put her away."

"That woman should be in an institution. She's clearly bat-shit crazy."

"True, but everything she did was carefully premeditated."

I sighed.

"So," Taylor said casually, "did you get anything when you touched her?"

"That was the point of bringing me, wasn't it?"

She looked embarrassed. "I didn't know what else to do. We need all the help we can get. Hell, I don't even know if I really believe all that shit, but you've got something. God's own intuition or something."

"I think it's *or something.*"

"Yeah. I figured you'd say that."

"Well, ask next time, okay?"

"Okay."

We sat in silence for a few minutes.

"Michelle?"

"Yes, Jessica?"

"*Did* you get anything?

I sighed. "Yeah, I got a head full of hate and fear and a terrible rage that was little too close to what's in my head all the time anyway. I got images of things burned into my mind that I never wanted to see. I can still taste…" I choked and gagged.

"Michelle!" Taylor sounded truly concerned now.

"I'll be okay. It's no worse than what was already in my head from working with the police on dozens of murder cases. Heather was just so intense. Her personality was almost overwhelming."

"I'm sorry. I won't ask you to do that anymore. I shouldn't have risked this. I mainly just wanted to talk to her. Hear her story for myself. See if anything came out that was missed in the original investigation."

"No, it's okay. I'll recover. I do think I got some useful information. I would recognize anyone she had known. I know the faces of all the people at that party she talked about. I even got a few first names."

"So we have some new leads," Taylor said quietly.

"Yes, and if we can stop people like her, then it will have been worth it. Now, if you don't mind, I'd like to get some sleep."

The next morning, we grabbed a quick breakfast before we headed back to Pikeville.

I hadn't gotten much sleep. I could still feel Heather's insanity clawing at my brain. My dreams that night had been worse than normal.

It was an eight-hour trip back to Pikeville, and I didn't feel like talking. I sat back with my eyes closed. Taylor wasn't a terrible singer, but I didn't think she should quit her day job. If she'd sung something other than country, I might even have enjoyed a bit of it. I'm not sure when I fell asleep. Sometime after lunch, I think.

I woke up as the car swerved, brakes squealing.

"Shit!"

"What?" I open my eyes and looked around, expecting an imminent crash. "What happened?"

"I don't know. Someone – *something* – ran out in front of the car. I barely avoided hitting them. It."

I looked out the back window. "I don't see anything."

"I don't know. Maybe I started to nod off or something."

"Maybe. Where are we?"

"Pikeville, near your hotel."

"Sorry about sleeping the whole way back. Are you okay to drive to your hotel?" I asked, yawning.

"I'll be fine. Listen, I have some things I'll need to do in the morning. Why don't we meet in the afternoon?"

"Okay. I have a few places I can look around town for someone who might be willing to answer some questions."

"Sounds good." Taylor pulled into the hotel parking lot. "I'll call you around three. How's that?"

"Good. Be safe." I walked into the hotel. I wasn't sure I could make my way up to my room, but I managed somehow.

My head still really hurt.

CHAPTER FORTY-THREE

I slept until ten in the morning.

It felt good to get some rest; I'd really needed it. I lay in bed, sipping a Coke from the machine down hall and reading through old police reports, until almost noon. Then I got up, took a shower, and dressed in jeans, tight tank top, and open button-up shirt. I was planning to scope out the college campus today and didn't want to look too out of place.

I put on all my jewelry and slipped my pistol into its shoulder holster. I put two spare mags in my purse. I wished I had some of my clubbing clothes, but I figured I'd be okay. I should have just the right look of casual and alternative. Hopefully, any guys I talked to would be too focused on my tits to think about how old I was -- not that I look my age. Normally, having guys do that would piss me off, but I figured I'd use the weapons I had available.

I didn't have any messages on my cell phone. I'd have to call Michael later and find out how his case was doing. I hoped he would have it wrapped up and be heading home soon. I felt as if I really needed to see him.

Downtown Pikeville was about as exciting as you might expect. A funeral home and a small high-rise apartment complex were all that broke up the monotony of run-down buildings and closed businesses.

It was depressing.

The community college was empty. It was a commuter college, so there wasn't a lot for students to do around the campus, and no one who went to that school had any money anyway.

I drove around downtown for an hour or so before finding the game and comic book store I was looking for. Heather had memories of that store; her friends used to hang out there. Those memories were a decade old now, but I was hoping some of her friends might still be around.

I parked outside and walked in. The front of the store held the now-usual racks for packs of collectable card games and boosters. The walls were lined with comic books, and small shelves held comic collectable figurines. Indexed boxes held a surprising number of comic books, as well. The counter was to the right as I came in. It felt odd, having memories of a place I knew I'd never entered before.

A greasy-looking guy in a faded Batman t-shirt was reading a comic book by the cash register. He looked up and frowned at me. He seemed irritated that I'd disturbed his reading time.

Great people skills, I thought.

"Something I can help ya find?" he asked. He looked bored.

"I'm fine. Just looking." I walked along the wall, looking at titles.

"Looking for something for your boyfriend?" he said with a sneer.

I was beginning to not like this asshole. "No, for myself. I don't have a boyfriend."

"Girlfriend, then?" He sounded a little bit hopeful.

I shuddered to think I'd be featuring in a masturbation fantasy for him soon. "No, I'm looking for *Sandman* collections and collectables. I'd also like to find the original *Death* comics."

He blinked a couple of times, maybe processing the data. It looked as if it hurt him, which pleased me. "Which *Death* series?"

"Gaiman's *Death*, not *Lady Death*."

"Oh, I doubt we have those, but you can look. They'd be down there." He gestured to a place where I would have to bend over, facing him. "They've been out of print for a while."

He wasn't someone Heather had known, so I didn't need him.

"Sorry, buddy. You'll have to get your kicks looking at someone else's tits."

"Not much to look at anyway," he muttered.

"More than you've ever seen, I'd say." Dude was an incel if I'd ever seen one. I'd already found the *Sandman* books.

"What is your frigging problem, anyway? Damn! Matt! I'm going on break. We got another dyke browser." He stomped into the back of the store.

A medium-height man in his early thirties came out of the back. He didn't see me at first; he was carrying a load of comics in plastic covers. He sat them down on the counter and then looked around. He did an almost silly double-take when he saw me.

He looked familiar. I flashed him a smile. *This* guy, I could work with. He knew what a woman could do for him. Not that he had a chance in hell with me, but as long as he didn't know that, I could use him.

"Is, ah...?" He glanced at the back of the store. "Is there anything I can help you with? Sorry about the mess." He had thick glasses and pale blue eyes. He was almost cute, and very familiar. Heather had definitely known him.

"I found what I was looking for, thanks," I held up a *Sandman* comic I'd just taken off the shelf.

"Oh." He sounded disappointed. "Well, if you need help with anything else, just ask. My name is Matt," he said hopefully.

I just smiled and went back to flipping through the pages. I admit, I really do like *Sandman*, but I already had them all, even the *Death* ones. Only comics I ever really got into.

"Matt," I called.

He jerked to his feet so quickly that he knocked over the comics he was pretending to look through. "Yes?"

This boy must be desperate. "Do you have any roleplaying games here?"

"Sure, we've got lots. What are you looking for?"

"I don't know. Could you show them to me and tell me what's

cool?" It was difficult, pretending to be meek; I've never been the docile type. I didn't want to overdo it, either.

"Okay." He came around the counter.

I was maybe an inch taller than him. He led me to a shelf full of game books, which I'd already spotted.

"Have you ever played any before?" he asked, sounding doubtful.

"I've played some *AD&D*, *GURPS*, and *Red Shift*, but not much else. I'm thinking about coming back to school up at the college this spring, but I don't have much to do till then. After my divorce, I been kinda lost, you know? Anyway, you don't care about that. Sorry. I thought about how I used to play RPGs in high school and thought it would be fun to play again. You know, kinda connect with people again."

"Where you from?" he asked.

"I was born in Wimson, but my family moved to Lexington years ago. I just moved back to Pikeville this summer. Trying to get back to my roots. My name's Rhiannon, by the way."

"No way! What's your real name?"

"I'm serious." I punched him lightly on the arm. I got a few unpleasant flashes from him. "I'll prove it." I got out my ID and carefully covered the address and date of birth.

"That is so damn cool. So what game would a hot chick like you want to play?" He pretended to study the shelf.

I'm good looking, but *hot chick* was pushing it. "I'd heard *Changeling* was kinda cool," I said.

"It sucks," he said bluntly. "Only flower-power girls and fags play it. The coolest game by far is *Vampire: The Masquerade*." He held out a copy.

I took it and looked through it. I bobbed my head vapidly. "Vampires are cool," I said. "I once knew this girl that used to cut herself a lot. Not me, though. I'm too squeamish for that. I faint if I even see blood."

That got him. I knew he'd want a chance to make me bleed. He was almost panting. He was the one who was going to be bleeding, though.

CHAPTER FORTY-FOUR

I pretended to keep looking through the book so he wouldn't notice that I'd seen the look on his face. "It looks hard to play," I said.

"No, it's easy. I learned it in minutes from reading the book."

Yeah, right, I thought.

"Of course," he added, leaning close enough for me to smell his sour sweat of excitement, "the easiest way to learn is to play."

"I can see that. That's how I learned those others. I never would've figured it out on my own. Everything is so much easier when you have someone to tell you what to do." I was going to enjoy breaking this guy. This was humiliating.

"Yes, I'll tell you what to do, then. How about you come down to our local game? We got a few open spots. I'm sure we can find something to do with you."

"I guess. When is it?" I didn't want to seem too eager.

"Tomorrow night, Friday. Here." He scrawled an address on the back of a business card. "Be there at seven PM, sharp." He tried to assume a tone of command, but I knew this moron had never commanded anyone.

"Okay, thanks. Should I still buy this?" I held up the book.

"Of course. You'll need to at least look over the rules. Not that I expect you to understand them." He walked over to the register and rang me up. He charged twice the cover price and showed me the price on the book as he did. "This one is a limited edition," he said.

He was testing me.

I handed him the cash without comment, and he pocketed the change.

"Remember, be there exactly at seven PM."

I brushed his hand as he handed me the book. Everyone else would be arriving there at six. I guess I was supposed to be the dessert. I had other plans. I held my head down as I walked out of the store. I could feel him watching me.

I sighed. *It will be worth it, if I can get a lead tomorrow*, I thought. I'd show up, but not as he expected. I smiled to myself. I'd take out my due in flesh if I had to. I'd... I stopped myself. My thoughts were getting a little dark, even for me.

I walked to my Jeep, watching shadows flit from door to door. I shivered as I drove back to the hotel. My head hurt. My thoughts were jumbled and confused. It was hard to concentrate on anything.

I needed to make some plans.

I also needed another shower to delouse.

I waited around the hotel for most of the day. I was bored and fidgety. Three o'clock came and went. Taylor didn't call. That was unusual. I started feeling nervous and found myself pacing. Finally, I got out my cell phone and called Taylor's number around four PM.

"Special Agent Mullins speaking," a man said.

My brain did a flip-flop. I knew I'd dialed the correct number. "Hello. This is Dr. Michelle Fredericks. I was calling for Special Agent Taylor."

"Can I ask your business with Special Agent Taylor?" He sounded suspicious.

"I'm working with her on a case, civilian consultant. She was supposed to have called me at three but didn't."

"Hold on a minute." I could hear him muttering to someone, and then he was back. "Did you say your name is Michelle Fredericks?" he asked.

"Yes. I've been hired as an occult consultant for the recent murders. Is everything okay?"

"Frankly, no. How soon could you get to Phelps?"

"Isn't that on the way to Majestic?"

"Yes, it is."

"I could be there in twenty minutes or so."

"Okay, I'll fill you in when you get here. You'll see a bunch of cars by the road. Park and ask for me. My name is Mullins."

"Affirmative. Be there soon."

I buttoned my blouse and pulled on a suit jacket. Then I ran out of the hotel and down to my Jeep. Something had gone terribly wrong; I could feel it.

I made it to Phelps in ten minutes, but I left rubber marks around every curve. I parked with the other cars. Taylor's car was in a ditch; the driver's side door was open. A tall man in a dark suit was talking to a couple of state police officers. Several other officers were looking around in the bushes nearby.

I recognized two of the police officers. They nodded to me as I walked up. The state police, at least, weren't as weird as the local cops. They were coolly professional.

"Special Agent Mullins?" I walked forward, my hand out.

He shook it briefly. "Dr. Fredericks," he said with a nod.

I glanced at the closest officer. "How is Sergeant Reynolds?" I asked.

He looked startled at first, and then he recognized me. "Sorry. Didn't recognize you without blood all over you. He's doing okay. The doctors say they think they can save his leg. You were up there with him, right?"

"Yes. Did you catch the guy?" I was anxious to know about Taylor, but it didn't seem polite not to ask about the sergeant.

He scowled. "No, not yet."

"Dr. Fredericks?" said Mullins. "Could I talk to you over here?"

"Certainly." I followed him around the car.

"Taylor spoke highly of you on the phone and in her reports. I hope you can help us with this. Local police found her car run off the road here, just as you see it."

I glanced at the car again. There were two bullet holes in the front and back windows. A tire had been shot out, as well. The door was open. I checked the inside for blood. Nothing.

"Okay," I said. I repeated my observations to him. "I would guess that she ran into the woods. She wouldn't have gone far unless chased."

"My thoughts exactly. We have a search party organizing right now. They've been out in the woods looking for that axe-man, so they're exhausted already. The county police will be able to get dogs over here by tonight. Taylor dropped her phone in the ditch after dialing our local number. We traced the call to here."

I nodded. "Has anyone checked out the car?"

"There's a team on the way. Do you happen to know what she was doing this morning?"

"I'm afraid not. She dropped me off last night at my hotel. She said she had some leads to check out this morning. I had a couple I checked out myself. We were going to get together and compile our findings this afternoon."

"Well, if she calls you, do please let us know. Until then, I guess you can continue with whatever you were looking into. I don't want to poke my nose into her investigation, but we're worried about her. Can I have your number? We'll let you know if we find anything."

I handed him one of my business cards.

He glanced at it and then placed it in his coat pocket. "We'll let you know if we find her."

"Thanks." I walked back to my Jeep.

There wasn't anything else for me to do.

CHAPTER FORTY-FIVE

I left the accident site and drove slowly back to the hotel. I stopped and got something to eat from a fast-food place. I hadn't eaten that day. You may have noticed that I have a bad tendency to get distracted by what I'm working on and forget little things like food.

I was worried about the bullet holes in Taylor's car. The fact that her car had been found by the local police wasn't reassuring; we'd had quite a few problems with them. I wouldn't put it past some of them to shoot at her and run her off the road. What really worried me was that they might have captured her. I liked Taylor; I didn't want her to get hurt.

The rental car was still gone. I got out my cell phone and called Lawrence, but he was out of the service area. I sighed and took my food up to my room.

I had just finished eating when my phone rang.

"Hello?"

"Hey, you," said Michael.

"Goddamn, it's good to hear your voice."

"I was just going say that. You must be psychic."

We both chuckled for a moment.

"How's it going up in the mountains?" he asked.

"Ugh. Not well. Agent Taylor went missing this afternoon."

"Shit, what happened?"

I explained everything that had happened since I last talked to him. I left out the worst of the details about Heather, though. He didn't need to know all of that. Hell, I didn't even want to think about any of that.

"Well, I can't condone what Taylor did to you with the convict, but I understand it. So what's this you plan to do tomorrow? It sounds dangerous."

"I suppose it is. That woman I told you about, Heather: I got flashes of the people she used to hang with. All I had to do was be vulnerable in the right place, and one of the guys swooped in. I have him hooked now. This guy and the cult he's part of think they've got a helpless woman showing up at seven tomorrow. I plan to show up in full battle gear and watch them as they enter the house. Then I'll go in and have a long talk with them. I'll use force if I have to. It's too much of a coincidence that Heather knew these people, and we have bodies showing up killed in a similar fashion."

"If you have to kill, don't leave witnesses."

"Ha! That doesn't sound legal, mister marshal."

He snorted. "You don't have the same protections a law enforcement officer has."

"Can you make me a deputy federal marshal over the phone?" I asked.

"I'm afraid not. Just be careful, okay?"

"I will be. How is your case going?"

He sighed. "It's just about wrapped up. I never did figure out what was going on with the neo-Nazis. They might have just been a crazy anti-government group." He didn't sound convinced. "I'm in D.C. right now. I have a couple of meetings next week, and then I'll be free. Maybe by next weekend, certainly by the middle of the next week."

"Are you going back to Cincinnati?"

"Yes."

"Can you be sure? They've screwed you over before."

"I'll be back. I promise."

"I doubt I'll have this wrapped up by then," I said miserably, "but maybe I can get away for a day." That was a long drive. I'd do it to see him, but I didn't want to.

"We'll work something out."

We talked for another hour or so before he had to go.

I plugged my phone into the recharger and lay back in bed. I was worried about Taylor. I was worried about meeting the cultists. I was worried about many things. This whole case was getting out of control.

That was the only normal thing about it.

I tried Lawrence again but couldn't get him. I left a message for his room with the hotel message service. I hoped he and Jean were doing okay.

I changed into pajamas and watched television for a while. I dozed off during *The Princess Bride* and had some *very* odd dreams.

CHAPTER FORTY-SIX

By the next morning, I was really starting to worry about Lawrence and Jean.

Neither of them had called me the night before, or the whole morning. The rental car was still gone. They must have stayed up in South Williamson. I was worried that their father had taken a turn for the worse. He was a good man. I had mixed feelings about his passing. On the one hand, I knew what it would do to my friends; on the other hand, I couldn't help but think it would be best for him.

I started getting hungry around noon and decided that I needed to get out of bed and get moving. I took a shower. Then I went through the hotel drawers until I found a phone book. I wrote down the addresses of two Army surplus stores. Then I looked them up on a map of the city. I didn't want to waste any more time.

I grabbed lunch out – I was eating too much fast food – and drove to the closest store on my list. The surplus store was a long, narrow building that looked ready to fall down. I parked in the gravel lot and walked into the store. Heaps of folded clothes covered tables, flaccid backpacks hung from pegs, and boxes of various military goods were stuffed under every flat surface. The place was perfect. I started browsing.

"Can I help you, ma'am?" An ancient-looking man limped toward me. He wore slacks and a plain, light-blue button-up shirt, but he had a few medals and campaign ribbons on the front of it.

I gave him a genuine smile; I got a good feeling from him. "Hello, sir, I'm looking for combat boots, size nine, regular."

He nodded. "Any special type? I can show 'em to you."

"Thank you, sir. I'm looking for black leather speed-lacers," I said. "Ro-search, if you have them." Modern combat boots were unisex, but I liked the older ones that were in men's and women's sizes.

"You don't have to *sir* me, young lady. I was no officer." I could tell he appreciated it, though. He probably didn't get a lot of respect from the younger people in town.

I met his eyes; they were a watery blue. "You fought in the Pacific, in the Second World War? You were a marine?"

He nodded. I noticed his fingers twitched, too. He had some kind of palsy, then. "I was," he said proudly. "Fought at Guadalcanal."

"Then it's a *sir* for you, I'm afraid. You'll just have to get used to it." I smiled again.

"Oh, you're a cheeky one. If I was bit younger…" He sighed.

I laughed, and he grinned.

"So…" He eyed me critically. "These boots for you?"

"For myself, sir," I said. "I also need black fatigues, Special Forces grade, if you have them."

"Hmm. You're not going hunting in that getup."

I decided to trust this man. "Well, yes and no, sir. I'm in town working with the FBI."

"Trying to solve them murders," he asked, "or looking for drugs?"

"Trying to solve the murders. Both the girls and ones they don't talk about."

He sniffed. "A lot of good old folks up in the hills have died in recent years. Didn't know any of the Feds cared."

"I'm not a Fed, and I'm planning to stop that, sir."

He squinted his eyes at me. "You don't look military, girl. I didn't think they let women fight yet."

"I had special training," I said quietly.

"You might have, at that. You got the look in your eyes. Don't go seeking death; you got a lot of life left in ya. Look at me – I'm ninety-one years, haven't gotten tired of it yet." He chuckled to himself.

I smiled again.

"Here are those boots. Try 'em on."

I sat on the bench. The boots fit perfectly.

"Okay, then," He looked around. "You needed black fatigues. You know your measurements, I suppose?"

"Yes, sir." I told him.

He sifted through the stacks of clothing until he found pants and a shirt. "Try these," he said.

I held the pants up to my waist. They looked good enough. They were adjustable anyway. I set my jacket and purse on the counter. Then I stripped off my outer shirt, down to my black sports-bra, and tried the shirt on.

"Lord above, woman! You're going to give me a heart attack. You got the shoulders and muscles of a soldier, I'll give you that."

I flexed my arms and moved a bit to check the fit of the shirt across the shoulders. It was good. "I'll take them," I said.

He was still chuckling to himself as he walked behind the counter. I'd probably just made his day, maybe his decade. He rang me up as I changed back to my shirt and put my coat on. I paid him and thanked him.

I checked my watch; I still had time to make some plans. I drove back to the hotel and parked. I got out and opened the cargo gate on the back of the Jeep. I keep a few cases of goodies under the seat for special occasions. I deemed this evening's activities special enough.

I carried my new clothes, boots, and two large metal cases up to my room.

It was two o'clock.

CHAPTER FORTY-SEVEN

I did tai chi for two hours and then took another quick shower.

I was in the proper state of mind now, coldly prepared for anything that I might have to do.

I dressed in my black sports bra and fatigues. My boots went on next, followed by the body armor Taylor had loaned me. It was also black, with a small silver *FBI* embroidered over the left breast. I thought about putting a piece of black tape over it, but decided against it. If I got stopped by the police, it might help.

I pulled my hair back tightly and braided it. Then I put on black leather gloves and opened the two cases. The first case held a large rifle. I hoped never to need that. It was a HK G3. Big and mean. I closed that case and slid it next to the door. I'd carry it down when I left.

The second case held a HK MP 5 machine pistol: a submachine gun, really. That could come in handy. I took it out and strip-checked it. It was good. I reloaded the two thirty-round magazines with standard jacketed rounds. I placed a retractable metal wand in my right hip pocket. The last thing I took out of the case was a set of military-grade night vision goggles. I adjusted the strap to fit my head but didn't put it on yet.

I shrugged into my shoulder holster and double-checked the mag on my Smith, still loaded.

It was time to go. I hoped I didn't run into any cops on the way to my meeting.

I parked my Jeep well away from the house, a full street over.

I felt weighed down as I crossed the road and jogged through the woods to the other street. I had my Glock on my hip and four extra pistol mags for it. I had a suppressor in my pocket for the pistol. The Glock was loaded with Teflon-coated, light armor-piercing rounds, courtesy of Julia's PMC. Those rounds would go through a vest like the one I was wearing. I was hoping the people I was about to drop in on didn't have any – vests *or* Teflon rounds.

I didn't think it likely.

I sat in the woods and watched for an hour as people arrived at the house. Then I waited. The windows of the house were boarded up on the inside. The lawn was not in great shape. I wondered how many young women they had lured here. I'd gotten the impression that I wasn't the first woman the guy from the comic shop had done this to. My grip tightened on the MP5.

I sighed and looked at my watch. It was almost seven. No one had shown up for half an hour. I had counted eleven people, including the two who had come to the door to let the others in. Three of them were women; the other eight were men. None of them looked over forty. The youngest had looked to be in her early teens.

Time to go.

I drew my Glock and screwed on the suppressor. I had eighteen rounds before I had to reload; I'd have to make them all count if it got ugly in there. I slung my machine pistol over my shoulder and jogged over to the front door. With my Glock held low to the side, I knocked.

A man pulled open the door.

I raised the pistol and shook my head as he started to shout. "I wouldn't do that," I said quietly. "Move."

He swallowed convulsively and moved back, away from the door. I could hear people talking inside. They sounded stoned.

I followed the scared man inside. The living room was just off from the entry hall. Most of the people were sitting around on the floor. I smelled incense and marijuana smoke. "Move," I said again. I gestured toward the living room with the pistol.

I followed him. The conversations stopped suddenly as we walked in. I glanced around the room. All of the people I'd seen come into the house were here. They stared at me with eyes wide.

"Don't anyone move. Is there anyone else in the house?" I asked.

Matt stood near the old, brick fireplace. "No," he said. "Hey! You're the girl from the store!" He looked shocked. "What the fuck?"

I smiled grimly. "Not the mouse you were expecting?" I looked around at the others; their face held varying looks of anger and confusion. "I want weapons piled on the floor by my feet."

"Fuck you!" said a teen. He was maybe sixteen.

I put a bullet into the bricks by the fireplace. Everyone jumped at the quiet noise from the gun and the sound of shattering bricks. A subsonic round with a suppressor is pretty quiet. "The next round goes through the head of anyone who speaks without permission. Now, weapons on the floor."

A couple of small knives skittered across the carpet.

"No guns? Everyone against that wall." I used the pistol to indicate the wall I meant.

They quietly lined up. No one gave me any trouble as I patted them down. I found some baggies of pot and lighters, but no other weapons. I backed away.

"Okay, everyone sit. Let's talk."

A girl with blue hair raised her hand.

"Yes?"

"Can I go pee?"

"No. Don't ask any more stupid questions."

She sat and squirmed.

"Matt, are you the leader of this little party?"

He shrugged.

"You'll do. What do you know about the disappearance of Special Agent Taylor?" I asked.

"Who?" He looked confused.

"Anyone else?" No one said anything. It had been a long shot anyway. Honestly, I was betting on the local police. "Now, Matt, you seemed to have a certain agenda when I spoke to you yesterday."

"I don't know what you're talking about."

"Matt, don't make me kneecap you." I aimed the pistol at him, and he flinched.

Suddenly I was knocked off my feet by two heavy blows to the back. As I fell, I heard the roar of a large-caliber pistol. I rolled over as I hit the floor and put two rounds through the head of an older man running toward me. He flipped back and fell heavily to the floor, twitching. He'd been carrying a small oil lantern. It burst as it hit the floor and began to burn. I ignored the flames.

I kicked the pistol from his very dead hand.

No one else had moved.

I was angry and scared, both. My back felt as if it had been kicked by a horse. I could barely breathe. I moved along the wall and rested against it.

Then I shot Matt.

CHAPTER FORTY-EIGHT

I hadn't intended to.

I didn't even think about it: He smirked at me, and I shot him.

Matt screamed and clutched his right knee, blood flowing between his fingers. Several other people began sobbing. My head was pounding. I didn't feel like myself.

"What the fuck kind of FBI agent are you?" the teen boy screamed.

"I'm the kind they don't talk about. Help him with his leg. He'll need a tourniquet. Now, I'll ask everyone again: Is there anyone else here?"

They all shook their heads. Matt was moaning. The blue-haired girl had pissed herself.

"If someone else takes a shot at me, I'll shoot four of you at random."

No one said anything. Several of them were staring in shock at the body in the hall. I think I may even have meant it when I said it. I was shocked at what I was doing, but my training had taken over, and there was no stopping the train at this point.

"It's like this," I said quietly. "I've had some bad experiences with cults. I don't like them. I don't like anyone who does things like this. When I get to feeling like this, I don't care about due process. I just want justice." I took out several of the crime scene photos from my thigh pocket and tossed the picture on the floor in the center of the room.

They each looked at the photos. Several of them looked as if they were going to be sick.

"I want to know who is doing this."

They just shook their heads.

I sighed. I pushed myself away from the wall and walked over to Matt. "Matt, don't pass out on me, lover-boy. You were thinking of raping me, and cutting me while you were doing it, yesterday. What made you think you could away with that? Who's covering for you?"

"I wasn't thinking anything," he said through gritted teeth. "How the fuck could you know...?" He trailed off and stared at me. "You're not FBI. You're psi-ops," he whispered.

Psi-ops was one of those conspiracy theories the internet wouldn't let die. The gist of it was that the government used specially trained people with psychic abilities to wage a secret war against the American people. I suppose that might have been what the project that had created me had been about, but I doubt it. If any of us were used against the public, it was the government using a handy tool.

"If that's what you think of me, then you had better tell me what I want to know, or I'll rip it from your skull," I said, playing along.

I saw his eyes suddenly widen, and I dodged to the side. The teen boy had taken a piece of brick from the fireplace. It grazed the side of my head, and I went down. He hit me again before I managed to open-palm him under the chin. His head snapped back with a loud crack. I rolled to my feet. One of the other guys was going for the pistol. I kicked him in the ribs as hard as I could.

The blow lifted him off the floor. He flew into the wall and slumped to floor, unmoving.

I reached down and carefully picked up my pistol. No one else moved. I checked the two bodies; they were both dead.

"That was really dumb," I said tiredly. "Nobody else here had to die."

"What are you?" whispered one of the girls.

I was getting tired of answering that question.

"Are you..." She swallowed convulsively. "A real vampire?"

"Vampires are a myth, girl. I'm real, and I'm really pissed."

"You're not human," said Matt. "You're too strong. The way you kicked Mark..."

I knew I was going to have to kill all of them, and it sickened me. I needed to protect the secret of the project, or I was dead. I shook my head. I couldn't do it. I can kill in self-defense, but I'm not a killer like Julia. I'm not.

"Who was the guy I shot in the hall?" I asked.

"He was our master," the girl whispered.

"He tell you he was a vampire?"

She nodded.

I dragged his body into the room so they could all see him. "He's just rotting meat now," I said. "Doesn't look like a vampire." I reached down and pulled false fangs out of his mouth. "Look: fake teeth."

They just stared at me.

"Anyone know anything know anything about those pictures?" I asked. "Matt?"

"Go fuck yourself."

"Wrong answer," I said. I shot his other knee. I knew he'd go into shock soon and be useless to me. "You have a lot of joints in your body, Matt. I have a lot of bullets. Do you want to see if I run out of bullets before you die of shock and blood loss? I'm betting I can keep you alive. Anyone else want to bet?"

No one said anything. A few sobs broke the silence.

"Tell me what I want to know, or I'll kill each of you," I screamed. I didn't want to be like this. It was too close to the madness that had been inside Julia. I couldn't stop myself now. It was taking control. I could feel Heather's insanity tainting me. It was too close to my own darkness.

This wasn't me. I wasn't like this. I took several deep breaths. I needed to calm this down.

"Okay, who here wants to live? Let's see hands." Everyone but Matt raised their hands, but since he clutching both knees. I'd ignore that.

I unscrewed the silencer and put the gun back in my holster.

"Okay, piss girl, come over here."

"What are you going to do?"

"Don't make me repeat myself."

She stood up hesitantly and walked over to me. I placed my hand on her head. She was easy to read. I didn't need to touch her, but that made it easier. She was only into things a little bit. She played the game and pretended to be a real vampire to freak people out, but she wasn't a killer.

"You understand that if you talk, I'll find you. You're marked now. Go." She ran out of the house. I waited for the door to slam shut before turning to the next person.

I repeated the performance with each of them. Only Matt had actually hurt women, and a few boys. Tonight was to be the initiation for the rest. They hadn't even known what was supposed to happen. Many cults are like that: They force you to be a part of something horrible, and then use your guilt to control you. I would have been the main course.

I let everyone else go. I heard cars peel out on the road. The flames were roaring in the hall. I'd have to go soon, if I didn't want to die. I didn't think I did, but I wasn't sure. I felt sick and dizzy from what I'd done.

I walked over to the window and ripped a board loose. The others were all gone. I concentrated, but I couldn't feel anyone else around. Matt and I were alone. I wasn't sure what I was going to do with him. I didn't want to kill him. Not anymore. I just wanted the night to be over.

Matt must have gotten ahold of one of the knives while I was distracted. He threw it as I turned back into the room. It hit me in the side of the head. Luckily, it had been poorly thrown. It hit hilt first, and it hurt, but not badly. I didn't even think about it as I saw Matt's arm come back to throw another knife: I shot him twice in the chest.

He sort of coughed and sagged back, blood pouring from his

mouth.

I hadn't meant to kill him. Not really. It was all reflexes. I rushed over to him, but he was already on his way out. Two in the chest, one through his heart, plus the leg wounds. It didn't take him long.

I held his hand as he died. Partly to comfort him. Partly to see what information I could pull from him before he completely expired. His dying thoughts weren't exactly coherent. They were a mixture of anger and confusion, with a lot of regret and guilt. He hadn't started off as a bad person. He'd just gotten drunk on the power he'd been given over those poor unfortunates that entered his circle. The man I'd shot on the stairs had been the ringleader.

As Matt died, I caught one clear image and thought. He was thinking that Reggie the Snake was going to be pissed at what had happened tonight. Matt was supposed to deliver me to Reggie once he'd had his fun. Reggie, apparently, was a broker for a human trafficker.

I left the house burning behind me. I was tired and felt dirty. I'd check tomorrow on the leads Matt had given me. I didn't have any real remorse over Matt's death, or the others. Not after what I had gotten from Matt. He was a murderer and a rapist. The others had sometimes helped him.

Matt had deserved what he'd gotten.

I wasn't too happy with what I'd had to do to get the information, but I had to have it. I had to stop those murders. Someone out there in the hills was just like the psycho, Heather. They may have even been the one who'd made her that way. I still had flashes of her memories in my head. She had such a strong personality; it was hard not to be influenced by her. She had grown up in those hills, with her family. Someone had killed them all in front of her, and they'd died hard. She'd been raped and left to play with her *dolls*, the stuffed skins of her family. No wonder she was nuts.

I wasn't trying to find excuses.

Not for her behavior or mine.

We make our own choices in life, no matter what has happened to us. Tonight was the first time I had killed someone in anything but the heat of the moment. It had always been self-defense before, much easier to rationalize. From one way of looking at things, it could be said that I had killed Matt to protect others, and that is true. His death would save many people, hopefully.

I even thought I saw something following me through the woods. Probably my conscience.

Tonight, I knew, I wouldn't sleep well.

CHAPTER FORTY-NINE

The next morning was rough.

My right foot was swollen and purple; I could barely walk on it. I didn't even remember hurting it, but I must have broken it when I'd kicked that guy who'd gone for the gun.

My back was one large, purple bruise. The muscles kept jerking spasmodically. When I peed, there was bright red in my urine; the lower round had hit near my left kidney. I felt terrible.

After debating with myself for over an hour about what to do, I finally called a cab to take me to the hospital. I didn't want to go, but I was having trouble breathing. It scared me. I waited a few minutes and then limped down to the elevator.

I waited for ten agonizing minutes in the lobby before the cab showed up.

"Pikeville Medical Center," I said as I got into the car.

Luckily, there wasn't a lot of traffic. The cabbie dropped me off at the door, and I paid in cash. I didn't want to wait for him to process my credit card. I was still thinking I'd be able to cover up what happened.

I limped into the emergency room. I signed in at the registrar and stood back to wait.

She looked up. "It'll be a few minutes, ma'am, if you'd like to take a seat."

"If I sit, I doubt I'll able to get back up," I said through gritted teeth.

"What's wrong with you?"

"I think I have a broken foot and maybe some broken ribs."

She got up and came around the desk. "Let's get you into a wheelchair and then get these forms filled out." She got me settled into a chair and went back to her desk.

I few minutes later, a nurse came through a door and called out, "Re, Ruh… Michelle Fredericks?"

I waved weakly. "It's Rhiannon, but I go by Michelle."

"That will be easier." She came around and pushed my wheelchair into a triage room. She put a blood pressure cuff on my arm and a thermometer in my ear. She made a few marks in the chart she held.

"So what brings to the emergency room today?" the nurse asked.

I repeated my list of injuries, including the blood.

"That doesn't sound good." She looked at me sympathetically. "Your man beat you?" She sounded bored, as if that happened all the time. She was writing down everything I told her.

I sighed. I suppose that would be the most common reason for injuries like mine in a place like Pikeville. "No, I'm in town working with the FBI. I had a close encounter with some bad guys last night. I didn't realize I was hurt this badly."

She looked at me quizzically. "Seriously?"

"I'm afraid so. I can show you my papers."

"That's okay. We'll get you fixed up. Wait here for a minute." She left by a different door. A few minutes later, she was back. "Okay, let's get you into an exam room and get you checked out."

The nurse wheeled me into the actual emergency room. The room was mostly open, with curtained beds in alcoves, and a few small private exam rooms. She took me to one of the private rooms.

"Do you need help getting undressed?"

"I hate to ask, but I think I could use the help."

She helped me get undressed and into a gown. She gasped when she saw my back. "That doesn't look good at all. Just try to rest. The doctor will be in soon."

I leaned back in the bed and propped my foot up. It was cold back in here. I'd sort of zoned out, but then a sudden knock on the door brought my attention back. The doctor came into the room, holding my chart. The nurse came in with him, but stood back by the door.

"Michelle? May I call you Michelle? I'm Dr. Thacker. Let's have a look at you."

I flinched when he said his name, but Thacker is a common name in this part of the state. I doubted he was closely related to Heather Thacker.

He looked at my foot first, pushing and prodding it with his thumb. I was barely able to keep from crying out.

"Well, you have bad bruising and maybe a couple of broken bones in there. Less swelling than I would expect, but we'll see. Let's look at your back. Lie down here on your stomach, if you can."

I carefully rolled over and lay on the narrow bed.

Dr. Thacker deftly untied the gown at the top and pushed it open just enough to see my back. He repeated his prodding there. I was gasping and shaking by the time he was done.

"So tell me how that happened. I'm not sure what I'm seeing here."

I got my breath under control. "I was shot in the back twice with a forty-five-caliber pistol, at close range."

His eyebrows scrunched together as he stared at me. "Pardon me for not getting that. You say you were *shot*? You don't have any bullet holes. A forty-five would have killed you."

I sighed. "I was wearing a level-three Kevlar vest."

"Ah, and how did you come by that?"

"Look, doc, I'm in town working with the FBI. Call them, ask for Special Agent Mullins, and ask him if he knows me."

"Oh, okay. Can I ask about how this came about? And when? You should have come here immediately."

"I'm working with the FBI on a criminal investigation. I can't tell you more than that about it. I was investigating some leads and was shot in the back while doing it."

"Okay, how did you hurt your foot?"

"Kicking the guy who shot me," I lied.

He stared at me for a moment and then started laughing.

I smiled hesitantly.

"Okay, I'm sure he got what he deserved. Let's see about getting you fixed up. We'll need to get you down to Radiology for some x-rays, back and foot. You said you were having problems with blood in the urine. Do you think you could pee in a cup for us?"

"If I had something to drink, I could."

"Okay, a tech will be in to take you down to Radiology. I'll see about getting a drink for you. It's going to just be water, I'm afraid."

I couldn't tell if he was joking. "That'll do. Thanks."

He started to leave the room but then paused. "You realize that we have to report this to the police? I'm sorry, but it's the law."

"I understand. Just call the FBI, too, if you don't mind. Ask for Special Agent Mullins."

He left the room.

I sighed heavily and lay on my stomach. *I should have thought of this.*

CHAPTER FIFTY

A nurse came in with two cups in her hands.

She sat the plastic cup with the lid on my bed. Then she handed me the cup of cold water.

I drank the water in one gulp. It tasted good. I hadn't realized how dehydrated I felt.

"This cup is for our sample. Whenever you need to go next, just make sure to save us at least half a cup, okay?"

When I nodded, she turned to go. "The x-ray tech will be here in a couple of minutes."

The doctor was talking on the phone and looking my way when they wheeled me down to Radiology. I had a feeling this was going to be a long day. The tech twisted my foot enough to make me cry out. Sometime, I don't think those people are human.

The doctor came in to see me when I got back from Radiology. "I made some phone calls. The police are sending a couple of officers over to take your statement. I also called the FBI. You're going to have a lot of explaining to do in a few minutes; I thought you should be prepared."

"Thanks, doctor."

"The x-rays should be developed soon. We'll see what we can do then to ease your pain."

I nodded.

A few minutes later, the nurse brought two police officers back to my exam room. She made the man stand outside while the woman officer came in to talk with me. That amused me, for some reason.

"Hello," the officer said. "I'm Officer Kelly. You're Michelle Fredericks? I understand you say you were shot?" She looked dubious.

I was sitting up on the bed. I smiled at her confusion. I hadn't even known Pikeville had female officers. How very progressive of them. "I'm working with the FBI. I took two shots from a forty-five in the back at close range. I was wearing a vest. I didn't see who shot me. We struggled in the dark. He thought I was dead at first. We fought, and I gave him a good kick but broke some toes."

Officer Kelly blew out a breath, hard. "Okay. You said you're working with the FBI? You're an FBI agent?"

"No, I'm a civilian attaché."

"Were you with an agent at the time of the attack?"

"Of course, she was, officer." Special Agent Mullins was standing in the open door. He held out his ID. "If I'd known she was hurt, we'd have come in last night."

I could tell Officer Kelly was nervous about having the agent standing there.

"Where did the incident take place?" asked Officer Kelly.

"Out of town along the highway," I said.

"Can you be more specific, please?" She looked annoyed.

"I'm sorry, officer, but I think that's enough questions," said Mullins. "You have the basics of what happened. This is an FBI matter."

"If someone is shot, we need to –"

"You need to back off and not overstep your jurisdiction. I said it's an FBI matter. End of discussion. Good day, officer." He held the door open for her.

She sighed and put away her notebook. "If you decide you want to press charges, let us know. Jurisprudence aside, if this guy comes forward and says you assaulted him, it's a good idea to have your complaint on file first."

"Thank you, Officer Kelly. I'm not worried about that." I really did appreciate her concern. She must have had a hard time working in that police department.

She left, and Mullins watched the officers leave the ER, then shut the door.

"Damn, that looks nasty," he said, looking at my foot. He came around and sat next to the bed. "You know, I'm almost afraid to ask you what really happened. Taylor said you had a penchant for getting into trouble."

I smiled. "She said that?" I sighed. "I don't suppose you've heard from her."

He shook his head.

The doctor came in and stared at Mullins. "Who are you?"

"Special Agent Mullins, FBI." He didn't get up.

"Oh, yes, we spoke on the phone." The doctor glanced at me. "Do you want him in the room for this?" He wiggled the x-ray film.

"If he wants to stay, it's fine by me."

"Okay." The doctor put the x-rays up on a light board and switched it on. He rubbed his face. "Okay," he began again, "you've got three broken toes, and two of the metatarsals are fractured. Oddly, the bones seem to be in correct alignment and fusing already." He scowled at me. "Are you sure this happened last night?"

"Quite sure, doctor."

He sighed. "You have four cracked ribs, two here and two here." He pointed to the ribs. "They are also starting to fuse. From the degree of bruising and the condition of the bones, I would have speculated that these were over a week old."

I was beginning to think that I should have had Mullins wait outside.

"What can I say, doctor? I heal fast."

Mullins cleared his throat. "I'm sure she didn't have these injuries yesterday when I saw her."

The doctor nodded slowly. "And of course, your agent was with her last night when she was injured."

"Of course."

"Okay, I don't know what we can do for you, Michelle. Once injuries have gone a certain amount of time since they happened, we can only patch you up. I'll get some bandages." He left the room.

"You heal pretty damn fast," said Mullins.

"I do," I said helplessly.

"Will you please tell me, after we leave here, what actually happened?"

I nodded. I could do that, at least. Mullins had kept me out of hot water with the police.

The doctor came back in with a nurse and a handful of bandages. The nurse carried a crutch. "Do you mind stepping out?" the nurse said to Mullins.

Mullins got up without a word and left the room. The nurse shut the door.

"Let's take care of this first." Dr. Thacker and the nurse carefully wrapped my foot up. It hurt, but not as badly as it had before. They taped my toes together, with cotton balls between them, before they wrapped the whole foot in an elastic bandage.

"We'll need you to remove your gown. Would you prefer I ask another nurse to assist, instead of myself?"

"I'm sure you've seen breasts before, doctor. I'm not real worried about it."

The nurse laughed.

"I'll just stand back here. By the way, your urine test is back. It had very little blood in it. You probably just took light damage to the kidney. You get a little blood in the urine from that."

"I know," I said without thinking.

He stood behind me and undid the gown. Then he and the nurse wrapped a wide elastic bandage around my ribs, tightly. It hurt.

"Damn, I've always hated these things," I said.

The nurse draped the gown across my chest, and the doctor came around. "Here are your discharge papers. I've written you a prescription for a painkiller and a muscle-relaxer."

"You can keep the painkiller, doc. I'll just take a couple of ibuprofen. The muscle-relaxer will be nice, though. I've had some nasty back spasms."

"Well, fill both prescriptions. You may be in more pain later. I wish you luck. Try not to get shot again."

"I don't plan on it."

"No one ever does."

CHAPTER FIFTY-ONE

Mullins offered to take me back to the hotel, and I accepted.

We stopped first by the hospital's drive-through pharmacy and got my prescriptions filled.

He didn't say anything to me all the way back to the hotel. He parked up front and came around the car to help me. We went up to my room, stopping only to pick up two Cokes for me from the machine.

In my room, I sat on the bed, and he sat in Taylor's usual spot on the desk chair. I suddenly realized that I missed her company; we'd quickly become friends. Mullins waited for me to take my medicine and get settled before he spoke.

"So... Would you like to tell me what really happened?"

"Honestly, no. But I will if you want. I have to warn you that you won't like what you hear."

"Does it have to do with Taylor's case?"

"Yes."

"Does it have to do with Taylor's disappearance?"

"Not that I know of. I was hoping..., but no."

"Damn." He got up and walked over to the table to look at the body armor. His fingers found the places on the back where I'd been hit. "You get this from Taylor?"

"The armor? Yes. She left it with me after the incident with Officer May," I said. "The bullets…"

He nodded and sat back down. "Dr. Fredericks—" he began.

"Call me Michelle."

"Okay, Michelle, I'm not sure if I *want* to know what is going on. Not right now, anyway. From what Taylor said, this whole case is like something from the *X-Files.*"

I wondered if *he* thought Taylor looked a dark-haired Scully, too, but I didn't ask.

He sighed. "Okay, if Taylor isn't found within three more days, I have to take over the case. I hope she shows up. She's a good friend, and a good agent. But if she doesn't, I'll need you working with me. Are you okay with that?"

"Certainly. I hope Taylor is found. I like her. But if she isn't, I'll work just as closely with you. I want to see this case solved."

"So do I." He frowned. "One other thing: If we do end up working together, I'll need you to be honest with me. I'll need to know everything that has happened so far in this case, if I'm going to be able to solve it."

"I have no problem with that."

"Okay, good. Try to stay out of trouble? If any new leads develop, call me first? I'll smooth things over with the locals before they get involved. You and Taylor have pissed off half this city so far. Let's give the other half a chance to avoid that. Okay?"

I smiled. "I'll stay out of trouble. I'd like to rest. Maybe take the weekend off. I came up here with friends last week, before I was called into this case. I'd like to spend a little time with them."

"Take as much time as you need. I'll be in touch." He stood up and moved toward the door.

"Mullins?"

He turned and looked at me.

"Thanks for trusting me," I said.

"I don't," he said frankly. "But I trust Taylor, and she trusted you. That's good enough for me, for now."

He turned and left the room.

I sat and watched the door slowly close until it clicked.

What a day, I thought.

Lawrence still wasn't answering his phone.

I called the front desk, but they hadn't seen him or Jean. I decided that I would make the trip to South Williamson in the morning and see if I could find them. I was sure they were all right, but it never hurt to check

I'd wait for Taylor or Mullins to check on the other leads in the case.

My foot and ribs were killing me. I took one of the pain pills the doctor prescribed me and slept through the night.

I had vague dreams of something trying to get through my window, but they were just dreams, right?

CHAPTER FIFTY-TWO

I was sore in the morning, but not as badly as I'd expected.

I unwrapped my bandages and took a hot bath. The water soothed my muscles, and I was finally able to relax. Once I was out and dry, my back only hurt when I moved or breathed. Like the old tired joke.

"So," I said to myself, "as long as I don't do either of those things, I'm fine." I made a face at the me in the mirror. I couldn't tell if she was as amused by it all as I was.

I bandaged my ribs back up. Then I carefully bent and taped my toes back together. Most of the bruising was gone; nothing was left except lines of bruises where the actual cracks in the bone were. I didn't wrap my foot back up. I decided to wear my new combat boots; they would be enough support. If I was going to be kicking people, though, maybe I should get steel-toed boots.

It wasn't as funny as it should have been. There were a lot of people in that county that I wanted to kick. Starting with most of the police.

I tried Lawrence's number again. Still nothing.

I got dressed and knocked on Lawrence's and Jean's rooms. Nothing.

I'd intended to leave my gun at the hotel, but I couldn't bring myself to do it. I'd leave it in the Jeep's console when I got to their parents' trailer.

The trip to South Williamson seemed to take longer than I thought it should. I shook my head. I'm always a little groggy after taking medication. That's why I hardly ever take it. Well, that and the fact that I have a high pain tolerance. Still, I probably wouldn't have slept much without the meds.

I was feeling tense as I drove up the narrow roads to their home.

The rental car was sitting in the driveway. I let out a sigh of relief. I parked behind the rental car and got out. The sun moved behind a cloud, and a dog started barking somewhere up the road. I felt a sudden chill come over me.

I moved as quickly as I could up to the front door and knocked.

Lawrence's mother answered the door with a scowl. I realized I didn't know her name.

"Hello, ma'am. I'm Lawrence and Jean's friend, Michelle. Could I talk one of them?"

"No. Go away. You aren't welcome here." She started to close the door.

I put my foot in the door and winced as it jarred the broken bones. "Please, I just want to make sure they're okay."

"They aren't here," she spat.

"Do you know where they are?"

"I don't know. They haven't called me or even come to see their daddy." She started to close the door again.

"Please, it's important. Lawrence and Jean could be in danger. Now, I'll ask you again. Do you know where they are?"

Lawrence's mother sighed. "I haven't seen them in two days. They left with Sissy one afternoon and ain't been back. You might ask her."

I'd do that. "Thank you." I moved my foot, and she slammed the door.

I limped to the next trailer over and knocked on the front door. I was thinking about what to say to her when Sissy answered it. She had a twelve-gauge shotgun in her hand.

"Get off my property, whore," she hissed.

This wasn't going the way I'd imagined it. "Look," I said, "I know you don't like me. I'm just looking for Lawrence and Jean. Tell me where they are, and I'll leave and never come back. I promise."

She seemed scared for some reason. I hadn't done anything to *her*. She hadn't gotten scared until I mentioned Lawrence and Jean.

"You got three seconds," she said. She stepped out onto her porch, the shotgun leveled at my chest.

Gotcha, I thought. I snatched the gun out of her hands and spun it around. I put the barrel to her eye before she could move or call out. "Now, let me ask you again. This is your last chance. Where are they?"

"The devil's got them, and he'll have you, too!"

"Wrong answer." I slapped her with my open hand. "I'll count to three, and then I'm going to redecorate the side of your trailer with the contents of your skull, family of a friend or not."

She clenched her jaw stubbornly.

"Three," I said and started to squeeze the trigger.

"Okay! Okay!" She cowered down. "I'll tell! Please God, just don't kill me!"

"Then tell me before I get angry and decide the shotgun is too quick for you, dammit!"

"They're in the basement of my church. They're awaitin' the preacher to pass judgment on them for their sins. Poor Jeanie's gotten herself possessed, being around people like you!" She spat on my boots. I ignored that; I needed to polish them soon anyway.

"Where's this church?" When Sissy didn't answer, I fired one of the two rounds into the air and pointed the shotgun at her head again. "Where?"

"At the end of the holler. It's the white building. *May God strike you down!*" she cried, pointing.

I just stood and smiled at her.

Her jaw dropped, and she looked at the sky. I think she really expected a bolt of lightning to blast me or something.

"Okay, inside with you." She didn't move, so I reached down and threw her through the door. I quickly followed. She was already going for the phone.

I shot it.

The blast was incredibly loud in the small room. Sissy cried out and flung herself back; a little of the buckshot may have peppered her. I didn't really care. I dropped the gun and picked her up again, holding her off the ground by the front of her shirt with one hand.

"What are you?" she wailed.

I smiled through the pain of my ribs, and spoke on impulse. "I'm an avenging angel sent down here to clean this mess up. Your 'preacher' is an agent of the devil," I said.

Her eyes got wide. *"No!"* She started sobbing.

"You'd better not be lying to me about Lawrence and Jean," I said.

"I'm not! Please God!"

I dropped her. She lay on the carpet in a crumpled heap, crying. I walked into the kitchen and quickly found some clothesline in a drawer. She didn't protest or resist as I tied her up. I think my comments about the preacher must have really hit home. It hadn't taken much for her to believe it.

I left Sissy in the bedroom closet and ran back to my Jeep. I needed to get to that church. I had a feeling I'd just found a big clue as to who was behind the killing of the girls.

I just hoped I wasn't too late.

CHAPTER FIFTY-THREE

I drove cautiously up the narrow road.

I tried calling Mullins but couldn't get a good enough cell signal. The feeling of urgency was too strong for me to ignore. I needed to get up to the church. A beat-up pickup truck with a gun rack in the window sat in the gravel parking lot. I couldn't help but think of Taylor being run off the road and chased. It could have been rifle shots that had gone through her car's windows. Black paint was smeared on the fender.

I was sure it would match Taylor's car.

I parked and walked around the church. I had my pistol in my hand. I didn't care who saw me. If anyone had confronted me, I would have shot them without even thinking about it. The church was a little, one-story building that looked as if it only had one large room inside. It was wood-sided and sat on a cement-block foundation. The basement probably leaked when it rained. The windows were narrow and filled with heavily frosted glass.

I took a deep breath and walked to the front of the church. I could feel Lawrence and Jean some place nearby. I carefully tried the door. It was locked. I could hear someone inside moving around.

I knocked on the door and stood with my gun out of sight.

A man in his forties, with salt-and-pepper hair, answered the door.

He was wearing a clerical collar and was dressed in black. He had a black eye.

"Can I help you? Services aren't until tonight."

"I was hoping you would do a special service for me, pastor."

He frowned. "I sorry, I don't—" He stopped speaking as I held up the gun.

"You can take me Lawrence and Jean, or I'll blow your fucking head off."

"I don't know what you're talking about! I'm calling the police!" He started to shut the door.

I shoved the door open and grabbed him by the back of his shirt.

He fell to his knees, praying.

I glanced around the church. It was empty. There were two closet-sized boxes sticking out from the wall up by the altar. The boxes had plywood doors, and they were padlocked. I thought one of those could be a stairwell.

I placed the gun against his head. "God helps those that help themselves, pastor. You have two people locked in your basement, don't you?"

He nodded slowly.

"Is there anyone else here besides them?"

"No, I swear to God. Please don't kill me."

"I won't if you do exactly as I say. Get up." I shut the door behind me and locked it without turning.

He got up and stood there, trembling.

"Are you the one that goes by the name *the Preacher*?" I asked.

"No, I'm just the pastor here. *He's* going to be here tomorrow."

"Good. I'm with the FBI," I said, just for the record. "Take me to them. If you try anything, I *will* kill you. Do you doubt it?"

"No," he said quietly. "I've heard about you."

"Is there a phone in here?"

"Yes, it's over here." He led me to the right-hand closet and unlocked it. There, on the shelf, was a phone.

"Dial this number and hand me the phone, *slowly*." I told him the number, and he dialed it carefully, then handed me the phone. "Stand there," I said. I kept the gun pointed at the pastor's head.

"Special Agent Mullins," he answered.

"Hello. This is Fredericks. I'm in South Williamson. I think you need to get out here as fast as possible, but be discreet."

"What is this about?" he asked.

"I think I just stumbled across one of our killers."

"Give me the address, and I'll be there as fast as possible. Don't do anything foolish."

"You know me," I said.

"That's what I'm afraid of. Give me the address."

I didn't know the address, but I gave him detailed directions and hung up the phone.

"Now," I said, "lead me to me Lawrence and Jean."

The pastor slowly walked over to the other door and unlocked it. Then he flipped a switch in the wall and started down the steps.

"Stop," I said. "Lawrence? Jean? Are you down there?"

Silence for a moment, and then, "Oh, my God! Michelle! Help! You've got to get us out of here!" Both of them were speaking at once.

I shoved the man in front of me. "Get moving."

We came to the bottom of the steps. Jean and Lawrence were chained to the floor. Lawrence looked as if he'd been beaten. They were both dirty and malnourished looking. I doubted either of them had been given food or water.

"Unlock them," I pressed the gun to the pastor's head.

He fumbled with the keys and unlocked them both.

I helped them up and gave them each a quick hug. "Let's get upstairs," I said. "More help is on the way."

We went up to the main part of the church.

I made the pastor sit by the door with his hands on his head.

Lawrence and Jean wanted to tell me what had happened. "Wait," I said.

We waited until I heard a car pull into the parking lot. I handed the gun to Lawrence. "Do you think you could shoot him if he moves or makes a sound?" I asked.

Lawrence smiled grimly. "I would have no problem at all with that."

I opened the door a crack.

Mullins was running up. I opened the door and let him in.

He stopped in surprise when he saw the tableau inside the church. I shut and locked the door.

"Fredericks, what's going on?" Mullins asked quietly.

I took my gun back from Lawrence and holstered it. "This is Special Agent Mullins." I pointed I named each person. "This is Lawrence, his sister Jean, and the local pastor. Why don't you each tell your story to Agent Mullins? Lawrence, you can go first."

Lawrence rubbed his face. "Okay. It might be easier to have Jean and me to sort of go at the same time. My sister, Sissy, told us that she wanted to talk to us both. To reconcile our relationship while our father was still alive." His voice broke there. "Sorry. Anyway, we walked over to her trailer, and she pulled out a shotgun on us. Then five men I didn't know jumped us and beat me unconscious. I fought back, but..." He shrugged. "That's how this guy got the shiner," he said, pointing to the pastor.

Jean took up the story. "They gagged us and took us out to a pickup truck. They threw us in the back and drove up here. Then they dragged us down to the basement and chained us up."

"When was this?" asked Mullins.

"Thursday morning. I'm not sure how long it's been."

"It's Sunday," I said.

"Oh. Well, this guy gave us water a couple of times. The rest of the time, we've been down there. He seemed to think I was possessed or something. He said *the Preacher* would deal with me and Lawrence." She started shaking.

"Down where?" asked Mullins.

"The basement is over there," I said.

CHAPTER FIFTY-FOUR

Mullins came back a few minutes later and sat down. "I'd like to know more about this Preacher, but first, how did you find them?"

"I was coming up to look for them. These are my friends I mentioned. I hadn't seen them in a few days. I drove up and saw their rental car in the drive at their parents' trailer. I asked their mother, and she said they had gone off with Sissy, and she hadn't seen them in a few days. I talked Sissy into telling me where they were."

"Is she still alive?" asked Lawrence.

I couldn't tell if he was kidding or not. "She's fine. I didn't hurt her. I said some harsh things to her, though, especially after she tried to shoot me with her shotgun."

Mullins shook his head. "You can't stay out of trouble, can you?" He turned to the pastor. "You're in a lot of trouble with the law. If you cooperate, I may be able to get your sentence reduced."

"Mullins," I said, "you might want to ask him about Taylor before you make any deals."

He looked at me and then back at the pastor. "Well, what do you know about a missing FBI agent?"

The pastor had been silent up till now, quietly wringing his hands. He sighed. "The Preacher told us that there was an FBI agent snooping around and that he wanted her taken care of. I had a few of the Hatfield boys go after her. They said they ran her off the road and chased her into the woods. They couldn't find her and didn't try too hard. She'd shot one of them. I buried him yesterday."

"So you say she was still alive when they came back?" asked Mullins. "Killing a federal officer is a serious offense. The criminals don't often make it to trial. I hope, for your sake, you're telling the truth." He looked at me.

"For what it's worth, I think he *is* telling the truth," I said.

"Okay, so tell me about this Preacher, whoever he is," he said tiredly.

"The Preacher is God's chosen envoy from Heaven," the pastor said fervently.

Mullins rolled his eyes. "What's his real name?"

"I don't know. He gave up his name to God."

"Go on."

"He travels through this region, passing judgment on sinners and healing the faithful. He's found many a sinner in these parts. He's even—" The pastor lowered his voice. "He's found demons possessing young girls." He made the sign of the cross at Jean.

"And what does he do to these girls?" Mullins asked.

"He frees them," the pastor said simply.

"How?"

"I don't know. I've not been blessed with the knowledge. I've failed him and the Lord," he said in a quiet voice. Then he began sobbing.

Mullins rubbed his temples. "Okay, I'll get the state police up here. We need to catch this preacher and lock him up. We'll get names and then catch the rest of them." He smiled at me. "Good work."

I waited for him to use the phone and make some calls.

"Do you need us here?" I asked.

"No. We'll need official statements from all of you at some point, but that can wait."

"Oh, Lawrence's sister, Sissy, is tied up and locked in her closet. I'd like to press charges for assault now. I may drop them later."

"Okay, I'll have her picked up. I'm sure this one knows where she lives."

We waited for the police to arrive and then left. Jean and I had to help Lawrence to my Jeep. Once I got them both in, I climbed in and started back down the hollow.

"Do you want to stop for the car or get it later?" I asked.

"Later," said Jean. "If you don't mind bringing us back up here sometime, that is."

"I don't mind. I'd like to see your dad again."

I drove us back to the hotel. They slept the whole way back.

We got upstairs to my room somehow.

I got clean clothes and towels for them and let them use my shower. They didn't want to be alone. I could understand that. Lawrence let Jean take a shower first, which showed how much he loved his sister. I ordered two pizzas and a couple of two-liters of Coke while Lawrence was in the shower. Jean lay on the bed and rested.

We were sitting and talking quietly when there was a knock on the door.

"Pizza," I said and opened the door.

It wasn't the pizza delivery person.

It was Taylor.

"Oh my god!" I exclaimed.

She almost fell into the room.

I caught her and carried her to the bed. Jean and Lawrence moved to let me lay her down.

She'd passed out.

I quickly checked Taylor over, but she didn't seem to be wounded. She looked haggard and tired; her cheeks were gaunt.

"She's been missing since Wednesday," I said quietly. "She must have walked back from where they ran her off the road."

I checked her pulse. It was a bit fast but steady. "Jean, would you mind getting her a soda from the machine? There's cash in the table."

"Sure." She grabbed a handful and started for the door.

Another knock came from the door before she could open it.

Jean opened the door. It *was* the pizza this time.

"What?" Taylor started.

"You're okay. I'm here. It's Michelle." I gently pushed her shoulders back down onto the bed.

The door closed.

I looked up.

"I just signed the receipt and handed him the extra cash as a tip. Is she okay?"

I laughed. "We've had a hell of a week, haven't we?"

Jean and Lawrence sat at the table, eating and talking quietly.

I helped Taylor get something to drink. After a few minutes, she was strong enough again to sit up and eat some pizza.

"You know," she said quietly, "when I said I wanted to diet, I didn't quite mean like this."

I smiled sadly. Four days without food had left her face too thin. I doubted she'd been carrying much extra weight before that. Once Taylor got some food and soda into her, she decided she was steady enough to take a shower, if I didn't mind.

"I'm just glad to see you again," I said. I got up and got some clean pajamas out of my suitcase. "Here, you can wear these. I think Mullins took possession of your things."

Taylor nodded. "Fred's a good guy." She went into the bathroom.

I finished eating while she was in the shower.

I tried not to laugh when she came out, but I couldn't help it. My clothes were huge on her.

"Laugh it up," she said, smiling.

I picked up my cell phone and called Mullins.

"Yes?" he answered. He sounded worn out.

"Hello, this is Michelle Fredericks."

"Oh, how are your friends?"

"They're fine. All of them. There's someone here I think you'd like to talk to."

"Who?" I heard him say as I handed the phone to Taylor.

She took the phone out into the hall to talk to him.

I let her back in a few minutes later.

She came into the room and sat on her chair. "Well, you've been busy. Do you really think this Preacher is the one who's killing the girls?" she asked.

I noticed Jean pale at the mention of killing. "I think so. There's a lot of evidence against him."

"Good. One down, then. How does one go about getting a hotel room here? I don't have my purse or wallet. Do you think they would take my word that I'm an FBI agent?" She grinned.

I shook my head, walked over to the phone, and called the front desk. "Hello, this is Michelle Fredericks in 316. Is 317 occupied?" I asked. "No? Good. I'd like to have it. No, I just want to add it to the other three. Okay, thanks."

I turned to Taylor, who looked amazed. "They'll bring up the room key in a moment."

The four of us sat and talked for hours before exhaustion and injuries forced us each to our own beds.

I had a good feeling about the way things were turning out.

I couldn't have been more wrong.

CHAPTER FIFTY-FIVE

Taylor woke me up by knocking on my door early in the morning. I rolled out of bed. It was only six o'clock.

"Yes?" I said blearily as I opened the door.

"Rise and shine," said Taylor. "We have real work to do today."

She was dressed in a dark suit.

"Wha'?" I wasn't awake yet.

Mullins peeked his head around the doorframe. "Get dressed. We have bad guys to catch, remember?"

I groaned. "Okay. I need to take a quick shower. Wake up Lawrence and Jean for me, would you? I promised to take them to get their car back. Might as well do it today and save a trip."

"Sure, but hurry," said Taylor.

I nodded and shut the door. It didn't take me long to take a shower and get dressed. I decided to wear the black fatigues and boots. I grabbed my gear and walked into the hall. Lawrence, Jean, and Taylor were talking quietly about the terrain up around the church.

"I'm ready," I said.

"Okay, we'll get rolling, then. Mullins is downstairs with the car. I'm going on ahead with him to get things moving. Meet us there, okay?"

We walked down the hall and got on the elevator. I went outside and started the Jeep while Lawrence and Jean grabbed a quick breakfast in the lobby. I pulled up to the doors and left it running; I grabbed a donut and an apple juice while the Jeep warmed up. The outside air was cold, and there was a light dusting of snow on the ground.

We didn't talk much as I drove to South Williamson. It was weird: the road was starting to feel familiar to me. The morning sun was just starting to brush the cliffs around us. It was beautiful in a rugged, harsh kind of way. I wondered about the desperation that had driven the original settlers into this region. It was an inhospitable place. The motivation had to have been the coal. Nothing else of value had ever been found in the place.

All was quiet when I pulled into the driveway next to Jean and Lawrence's rental car. There weren't any lights on in the trailer. I parked and looked around.

"Are you guys going to be okay?" I asked.

"We'll be fine," said Lawrence. "We're just going to stay here until you finish. Visit for a while. We need to talk to Mom anyway."

Jean nodded.

"Do you want me to wait? What if the door is locked? Do you have keys?" I felt nervous, and I realize the old watched feeling was back. Something was wrong in the woods today. I had a feeling that something was getting tired of the cat-and-mouse game. *Good*, I thought. *Time to get it out of the way.* I was tired of the game, too.

"We'll be fine," Jean said. "There's a spare key under the mat. My purse is next to the couch, with the keys for the car. Just hurry back." She glanced into the woods.

I sensed that she could feel it, too. I'd have to have a long talk with her about psychism sometime soon. She might have useful skills. If so, I could definitely point her toward a lucrative career as a consultant.

They got out of the Jeep, and I watched them until they retrieved the key and, waving, entered the house. I watched the trailer in my rearview mirror as I drove up the hollow. They would be fine. I needed to worry about myself now.

I pulled into the parking lot for the church and felt human eyes watching me. As I parked, an officer in full SWAT gear appeared next to the car. He carried a HK MP5 slung low. I approved of his choice of weapon even as I detested it being pointed at me. I kept my hands visible until he indicated for me to roll down the window. I moved slowly and carefully.

"Name?" he said quietly. He had a hands-free headset on his helmet.

"Dr. Michelle Fredericks," I said.

He nodded, no doubt getting a verbal description. "You're cleared, ma'am. You can gear up here. Then you're requested to meet with Special Agents Taylor and Mullins in the church."

"Thank you, sergeant." I'd noticed his blackened rank insignia as I waited.

I got out of the Jeep and put on my ballistic armor and weapons. Other than not having a helmet, I wasn't dressed that differently from the sergeant. He escorted me to the church doors and waited for visual confirmation of my identity before leaving.

These people were serious.

"Fredericks, good. Come on over." Mullins waved to me from the front of the church.

I walked over to Taylor and Mullins. I noticed that my foot was feeling better; it had a bit of an ache, but not much. I just hoped I didn't stub it or drop something on it. I was grinning at that thought as I walked up.

The agents had a small table set up. It looked like a folding card table; it held spread-out maps and a handheld radio. Styrofoam cups held old coffee.

"Sorry about the treatment when you arrived," said Taylor. "We're screening all the traffic up here this morning. We want to take this guy alive." She looked grim.

"What's wrong?" I asked.

"The pastor killed himself last night. He chewed his wrists out. They found him dead just a few minute ago," said Mullins.

"Shit." He was our best witness.

"We still have Sissy Anderson's testimony, but it's mostly hearsay.

She is not exactly a credible witness, when she helped kidnap her own brother and sister."

I nodded; I hadn't known Sissy's last name before. What Mullins said was not exactly unexpected. I hadn't been counting on Sissy's testimony anyway.

"Basically," said Taylor, "all we have is hearsay evidence so far. Even Lawrence and Jean were only told that something was going to happen to them once the preacher arrived. They were not told that the preacher was the one who was going to do it."

"There has to be something," I said desperately.

"Oh, there is. If the preacher is coming up here expecting to kill Lawrence and Jean, he'll have a nice set of branding irons with him."

I shuddered. I hadn't thought of that.

"You're looking and moving better today," said Mullins.

I shrugged. "I still have a few twinges, but not much."

Taylor looked at me. "What's wrong with you?"

I glanced at Mullins; his eyes were shining slightly in the dim light. He hadn't told her anything yet. I sighed. "It's a long story. I didn't want to get into it last night. The short version is that I have a possible lead on the other murders."

"So what's wrong with you?" she repeated.

"I broke my foot and took two forty-five rounds in the back getting that lead."

"What?" she exclaimed. "When was this?"

"Friday evening."

"Michelle, you shouldn't take chances like that. What happened to the shooter?"

"I'd rather talk to you about that later," I said. "Maybe after this immediate problem is taken care of."

Something in my voice must have convinced her. "Okay, but we will be talking about it later. I want the full story."

"You'll get it. I'll tell you everything."

CHAPTER FIFTY-SIX

Taylor met my eyes.

She knew I meant more than just the story about the other night. She sighed. "Okay, let's concentrate on this problem first."

Mullins had watched the whole exchange with interest.

Too much interest, I thought darkly.

There actually wasn't a lot to do. The state police SWAT team intercepted all the cars that pulled into the lot. There weren't many; the little church didn't have many attendees. As they were taken, they were brought into the church under guard. It was getting close to ten in the morning before the SWAT team reported another car coming up the road.

It was a limousine.

"That has to be him," said Taylor.

I nodded. I couldn't imagine driving a limousine up that road.

Mullins got on the radio. "This is Mullins. Let them pull in. They'll probably drive right up to the front doors. Let them. I want a full welcoming committee. This is probably our man. Remember, we need him alive."

We heard the limo pull up front, and then a commotion as the preacher was intercepted by the team.

"Got 'em," Taylor said with a grin.

The sergeant reported two men in the limo: a driver and a young man in the back.

"That's odd," I said. I'd expected the preacher to be older.

"Let's go take a look," said Mullins.

We walked outside. The SWAT team had two men standing to the side of the limousine. The rest of the team was still watching the road.

We walked over to the men. The young man was sandy-haired and wore a white Armani suit. He was maybe twenty-six, of average height and build, with blue eyes. The other man was built like a football linebacker and looked about forty; his eyes and hair were brown.

Taylor walked up to the young man. "Are you the one they call *the preacher*?" she asked.

"Yes. What's this about, ma'am? Why have we been harassed and humiliated this way on the way to church? This is an infringement of our civil rights."

"We'll get to your rights in a moment," she said. "You might not want to say anything else until you get a lawyer. This your car?" she asked, indicating the limousine.

"It belongs to God, through our ministry." His voice was soft and melodious. The sound of it sickened me.

"Right, well, I swore my oath before God," said Taylor, "so I don't suppose he'll mind if we look through his car."

"Do what you feel you must," said the preacher.

"Sergeant, check it out."

The SWAT team officer organized two of his men to strip the vehicle. It wasn't long before he called to us. "You might want to take a look at this, ma'am."

We walked over to him.

He was by the trunk of the limo. There in the trunk were three thick, old-looking books, an opened leather bag, a box with a brazier, and a bag of Kingsford charcoal. The bag held a selection of long, iron rods with glyphs shaped into the ends. Branding irons with zodiac signs.

I felt a wave of nausea.

"Sergeant, please ask our fancy young guest to come over here." I could hear the anger in Taylor's voice. I felt that same anger myself.

When the preacher had been brought over, he just stood and smiled at us pleasantly. I could sense the enmity coming from him. He was pure evil. He was worse than Heather Thacker had been. She was crazy. This man was quite sane... and evil.

"Young man," said Mullins, "would you like to explain this?" He gestured to the trunk.

"Explain what?" the preacher said blandly.

Taylor stared at him. "What are these things doing in your trunk?"

"It's God's trunk," he said quietly. "I have no idea what those things are. For all I know, you have just put them there to frame me."

"Frame you for what?" pounced Taylor. "We haven't said anything about them."

I was starting to get a bad feeling about this. I could sense the preacher laughing at us. My fingers itched to wrap themselves around his neck. It took all of my control to stand still.

"I read the papers," he said scornfully. "I don't know how those things got there. You might ask my driver if he knows."

Taylor and Mullins exchanged glances. This wasn't going the way they'd expected. Taylor nodded to the sergeant. He brought the driver around to the rear of the vehicle.

"These good people would like to know if you know anything about these things," said the young man, gesturing to the tools.

The driver straightened his shoulders. "Those are mine. The Preacher knew nothing of them. After the Preacher blessed them women and cleared them of being possessed, I wasn't convinced. I performed a ritual I learned from my grandfather to keep the demon from ever hurting anyone. I was trying to save the girls' souls." It sounded rehearsed.

"*Goddammit!*" yelled Taylor.

"I'll ask you not to profane the Lord's name in my presence."

"Arrest them," Mullins said quietly. "*Both of them.* I want the other people brought down for questioning, too. Get a forensics team on this vehicle now. If there is so much as a single skin cell of yours on these tools, you're going down. Do you understand me?"

"I'd like to speak with my lawyer," the preacher said. "I'm *not* going down. My place is assured in heaven, for I am God's messenger on Earth. You will never be able to stop God's message from spreading. It's *you* who are going *down*." His eyes gleamed with religious fervor. Maybe he was insane, after all.

"Get him out of my presence, sergeant."

"Ma'am."

The preacher and driver were taken to the side and cuffed. An officer read them their rights. The preacher smiled the whole time.

CHAPTER FIFTY-SEVEN

I drove back down to the trailer. My thoughts were in turmoil. I knew that the sick bastard was going to get off. We just didn't have enough evidence against him. They probably wouldn't even be able to hold him overnight.

Jean was sitting on the trailer's porch.

She looked terrible, as if she'd been crying. After one look at her face, I forgot everything I'd been going to say. I parked and ran up to her.

"Jean? Jean, honey, what's wrong?" I squatted down in front of her.

She wiped her face before raising her swollen eyes to meet mine. "Daddy died this morning, just after we got here." She broke down and started sobbing again. I moved next to her on the porch and held her.

"Where's Lawrence?" I asked gently.

"He's inside, being strong for Momma. He's doing what needs doing." Her accent was much thicker than usual; it was hard for me to understand her. I rocked her until she calmed down.

Lawrence came out and sat on the other side of Jean. She let go of me, clung to him, and started sobbing again. I saw tears running down his face, but he didn't break down. He just held Jean and let her cry herself out.

I could have really used a brother like him.

I waited there with them until the hearse and medical examiner arrived. The home healthcare nurse who had been coming in regularly also showed up. Lawrence spent most of the time inside with his mother.

I wondered where Mabel was, until I realized that she and her husband must have been taken in for questioning, too. I'd forgotten they all went to the same church. I wondered if Jean had ever gone to the church with them. Had she known and trusted the pastor who'd locked her an Lawrence in the basement?

After the medical examiner left with the body, Lawrence came out and sat down next to us with a sigh.

"How's Mamma doing?" Jean asked. She'd gotten a bit of her composure back.

"She's coping," he said softly. "Blaine is coming up to stay with her. I don't like him, but he's always looked out for Mamma."

Jean nodded.

"We'll wait for him to get here," said Lawrence.

"Would you like me to stay?" I asked.

"It might be best if you didn't," he said. "I'm sorry."

"No problem. I'll head downtown and see how things are going with the police. You two be safe. I'll see you tonight. Want to have dinner together?"

Jean smiled. "That would be great."

Lawrence nodded.

"Take care," I said. I gave them each a quick hug and then got into my Jeep. My heart ached for them. Losing a loved one is never easy. I was sure they would be okay, though. They were tough.

I drove back to the Pikeville, feeling odd.

I realized that along with Mark and Jen, I'd taken Lawrence and Jean into my heart as family. I didn't have anyone else. I wanted Michael to be there, too, although in a different role. I smiled to myself. My thoughts turn to him whenever I find myself needing comfort, and I needed him with me.

I went to the hotel and changed clothes before calling Taylor.

"Taylor," she answered. She sounded tired and pissed off.

"Hey, it's Michelle. I just wanted to let you know I'm back in town."

"Good. Listen, do you mind coming over here? There's a shit storm coming down, and I could use some counsel."

"Sure. Are you at the Pikeville police station?"

"No, the state police. It's down the road from you. Do you know where the Big Lots is?"

"I think so. Down toward the Windmill, but on the other side of the road?"

"You got it. The police station is on the same side, a little farther. It's a brown building with a sign. Get here as soon as you can."

The drive took me only a few minutes.

An officer led me through the building to a conference room. Taylor and Mullins were discussing the case with a police lieutenant; none of them looked happy. Pictures of the victims and crimes scenes were strewn across the table.

"Dr. Fredericks," the trooper announced and then left, closing the door behind him.

I was introduced to Lieutenant Scott, a tall, well-built man with receding gray hair, as a special occult consultant assigned to the case. Then we all shook hands. Mullins winked at me as I sat down.

"The problem," began Scott, "is that we can't hold Mr. Smith. His lawyer is one of the biggest criminal defense lawyers in the state, and he knows what he's doing. We've got no reason to hold this guy. His alibis are airtight. We've only had him in custody for three hours, and we already have signed affidavits from over a hundred people as to his whereabouts on the dates in question. He's even got the damned families of the dead girls on his side."

"He did it," I said quietly. "We can't prove it, but we know it."

"Then it's useless," said Scott. "And just because you think he's guilty, doesn't mean he is."

"Damn it to hell!" Taylor said. "We had a witness who told us all about it!"

"A witness who killed himself and wrote a note in his own blood saying 'Please forgive me, I lied'!" replied Scott. "Look, we can only hold Mr. Smith for questioning so long. It's just a matter of time before that fancy lawyer of his shows up with a court order."

"From a judge who's probably a follower of this man," I said.

He sighed. "I'm on your side in this, okay? The man is dirty – anyone can see that – but you've *got no case.* We have a man in custody who admits to the crimes. He can give details, names, and dates. He's even told us about two more in other states. He was in the right places at the right times to be the murderer. As far as any court is concerned, he's the killer. We don't even have enough to charge this so-called *preacher* with conspiracy, much less as an accessory to murder."

"Can't we hold him until the analysis comes back from the crime lab?" asked Taylor.

"The preliminary analysis showed no prints or fibers on any of the stuff. We've got nothing. If you had his fingerprint on anything that was in that truck, I'd say yes, let's hold him, but you don't." He sounded sincerely upset. I could tell he wanted to take this guy down and knew it wasn't going to happen. To keep trying would only jeopardize his job.

Taylor started to argue again, but Mullins placed his hand on her arm. She shut up.

"So what happens now?" asked Mullins.

"We release him. With a formal apology."

Taylor made a growling noise under her breath.

"I'm sorry. I really am. We got nothing." Scott got up and left the room.

Taylor looked ready to cry.

"I'm sorry," I said. "I really thought we had him."

She took a deep breath. "We all did." She glanced at Mullins. "We all did."

"At least we have his tools and books," said Mullins. "It would be hard for him to replicate them. We've also scared him. He knows that we know. We'll be watching him." He shrugged. "The important thing is that the murders stop. We made sure of that. Take what consolation you can." He left the room.

"I can't let him get away with this," Taylor said quietly.

My mind was racing. I could feel what she wanted to do. She was thinking of getting up, and going and shooting the preacher. She'd throw away her whole career to take this guy down. I put my hand on her arm.

"Jessica, don't."

She stared at me and then at my hand. She tried to pull away. I held tight.

"Jessica, let it go for now. Later," I said. "He'll be vulnerable later. We'll find him then and do what we have to."

Her eyes met mine and held them for a long time, and then she nodded. A slight smile touched her lips. I let go of her arm; she'd have bruises there later. She looked thoughtful.

"I forgot what you'd told me before," she said.

I smiled mirthlessly.

Yes, I thought to myself. We'll find him later and do what has to be done.

CHAPTER FIFTY-EIGHT

I hadn't slept well the night before.

I couldn't remember when last I had. Lawrence, Jean, and I sat up late talking about what had happened with the preacher, and their family. We talked about growing up, family, and funerals. I'd been to quite a few of those. All of my blood kin were dead, except for a couple of great aunts. I hadn't had anyone to turn to when my parents died. Lawrence's father dying had brought up a lot of old pain that I'd thought long buried. I wasn't dealing with it well.

I couldn't even find comfort in my job. I hadn't been able to get enough on the preacher to put him away. I'd sworn to Taylor the day before that I would take care of it someday, but I didn't know how or when. He'd be on guard for a long while. Mullins had been right in saying that the most important thing was to make sure he didn't do it anymore. The families of those girls were just as responsible for their deaths as the man who had actually killed them. Hell, for all I knew, his driver might have been the killer.

I just didn't know enough.

Taylor and I were planning to meet at the Windmill for breakfast again. We still had another killer to find. I had also promised to tell her about what happened last Friday. I wasn't sure how she was going to take it. I could easily find myself in jail by the end of the day.

I sighed. Nothing I could do about that. I'd committed myself to finding and taking down the cult responsible for monsters like Heather and for the deaths of the innocents in the hills around here who never have anyone to take their side. People like that sit outside normal society, and society sneers at them. I would do whatever it took to protect them, even if it took my life.

Maybe I should have been a cop, I thought ruefully.

Taylor was steadily drinking coffee at the far end of the restaurant. She'd had the waitress leave the pot. I smiled as I walked up and sat at the table. There were only a few other people in the restaurant. From where we sat, I could see that the restaurant had placed small flags for all the local school sports teams on one wall.

"Good morning, Jessica," I said.

She glanced at me and took another drink of coffee. She didn't look as if she'd slept at all the night before.

"Is it?" she asked.

I shrugged. "It could always be worse," I said.

I ordered a Coke when the waitress came up.

"I don't know, Michelle. I mean, this isn't the first time I've had some dirtball get away from justice. I don't know why this is getting to me so badly."

"Yes, you do," I said. She looked up and met my eyes. "You've never had a *serial killer* get away before. It doesn't happen. They usually *want* to be caught. The difference is that this time, the killer didn't think he was doing anything wrong. I really think this asshole believes he's doing god's will."

She nodded slowly. "You're probably right. I still don't like it."

"He'll get his eventually."

"Just what does that mean?" she asked.

I shrugged.

Taylor sighed. "Okay, I'll let it go for now. I'll just add it the *weird shit* list I keep of things I have to talk to you about."

I grinned.

We ordered breakfast when the waitress brought my Coke.

"Okay, now that that's out of the way... Tell me about what happened while I was incommunicado last week."

I'd known this was going to come up. "Last Thursday, early afternoon, I decided to follow some of the leads from the information I got from Heather."

She looked blank for a moment. "Oh, the psychic information, right. I was sitting here trying to think about what we could have learned that was useful. I knew before we went to see her that she was connected somehow."

"Yes. I got pictures of people she'd known," I said. "Some of the psychic flashes were about a store."

"An occult shop?" asked Taylor.

"No, a game and comic book store. *Is* there an occult shop in town?" That would have been a good lead if I'd thought about it. I couldn't imagine a shop like that operating opening in a place like Pikeville, though.

"Not that I know of."

"Oh, okay. Anyway, I went there and met a guy who talked me into coming to a little get-together at a friend's house to play the *Vampire* roleplaying game. He had more in mind than games. I sensed torture and rape on his mind when he handed me the book I bought."

Our food arrived, and I stopped talking.

"That was quick," said Taylor.

I continued my story between bites. "Heather had known this guy. I just played up the *college girl, new in town, don't have anyone to miss me when you kill me* angle."

Taylor laughed. "Damn, Michelle. I just hired you to give me information on how cults think, not get yourself killed."

I sighed. This was not going to be easy. "I know, but it's gotten a bit personal."

"Yeah." She chewed thoughtfully.

"Anyway, I found out that you'd gone missing that afternoon. I was worried and sort of fell back on my training for what to do. I thought this guy and his cult might have information about where you were."

"Okay."

"I picked up some fatigues and boots from an army surplus store."

"I'd wondered about where that came from. I almost didn't recognize you yesterday morning. I kept wanting to ask about that machine pistol you had, and things kept coming up. You looked like one my SWAT team."

"Remember what I told about the stuff last month?"

"Yeah, not so much."

"I told you that the fugitive, Julia, had a little mercenary company of ex-CIA and Special Forces people."

"You *might* have," said Taylor. "Yeah, you sort of implied it, I guess. You said she worked for, or had, a private military company or something."

"Well, I liberated equipment from some of her men who tried to kill me: guns, computers, night vision equipment, that sort of thing."

Taylor looked at me oddly. "By *liberated*, do you mean that you stole it from them, or...?"

I shook my head. "I mean that, after they tried to rape and kill me, and I dealt with them, they didn't need their gear any longer." I still found the memory oddly painful.

She put her hand on my arm. "Sorry."

"I'm fine. I'm explaining how I got the gun."

"Okay... So what does this have to do with our case?"

So far, so good, I thought. "It meant that I had the equipment needed for a surgical insertion into the cult, to excise the information I needed and get out with the minimum of collateral damage."

Taylor narrowed her eyes at me but didn't say anything.

Get it over with, I thought. I told her the whole story of that night with the cult, and what I had done to Matt. I left nothing out. Then I waited for Taylor to say something. Her only response at first was to push her half-eaten meal away.

"What the hell am I supposed to say to that, Michelle?" She rubbed her temples.

I didn't reply.

I'd apparently said too much already.

CHAPTER FIFTY-NINE

I sat quietly, watching her work through it in her head.

"Damn," Taylor muttered. "I'll need to think about this. What about the other stuff? Will you tell me what happened last month, so I can put this in perspective?"

"I'll you anything you want to know," I said. "But I don't think this is the right place for it."

"No, I suppose not. Okay, let me take care of the check. Then we can go back to the hotel and talk. You will go straight there, or I'll have to assume the worst."

"You can follow me."

She paid the bill, and we walked out to the cars. She then followed me back to the hotel. I hated to think that she'd lost so much trust in me, but I understood why she might feel that way. We walked into the hotel and rode the elevator upstairs together.

"My room," she said.

I walked with her down the hall, trying to put all my thoughts in order. They were a mess.

"Have a seat," Taylor said as she opened the door.

I sat at the table.

She locked the door and sat across from me. "Okay, talk."

I told about what had happened last month, starting with the first attack by Julia's men and ending in the hospital when Michael told me he was being reassigned. Then I waited for Taylor to digest the information. It was late afternoon; I'd talked for hours.

"I wish I could talk to someone and confirm all of this," she said finally.

"I've often wanted to be able to do that myself."

"I'm sure. So Henderson is actually working for some other agency, maybe the CIA. *That* doesn't really surprise me. I'm still not sure why he recommended you for this job. I would think that he wouldn't want you to get a lot of attention."

"I don't know anything about his motivations. Sometimes I think he like to push buttons, just to see what happens. It's also possible there's a connection I haven't seen yet." I thought about Julia and her brother Victor.

"What is Michael's last name?" she asked me.

I sighed. "Delling."

"And he really is a deputy federal marshal?"

"That's right."

"Well, I can contact him through the Marshal Service. That will prove a certain part of your story. Michelle, I want to believe you. I like you, but you have sat here and told me about killing people, some brutally, with little or no emotion in your voice," she said. "You're dangerous. I just don't know to whom."

"I understand that. You can be certain that I didn't want to believe it, either. For days after I killed those men, I threw up whenever I thought about it. Then later, when the memories came back, I knew that killing is what I'm good at, what I'd been trained for, and that I'd done it many times before."

"Jesus Christ, I wish I knew what to believe."

"I only kill in self-defense or the defense of others," I answered.

"You call what you did to this Matt guy *self-defense*?"

"I call it the defense of others," I replied coldly. I was getting angry.

We faced each other for a few minutes. I realized that we were both standing. Taylor was looking at my hands; I was gripping the table so hard that my fingers had sunk into the metal surface. I forced my hands to relax.

Taylor walked around the table and ran her hand lightly over the pits in the surface.

"Just how strong *are* you?" she asked quietly.

I took a deep breath to steady my voice. "I don't know. Michael says we're as strong as we need to be. I know that I'm a lot stronger than I look."

"*We?*" asked Taylor.

"The survivors of the project."

She sat back down in her chair. "Everything you say makes sense. I usually know when people are lying to me. I've never felt that way with you. Even with your crazy psychic shit." She met my eyes. "I'll track down Marshal Delling. If he confirms what you say, I promise I'll believe whatever you tell me from now on, okay? But you need to promise me you won't kill anyone else."

"You know I can't do that. *You* couldn't do it. We live dangerous lives. Sometimes people die. I'm getting better at controlling the rage and my instinctive reactions. I didn't kill Lawrence's aunt or the pastor when I found Lawrence and Jean locked in that basement. I didn't kill the preacher, and believe me, I wanted to."

Taylor laughed and shook her head. "How do I know you won't try to kill me?"

"If I wanted to kill you, you'd be dead," I said seriously. "Don't try to kill me, and we won't have to find out.

"You are seriously scary – do you know that?"

"Yes. If it makes you feel any better, I'd never kill you. I like you too much, and I don't like many people."

"Even if I tried to arrest you?"

I held out my hands, wrist together. "Go for it."

"You might be weirder than that ex-CIA guy in my boot camp cadre," Taylor said with a laugh.

I smiled. "Maybe he was related to me. You'll have to tell me about him sometime."

"Related to you? Oh, you mean… Yeah, I suppose he could have been, at that. He was about the right age. My worldview has been seriously altered."

"Talk to Michael. He's saner than I am. He'll confirm whatever you want to know."

My cell phone rang. I wondered if it could somehow be Michael; he tended to know when I needed to talk to him.

It was Lawrence. "Hey, Michelle. Are you wanting to attend services tonight?" he asked.

I'd gotten distracted and forgotten about the funeral. "Let me see if I can get away. Hold on." I met Taylor's eyes. "Do I have parole to go to Lawrence's father's service tonight?"

"Go. I'll sort this out. I still trust you, in spite of my common sense."

"I'll be there," I told Lawrence. He gave me directions to the funeral home, and I disconnected.

Taylor was rubbing her temples.

"Taylor?"

She looked up.

"Thanks. I'll be back in a couple of hours. You might want to talk to Lawrence, once all this is over. He's still trying to sort through the data on the computers. He met Julia once. He might be able to help put everything I told you in perspective, a little."

"I might, later. Get going, or you'll be late."

CHAPTER SIXTY

I stopped by my room and showered and changed clothes, then headed out the door. I left my pistol under the pillow. I had another pistol in the Jeep's glove box, but I didn't want to carry a gun into a funeral home. It didn't seem right.

The services were downtown at the funeral home I'd passed while looking for the game store last week. The psychic pressure from the place was strong, and foul. I hated funeral homes. I had to unclench my fists after I parked. This was going to be rough. I'd left most of my jewelry behind; I thought it was tacky to wear too much jewelry to a funeral. I had earrings, necklace, and bracelets. I hadn't worn any rings.

A tall, cadaverous man with a large, friendly smile was greeting people at the door: the funeral director. I managed to get past him without shaking his hand. A handwritten sign directed people farther back into the building.

The long hallway opened into what appeared to be an office breakroom. The room held a few round tables surrounded with folding chairs. More chairs were in ranks at one end of the room. Most people were just milling around the room. I didn't recognize anyone.

Several people were smoking. *Smoking.* At the funeral of a man who'd died of lung cancer. Unbelievable. I avoided everyone and waited near the end of the room, nodding to people I didn't know and trying to be inconspicuous. When I saw Blaine walking toward me, I stiffened.

"Michelle, right?" He held out his hand.

I blinked and then carefully shook his hand. I didn't detect anything but genuine grief.

"I want to apologize," he said carefully. "I'd been drinkin' that day, and, well, I got no less than I deserved. I just wanted you know that."

"Thank you," I said. I would never have expected that.

"You got a mean punch, woman." He grinned.

"I took martial arts from a young age."

"You must have." He sighed. "Do you know anyone else here?"

"No, just Lawrence and Jean," I said. "And your sister."

He shook his head. "She'll come around. Jean leaving was a shock to her."

"Will she be okay?"

"Oh, I think so. Jean's a good girl. She's needed to get out this damn part of the country for a long time now. Lawrence had the right of it."

Jean came down the hall from the chapel. Her eyes widened when she saw us together, and she hurried over.

"Michelle," she said as she came up.

"There ain't no need to be worrying, girl. I haven't bit anyone in days. Besides, this gal can take care of herself." He winked at me. "See ya around." And then he walked off.

What an odd man.

"Jean," I said, giving her a hug.

"Are you okay? Was he being mean?"

"No, actually, he was really nice. He even apologized for the other day."

"Now I've heard everything," said Lawrence. I hadn't seen him walk up. He gave us both a quick hug.

"It's good to see you two," I said. It was; I felt at home again.

Jean grinned shyly.

I could tell she'd been crying a lot. Her eyes were puffed up, and her nose was red. Lawrence looked as if he was keeping his emotions together well. I told him so.

"Well, it's only on the outside. Besides, it's not like it was unexpected. It was a mercy that it came as it did. He went quietly."

I nodded. Death is never easy.

He looked away and wiped his face. "I guess we should go back in there. Let you pay your respects."

We walked down the hall to a podium. The podium held a small lamp and a guest book. I signed the book. Then Lawrence and Jean led me up to the front of the chapel, to the casket. I felt lightheaded from the emotional overload: so many people had been in this room, grieving. My head started to throb.

The casket was half-open. Their father lay there, at peace. With his face relaxed in death, it was easier to see the resemblance to both Lawrence and Jean. They both took after their father in looks. He had been a handsome man, although years of working in the coal mines had left his skin permanently marked. The black pores couldn't be completely hidden with makeup. It was somehow fitting that they should show, the battle scars of fighting for a life in such a hostile place.

I thought of all the people I had met since I'd arrived in Pikeville with Lawrence. Suddenly the aberrant behavior made more sense. People in battle always break down. It made the good people I'd met that much more amazing. Here were people who faced hell every day, and stayed sane and good to one another. I wondered if I would've had the strength to survive in the hills around here. I didn't like the answer that seemed obvious to me.

I found myself crying. I couldn't remember the last time I'd cried. I just shook quietly until I felt Lawrence put his arm around me. He was saying something I couldn't quite understand, but the emotion came through. We moved off to the side and sat down, Lawrence on one side and Jean on the other.

I wiped my eyes. "I'm sorry," I managed.

Lawrence snorted. "When was the last time you cried?"

"Nineteen eighty-six," I said with a small smile.

Jean chuckled. "Crybaby."

I put my arm around her. I'd always wanted a little sister.

CHAPTER SIXTY-ONE

A stocky man in a dark gray suit gave a short sermon.

It was simple and dwelled mostly on the process of grieving and moving on. I was surprised; I'd expected something more fire-and-brimstone. Lawrence said his father hadn't liked that sort of thing and had asked this minister to do the service. I thought it odd to think ahead about your own death like that, but Lawrence's father had known for some time that he was dying.

After the service, friends of the family moved forward and paid their respects before leaving. I thought the funeral was over, but some people stayed behind and just sat there. We stood up and moved out to the lounge area. Someone was making coffee. A wide variety of food had been laid out on a back table, from fried chicken to soup beans and corn bread.

Young kids played in a corner, supervised by a couple of surly-looking teens. The kids were playing some kind of odd game with matchbox cars and a couple of large robot toys. The children didn't seem to know each other well. They kept stopping to discuss what a certain car or robot could do.

My eyes were drawn to a pale girl sitting on a bench and reading a book. She was dressed in black, and that looked as if it was her normal attire. The other people at the funeral left a pocket of empty space around her, as if they didn't want to get too close to her. She had dyed dark-red hair. Small round glasses sat on her nose, making her look like some sort of gothic John Lennon.

"Who's that?" I asked Jean. Lawrence had gravitated toward the coffee pot.

"Hmm? Oh, I'm surprised she's here. That's Mabel's daughter, Arlene."

Jean walked over to her and tapped her book. The girl looked up with an irritated look on her face and then grinned when she saw Jean. She stood and gave Jean a bear hug. Jean said something to her and then led her over.

I decided to reappraise Arlene when she got closer. She was carrying a copy of *The Return of the King*. Anyone reading Tolkien openly in Pikeville was worth knowing.

"Michelle? This is my niece, Arlene."

"Hello," I said, holding out my hand. She was almost five feet tall, in heels. She looked too old to be the niece of someone in their mid-twenties. Then I remembered that Kentucky has an insane law that people can get married at thirteen, with parental consent. Many girls do, and are having babies at fourteen and fifteen. It was hard to imagine.

She shook my hand lightly. "How are you?" She was looking at me curiously. "You're not from around here."

I smiled. "No, I'm from Northern Kentucky, up near Cincinnati."

"So how did you meet Beanpole, here?" She grinned up at Jean.

If she thinks Jean is tall, she must think I'm a giant, I thought. "I came down with Lawrence," I said. "As a friend," I added at her scowl.

Jean laughed. "You'll have to excuse her, Michelle; she's had a crush on Lawrence since she was a toddler."

"How would you know?" said Arlene. "You're, like, three minutes older."

"Years," Jean corrected.

"Whatever." Arlene waved her hand at Jean.

"Witness the feeding frenzy," Lawrence said as he walked up. "Let's move before they stray."

We moved out into the hall, away from the noise, smoke, and press of bodies. We settled into a little alcove with couches and an overstuffed chair, and tried to relax. We were out of sight, and sound, of everyone else.

"How are you doing, Arlene?" asked Lawrence.

"I'm doing well, thank you."

I noticed she had less of an accent than anyone else I had met from Pikeville. *I bet she's worked hard to get rid of it*, I thought. *Good for her.*

"So what do you do for a living, Michelle?"

Lawrence answered before I could. "Arlene, don't you ever talk to your mother? If you did, then you would know that Michelle is a well-paid whore." He winked at me.

I suppressed a grin.

"Lawrence!" Jean glared at him.

"Okay!" He acted as if he was warding off her glare. "She's a well-paid actress pretending to be my friend."

"You're hopeless," said Jean.

"I'm a criminal anthropologist," I said.

"Oh," said Arlene. "Just what does an anthropologist have to do, to be labeled a criminal?"

I laughed. "The usual: murder, mayhem, atheism."

"She's a psychic detective," said Lawrence.

"Really?" Arlene stared at me. "Or is Lawrence here pulling my leg some more?"

"Someone needs to pull your leg once in a while," he said. "Then you wouldn't be such a shrimp."

She kicked him.

"I'm a specialist in occult crimes," I said. I glared at Lawrence.

"Cool," said Alene.

Jean grinned. "She's the one that got your mom locked up."

I glared at her.

Arlene laughed. "Okay, that's it: you're a friend for life."

I just shook my head. I could understand how this free-spirited girl wouldn't get along with her mother. I couldn't see her growing up around those people. She must have been miserable most of her life. Maybe having Jean and Lawrence nearby had helped.

We talked for about an hour. I was conscious of the passing time and knew I needed to get back to Taylor. I hated to break it off. I was having fun, as strange as that seemed.

I stood up.

"Time to go?" asked Lawrence.

"I'm afraid so. I have to get back to work. Call me if you need anything."

I gave him and Jean a quick hug.

"Arlene, it was nice to meet you. I'm sorry I have to rush off."

She stood up and gave me a surprise hug.

I quickly said my goodbyes and headed out to the Jeep.

CHAPTER SIXTY-TWO

The wind was up, and the air was bitterly cold. The low clouds couldn't seem to decide whether they wanted to rain or to snow. I drove as fast as I could back to the hotel. The Jeep was just getting comfortably warm as I parked. Some of the bulbs were out in the lights over the parking lot. The pool of darkness under the closest one was darker than the others; it seemed to move and call to me.

I shook off the feeling and rushed inside.

I went straight to Taylor's room and knocked on the door. She opened it and let me in without a word. I sat at the table again.

"How are your friends doing?" she asked.

"Okay. As well as can be expected. It was a funeral, after all."

She nodded. "Well, I got ahold of Delling." She shook her head. "I'm glad you told him good things about me. I thought he was going to come over the phone line after me."

I smiled. That sounded like him.

"You've had a rough life, Michelle. I'm not going to make it any rougher. I still don't like what you did the other day, but I guess I might have done something similar in the same situation. I don't know – I've never really found myself in that sort of situation."

"I don't make a habit of hurting people. I'd love to just spend my time sewing and going to Renaissance festivals. But working as a police consultant is rewarding. Maybe I should have gone into law enforcement, but I don't know. I only know that if I can do something to help someone, I will."

"Well, those bastards probably all deserved it anyway. You should be careful, though. You might make a mistake, one of these days."

I nodded solemnly.

"Okay, so how about this case? How are we going to get these sons of bitches and put them away?"

I smiled. Taylor was practical; she wouldn't discard a valuable tool just because it might be dangerous. I liked my analogy, even if that did make me a tool.

"I'm not sure," I said. "We need to find the guy Matt told me about, Reggie the Snake."

"Do you think he could have been…? Never mind. Okay, we'll need to write down everything you can remember about what Matt told you. Then I guess we get the police looking for him. Maybe we'll get lucky."

We spent the rest of the evening discussing the case. She acted as if there had never been anything strained between us. I was glad. I truly, honestly liked Taylor. I hadn't wanted to lose her as a friend.

She faxed the information on Reggie off to the local and state police departments. We would go in person tomorrow and make sure that they were working it. I left her room and walked next door, feeling content. I'd get back to work in the morning and maybe save some lives.

CHAPTER SIXTY-THREE

Taylor woke me up with her usual early-morning phone call.

"Yes?" I said irritably. I was getting as bad as Mark; I'd known the call was from Taylor before I picked up the phone.

"They caught him!" she said excitedly.

I was suddenly wide awake. "Reggie? Already? When did they get him?" That was damn fast for the police.

"No, not Reggie. The guy who took the axe to Sergeant Reynolds."

"Oh. Oh, okay. Sorry, took me a minute. I didn't think they could've found Reggie already. How did they finally get the axe guy?"

"They were watching the old ladies' hut. He wandered back there. He wasn't armed and came peacefully."

"Are they sure they have the right guy? Where is he?" I looked around my room for the clothes I'd left on the back of the chair.

"He's on his way to Pikeville; he's in state police custody. We'll have an opportunity to question him as soon as he arrives. So get dressed fast."

"Okay, let me get off the phone," I said.

Taylor hung up.

I got dressed in a hurry, and brushed my teeth and hair. I pulled my hair back as I was opening my door. Taylor waited impatiently outside.

"Come on." She grabbed my arm and pulled me along the hall.

She danced from foot to foot while waiting for the elevator.

"You okay?" I asked on the way down.

"The guy they're bringing took an axe to a cop. I want to make sure nothing happens to him."

I hadn't thought of that.

Taylor had her car warmed up and waiting at the door of the hotel. A thin layer of ice and snow covered the ground. It was *very* cold outside.

We got in the car, and she pulled out from under the covered drive. The parking lot was icy. I wondered if I should have driven. The main road was clear, though. I stuck my pistol in the glove box. I kept forgetting that law enforcement types frown on a person carrying a concealed weapon into a police station.

We pulled around behind the state police post and hurried inside.

Lieutenant Scott took us back to an interrogation room. The first thing I noticed about the suspect as we entered was the smell: an overwhelming combination of urine, feces, and skunk. He had the distinct underlying odor of decay, too.

He *really* needed to bathe.

The police officer standing guard in the room didn't look happy to be here. I didn't blame him. I wondered if the police had a shower someplace that we could use for the suspect. The poor man couldn't be happy with how he smelled.

The suspect had wild eyes and hair, both brown. His skin had that rough, weathered look of someone who spends all of their time outdoors. The state police had the man in wrist and ankle restraints, which was odd for someone they said had come peacefully. He looked scared; he was shaking.

Taylor frowned and turned to Scott. I didn't hear what she said, but Scott immediately ordered the guard to remove the restraints. The guard complied, but with as little contact with the prisoner as possible.

I noticed a rough bandage on the man's leg. If he was this dirty, what was his wound like?

"Taylor," I said, "I think this man may require medical attention."

"What?"

I pointed out the bandage. "He'd been shot that day out in the woods. The officer hit someone. We found blood, remember? This man's gone eight days without treatment."

I walked closer to him. I didn't sense any intent to harm me. "Are you okay?"

"Don't rightly know, miss. Been feelin' shaky," he mumbled. "Ain't et much, though."

"Does your leg hurt?" asked Taylor.

"Hurt bad at first, still does sometimes. Burns now a bit."

"Can I look at it?" I asked.

He met my eyes. "You not be a-hurtin' me?"

"No, I just want to see if you need medical care."

He nodded and continued to shake.

I realized then that the shaking could be from fever.

I knelt down next to him. Lieutenant Scott tensed up as I got close to the man. I carefully removed the bandage, which looked as if it had been torn from a shirt or something. A sickly sweet smell came from the wound, and I knew it had gone bad. The last layer of bandage was covered with pus and blood. The wound was gray-green, with dark lines radiating away from it. The signs of infection were duplicated on the other side of his calf, where the bullet had come out.

I sat back and looked at Taylor. "We need to get him to the emergency room. He's going to need some of the tissue removed and a broad-spectrum antibiotic, if he's going to keep the leg."

Lieutenant Scott sighed. "I didn't realize he was that bad off. He said he was okay." He turned to the guard. "Let's get him over to the hospital."

"We'll follow you to the hospital and ask him questions there," said Taylor.

Scott nodded. "That's fine. You want to ride over with him or meet us there?"

"We'll meet you there."

"Okay."

We walked back out. I stopped to wash my hands, and then we sat in the car and waited. The officers brought the suspect out after just a few minutes. One of the officers was helping him walk. They got him in a car and headed for the hospital.

We followed.

CHAPTER SIXTY-FOUR

The police must have called ahead, because the hospital staff took us straight back into a small exam room. As I entered the exam room, I couldn't help but glance into the room next door, where I'd been seen after my close call with the cultists.

Doctor Thacker, a nurse, and a couple of techs got the man undressed and into a gown. Then they scrubbed him clean. He mumbled about not being able to bathe on the run.

I heard Taylor chuckle. I guessed she knew a bit about not being able to bathe.

His name was Sam.

He didn't know or didn't remember what his last name was, or if he'd ever had one. He'd lived up in the hills all of his life. It was all he knew. He'd heard about cars and towns and the modern world in general, but it had never been a part of his life.

The hospital staff got Sam's wound cleaned out and some antibiotics going into him. He seemed fascinated by the IV. Dr. Thacker wasn't optimistic about the chances for saving his leg. They'd wait a few days and see if the infection diminished. If it didn't, they'd have to do surgery.

I couldn't imagine growing up without any modern things. Sam's clothes were all hand-sewn; even his boots were handmade. He lived somewhere to the east of Pikeville. He didn't know if it was in Kentucky or not. None of us recognized the name of the creek he said he lived near.

The two old ladies in the hut had been his aunts. He visited them regularly with rabbits he had hunted, and got herbs and such to take to his other relatives. It was as if he had walked out of the seventeen hundreds.

"Why did you attack the police officer with the axe?" asked Taylor.

"I didn't know who he was. I'd seen them men take my ma's sisters. I di'nt know what to do. When them men started chasing me, I ran and then hided wit' the axe."

"What's this all about?" asked Dr. Thacker.

"Maybe we should talk outside," I said.

Taylor nodded, and we led the doctor out of the room. The nurse and registration clerk were talking to Sam and trying to work things out for the hospital. He was a write-off, for sure. He didn't know about the modern world, so how could he have insurance?

"Last week, some hunters found two women who had been killed in a ritual murder in the woods out by Majestic," Taylor began.

"Hmm," Thacker said. "You think that this man…?"

"No." Taylor shook her head. "We think they were his aunts. He says some men grabbed them."

"Oh."

"A state police officer was attacked with an axe while we were investigating a small hut near there," I said.

"Wait," Thacker said. "Okay, leg wound. I remember: we sent him on to Lexington."

"Right," said Taylor. "The officer shot at his attacker."

"And hit him in the lower leg," he finished.

"Exactly."

"Well, that certainly makes things difficult for you. I imagine that a lawyer will get him off without charges, based on reduced mental capacity and the self-defense plea. Additionally, you said he hit the officer in the leg. No intent to kill there."

Taylor nodded. "Right now, he's our only source of information into the other killing. I'm going have the police post a double guard on him."

"You're afraid he'll try to escape?" asked Dr. Thacker.

"No, I'm afraid someone will try to kill him."

CHAPTER SIXTY-FIVE

Taylor dropped me off at the hotel and drove down to talk to Lieutenant Scott about getting guards posted. Sam was being admitted to the hospital. They'd sedated him before we left. I'd hoped that we might get some more information, but Dr. Thacker wanted him to rest. We'd be back in the morning to talk to Sam again.

The doctor had made some pointed comments about my 'miraculous' recovery. I told him I'd seen a faith healer over the weekend. That had left him confused enough for me to slip away.

A light snow was falling, blending with the snow and ice already on the ground. The cliffs had disappeared into the clouds, shrouded in the white glare. I went up to my room, took a shower, and changed into a clean suit. I'd had the hotel laundry service wash my clothes and dry clean my suits. The price was nothing short of ridiculous, but I'd needed to get everything cleaned. I had no idea how long I was going be stuck up here in the mountains.

I stopped and picked up a quick lunch at a regular restaurant. I'd been eating too much fast food. At least I was missing meals and staying active. I felt more like my old self, but I'd gotten out of the habit of working out every day. I needed to get back into it. I'd felt slow the other day against Matt and the other cultists.

I was feeling my age this morning.

I shrugged it off. The weather was probably just getting me down. That, and the pervasive feeling of despair always lingering in these low Eastern Kentucky valleys. I would need to take a long vacation after this. Maybe I could talk Michael into taking one with me, and we could travel out West to search for his sister or something. That would be cool.

I drove by the site of last week's incident. Yellow police tape surrounded the burnt shell of the house, but that was nothing odd. I remembered that strange feeling when I walked through the wood after I'd fled the blaze. I was going to have to make time to face whatever it was that I kept feeling watching me. I'd begun to suspect what it was, and the thought was not pleasant.

My cell phone rang.

"Fredericks," I answered.

"Michelle?" said Lawrence. "Would you mind swinging by the service early today?" He sounded upset. I could hear sobbing in the background; it sounded like Jean.

"What's wrong?" They'd been dealing with their grief quite well yesterday.

"We have an unwelcome guest. Please, I'll explain more when you get here."

"I'm on my way. Give me about five minutes."

"Thanks," he said.

I drove as quickly as I dared. Sand had been poured on the main roads. It helped with the ice. Salt would have been better, but I supposed it was too expensive for a county as poor as Pike.

A fair number of cars were parked at the funeral parlor. I was surprised to see so many. Once I went inside, I saw that there was another funeral going on at the same time in another part of the building. That seemed indecent to me.

Lawrence and Jean were waiting for me just inside the hall. They both looked upset, and Jean had definitely been crying again. I embraced both of them.

"Okay, what's happened?" I asked softly.

"They added a three-o'clock service on today."

I glanced at my watch. It was almost four o'clock. Where had the time gone?

"That *preacher* gave the service," Jean sobbed.

I stiffened. "Is he here now?"

Lawrence nodded. "I think he was with the other funeral. I'm not sure who added the service on. I haven't seen the funeral director yet to ask."

"So what happened?" I could guess, but I needed to know.

"He started spouting all this crap about sinners and hellfire. Some of the people at the service started egging him on, and he went pure evangelical. He sounded like one of those guys on TV." Lawrence closed eyes against the remembered pain.

I blew out a breath I'd been holding. "Oh, gods." I shook my head. "What happened then?"

Jean smiled up at her brother. "Lawrence stood up and told him to shut up. He told him that it wasn't what Daddy had wanted. That cut down the ones who'd been shouting. Lawrence told the preacher that he wasn't going to let him say things like that, and that if he knew what was good for him, he'd stop."

Lawrence shook his head. "He just stood there for a second, and then people started to mutter. So he walked out. I wish I could say that I'd won, but most of those mutters had been about me. I think I alienated just about everyone I'd known up here, but..." He shrugged helplessly.

I gripped his arm. "You did the right thing, Lawrence." I took a deep breath. "Is he still here?"

"Yes," Jean said quietly.

"Then let's see what we can do about that." I moved past them and headed for the area with the chairs.

"Michelle," Lawrence called quietly, "don't get yourself arrested over this."

I smiled grimly. "Don't worry about that. Come and watch." I walked on back to the parlor where they'd held the service. Most of the people were just standing around talking. Again, some of them were smoking. I could see the preacher moving around, working the crowd. I placed myself along his path. I was aware of Jean and Lawrence moving to see what I was going to do, from across the room.

Then the preacher was in front of me. He smiled and held out his hand. He didn't seem to recognize me without my fatigues and body armor. That was fine by me.

I gripped his hand tightly.

He flinched and tried to draw it back.

I smiled and squeezed until I felt joints pop and crack. "What's wrong, *preacher*?" I spat the word.

He tried again to remove his hand. "You seem to have a rather strong grip, young lady. I'm a man of God, not action."

"Some actions speak for themselves. How's your driver?"

People were watching us now; I could feel them wondering why he was holding my hand. Conversations were starting to falter.

"I'm sorry? Who?" He looked panicked.

"Your driver. The one you claim you didn't realize was brutally killing young girls. Did you know those girls had been raped first?" I was going on impulse. He had a lot of self-control, but it was slipping, and I was starting to get flashes of information from his mind. He'd raped all those girls himself before holding them down for his driver to burn and cut. I felt sickened, and I allowed myself to broadcast that feeling to the people around me.

I wanted *everyone* to know about this scum.

CHAPTER SIXTY-SIX

The preacher tried once more to pull his hand back, but it might as well have been in a vice.

"I'm not sure I know what you're talking about," he said "May I have my hand back?"

"Did you know that the families didn't want autopsies? They claimed you told them not to get them. That seems odd. Did you know that they found some *interesting* DNA evidence on several of the bodies? The coroner's reports were very enlightening."

"Liar! I had those reports taken—" He broke off as he realized that I'd tricked him.

I jerked his hand, and he stumbled toward me.

That got just the reaction I'd wanted. I let go of him just as he raised his hand as if he was going to hit me. It looked to everyone else as if he'd attacked me.

"Witch!" he hissed.

Several people grabbed him and pulled him back.

"You weren't planning on trying to rape me just now, were you?"

He struggled in the grip of the men who held him, but they didn't let go.

One of them was Blaine. "Time for you to leave," Blane said to the preacher.

"She's a demon! A succubus! You saw her! She held me, and I couldn't escape!" he cried. "You must have seen her!"

"Why, preacher," I said loudly. "Why would a man of *god*, favored as you claim to be, be afraid of a demon? Or are you really afraid of ghosts? Maybe you should tell people your real name, and what happened to your sister. How about telling them about the six years you spent in prison for raping and murdering her when she was just eleven years old?"

Everyone was quiet.

The preacher just stared at me. "You couldn't possibly know...," he began.

"Xavier Bradley," I said quietly. "That's your real name. Not Smith."

He turned and pushed himself out of the room, almost running. Everyone moved quickly out of his way. They might not have understood exactly what had just happened, but they understood that he was somehow out of favor. As soon as he was gone, everyone began talking loudly.

I found Lawrence and Jean, and led them back to the little alcove we'd sat in last night. They collapsed onto the couch. I held up my hand to forestall questions and took out my cell phone. I need to tell Taylor what had happened.

"Taylor," she answered.

"It's Michelle. I've got something for you."

"What? I hope its good news."

"The preacher's real name is Xavier Bradley. He raped and murdered his eleven-year-old sister ten years ago. He served six years in prison for it. He escaped three years ago." My heart was pounding. The man was disgusting, and I felt tainted by touching him, but it had been worth it. The preacher was publicly humiliated here.

"*What?* How can you know that? He didn't even show up in our system! Where are you?"

"I'm at Lawrence and Jean's father's funeral," I said. "*He* was here. He didn't recognize me, and I shook his hand. Look him up. He's a fugitive, and you'll have something to pin on him. He killed his sister the same way, but the tools were never found. He'd hid them in a well."

"Hot damn! We have him! Let me get back to you. I'll get the state police on this." She disconnected.

"Do you really think you can get him?" asked Jean.

"Yes. If he doesn't get out of town before the police go after him, then he'll be caught and sent to prison."

"What happens if he doesn't get caught?" said Lawrence.

I smiled. "Then I find him and take care of him myself."

I saw approval on both of their faces.

By the time I met Taylor for dinner that night, we knew the preacher had escaped.

The police had found his limousine abandoned near the edge of town. No one had reported a stolen car yet, but that was the best guess. He was probably heading for Virginia or West Virginia. The Marshal Service and the state police in both states had been alerted.

I wasn't confident about them finding Bradley anytime soon. There were many places to hide in these mountains. I'd find him, though. When I did, I wouldn't be turning him over to the police.

CHAPTER SIXTY-SEVEN

The snow had stopped falling during the night.

The day was clear and cold.

It's a good day for a burial, I thought as I stared out the window. *As good a day as any.* My breath turned to frost on the windowpane, and the world blurred out of focus.

I'd wanted to call Michael but didn't have the chance the night before. I'd been trying to get my thoughts straight on everything, but my mind kept slipping into old habits, and I couldn't think of anything but my job. Michael said he would be back in Cincinnati by the middle of the week, but I hadn't heard from him. I wanted to talk to him, but I didn't want to bother him at work. I'd call him later and apologize for not being home. I missed him.

The funeral was supposed to start at one o'clock.

I lay in bed late into the morning. That wasn't like me; I'm usually pretty good about getting up. I knew it was going to be a long day, though. I think I was emotionally overloaded. Too much had happened. The incident with the preacher had just numbed my brain. My hand still itched and felt dirty where I had touched him. No amount of scrubbing would fix that. I was just going to have to live with it until it faded.

I got out of bed.

I knew I should eat breakfast, but I couldn't bring myself to do it. I just wanted the chaos and pain to be over and my life to go back to some semblance of normalcy. I was tired of having my brain squeezed by the psychic pressure. I wanted to go home and curl up with a cup of hot tea and my cat. Northern Kentucky has its own problems, but I grew up with those. I know how to block them out.

I started getting ready at eleven AM.

I'd told Taylor that I wasn't up to working that day. I'd done enough recently. She told me to take as much time as I needed. What I needed was a break. I wanted to get away from this kind of work for a while. I'd had a busy autumn. I also didn't want anything to interfere with the funeral. I needed to be there for Jean and Lawrence.

They were my family now.

I met them in the lobby. Jean hadn't been sure she'd be able to drive, so they were riding with me. We hadn't talked a lot about what we were going to do afterward. I thought they might head to Cincinnati. Jean would be able to stay with Lawrence until I finished in Pikeville.

We drove over to the funeral home in silence and parked in the area in front of the building. A couple of other cars were already there. Blaine's truck was up front. He'd be taking Lawrence and Jean's mother in the processional. One of the funeral director's sons placed a small magnetic flag on the hood of the Jeep and walked on by.

We got out of the Jeep and went inside. The inside of the building was crowded. Many of the people here could only take off work for the funeral itself, and not the visitations. We walked around and talked quietly to people. The minister gave a brief sermon, and then we filed out. I waited with Jean outside. The funeral director had to close the casket, and then the pallbearers would bring it out and place it in the hearse. Lawrence and Henry were pallbearers, along with Lawrence's father's surviving brothers, and Blaine.

"Michelle!"

I turned and saw a couple of familiar faces that were dear to me.

"Mark!" I cried. "Jen!"

I found myself suddenly engulfed in hugs. I hadn't expected to see either of them.

"How did you guys get off work?" I asked.

"Magic," Mark said with a grin. "We brought someone with us."

"Who?" I asked, clueless.

He gently took my shoulders and turned me around.

Michael.

I just stood and gaped as he lifted me off the ground with his embrace, and our lips locked for what seemed simultaneously both an eternity and not nearly enough time.

"How?" was all I could manage as I gasped for a breath.

He gently set me down and pressed his forehead against mine so he could look into my eyes. I felt lost in the green depths of his. He closed his eyes and kissed my nose. Then he grinned. "I missed you – could you tell?" As close as he was pressed to me, I could tell he'd missed me a lot.

"I missed you, too," I whispered.

I wiped sudden tears from my face. It was so good to see my friends again, and to be in Michael's arms. I introduced Jean to them, and we waited together for Lawrence. I couldn't bring myself to let go of Michael's hand.

"Did you drive down?" I asked him.

"No," he said. "I rode with Mark and Jen. I figured you wouldn't mind giving me a lift back when you go home."

"Michael," I said, "I might not be going home for a while. There's still a lot to do here. What about your job?"

He pressed a finger to my lips and smiled. "I'll tell you about it later."

I nodded, confused. Lawrence and the casket came out then, and we waited for the pallbearers to load it. Lawrence came over, and I hugged him again. Tears were running down his cheeks, but his voice was steady.

"I'm okay," he said. "Good to see you again, Michael."

Michael embraced him quickly and then gripped his arm. Lawrence nodded to the unspoken words.

We walked back to the Jeep. Michael sat up front with me, and Lawrence and Jean sat close together in the back. Michael held my hand again as I drove. It felt so good. I could sense a deep uneasiness in him, though. Michael's mission in Seattle must have gone badly, and then his debriefs in Washington, D.C. He met my eyes and gave my hand a squeeze. He knew I was probing a little for information, but he wasn't giving anything up. He was almost impossible to read.

The procession wound through the city and up into the mountains. Every time we made a turn, I'd think that this would be the end of the drive, but then we would drive farther. We ended up on a narrow road that crept up the side of mountain at a steep angle. I wondered how some of the cars behind us would be able to make it. At the top, the trees faded back to reveal a small area of unnaturally flat land, the graveyard.

I was wondering why we were in such a remote area when I suddenly realized the answer: Land is at such a premium in the mountains that only the small patches near the tops of them are still available for any kind of development, and cemeteries take up a lot of room. Strip mines in the area commonly took the tops off the surrounding mountains.

I parked on the circle, and we got out. Lawrence went up to wait by the hearse. Jean stood on one side of me, and Michael on the other. I was aware when Mark and Jen came up and joined us, but most of my attention was on the graveyard.

It was still and cold up here. The ground was covered in a deeper layer of snow than we'd gotten down in the lower areas. An occasional blast of wind sent needles of ice to strike against my exposed skin. The whole area had a strangely peaceful quality, though. I normally hate being in such places, but this one held only a muted feeling of grief. Maybe it was so remote that people didn't get up here much.

Lawrence, his brother-in-law, and uncles took up the casket and walked down to the waiting grave. The funeral home had set up a small pavilion over it with chairs, but the wind was so strong that the chairs had all fallen over. No one seemed inclined to use them, and the funeral director ended up moving about and quickly folding them. His son helped move the folded chairs to the side.

The minister said a few brief words, and then it was over.

CHAPTER SIXTY-EIGHT

Michael and I waited by the Jeep while Jean and Lawrence were embraced by family members and made sure their mother was doing okay. Blaine had said she was going home with him. He'd help her through her grief, and she'd help keep him off the booze, he quipped. I wished the best for her – for them all.

Finally, everyone was leaving. We stood and talked about what to do, and decided to meet in town. We'd all have dinner and talk together. I started the Jeep, and we left. I was glad I'm good with directions. It was hard to figure out how to get back out of those hills.

We met in the parking lot and went in together, the six of us, my whole family.

I had a steak for dinner, and it was good. I was trying to remember why I hadn't eaten at this place yet, but I wasn't sure I'd even noticed it was here. I'd been correct about my earlier surmise that Lawrence and Jean were leaving to go back to Cincinnati. They were leaving that night. I was sorry to see them go, but I knew they would be happier and safer there. Mark and Jen were going to give them a ride back. They'd get their stuff out of the hotel and then drop off the rental car after dinner.

Michael was staying in town, but he still wouldn't tell me how he had gotten off work.

"I'll tell you later. If you don't want me here, I can go back to Cincinnati," he said jokingly.

I glared at him. "Don't even think about it."

Lawrence, Jean, and I had a tearful goodbye in the parking lot. Then I was suddenly alone with Michael, and shy. I wasn't sure exactly what he had in mind when he said he wanted to stay with me. Was he getting his own room? Sharing mine? I wished I knew.

We put his bags in the back of my Jeep and got in. After starting it, I sat for a minute, suddenly nervous.

"Are you okay?" he asked quietly.

I nodded. "It's just all so sudden. I've been aching to see you, and now suddenly you're here, and I don't know what to say or do. I just know I'm happy to see you again, and I can't stand the thought of you leaving."

"Well, I'm glad to see you, too. You weren't in the best shape the last time I saw you," he said.

I'd been in the hospital recovering after Julia tried to kill me.

I looked out the car window at the snow and mountains. The sun was going down, and the sky was clouding up again. It felt like more bad weather was on the way. I didn't know what to say. I wasn't sure where our relationship was headed. He'd pushed me gently away once before when I had wanted to go farther.

"Michael," I started.

He shushed me. "Don't say anything yet. Let's get settled, and then we can talk. It's cold out here, and there's something watching us. We'll be safer inside."

I stared at him. I'd been aware of whatever it was watching again, but I'd gotten so used to it that I was ignoring it. I'd also forgotten that he, too, had hidden abilities. I tended to just think of him as a marshal and not think about what else he might know.

I pulled out of the parking lot and drove over to the hotel.

Our friends were gone. Jean and Lawrence must have already packed. I wondered if Lawrence had known that Mark and Jen were coming. Probably. He could have told me, but then, he'd have wanted me to be surprised.

We carried Michael's bags up to my room. He didn't stop at the desk. We didn't say anything on the elevator. I was starting to get very nervous by the time we made it to my room. We went in and sat his bags on the floor.

I heard the door click behind me and turned. Michael pinned me to the wall and crushed his lips again mine. I was surprised at the sudden assault, but too aroused to resist. I wrapped myself around him, and he held me there, kissing, melting into one another.

I felt him pull back and responded by shoving him down onto the floor. I found myself on top of him, kissing him and pulling at his clothes. I never gave him a chance to say whatever it was he'd been about to say.

I wasn't going to let him back off this time.

I awoke in the darkness later.

I was startled by the quiet sound of breathing, until my confusion melted away and I realized it was Michael in the bed next to me. It hadn't been a dream. I reached out and ran my hand across the line of his jaw, his chest.

He was real.

He was awake. I could see his eyes gleaming slightly in the light that leaked past the curtains. He reached out to me, and I snuggled into the curve of his shoulder. It felt so good to be held. He kissed the top of my head, and I fell back asleep to the rhythm of his heart.

CHAPTER SIXTY-NINE

I woke up the next morning to the smell of croissants, eggs, and bacon.

As I sat rubbing my eyes, Michael grinned at me from the side of the bed. He was fully dressed. Breakfast was sitting on the table. He must have just gotten back with it.

"Good morning, beautiful," he said softly.

I felt myself blushing and realized that a lot more of me was turning red than I normally exposed. "Good morning," I said. "I seem to remember it was a good night, too."

His turn to blush. Payback is hell.

He handed me a shirt and got up to set out breakfast. I quickly dressed in my pajamas. Not only was I strangely shy, considering the night before, but I was also *really* hungry.

He'd gotten me a Coke to go with breakfast. He knew me so well already. I grinned at him across the table. It looked like he'd shaved and showered this morning, too. I must have been really exhausted. We sat and ate without talking. Afterward, he cleaned up the trash and then sat back down, sipping his coffee.

"I find myself at a loss for words," he said.

"I know a few that always sound good," I replied.

He gave me that grin of his, and I felt my pulse quicken in response.

"Okay, how about these." He took a deep breath. "I love you. I've loved you since we were back in the project together. When I met you again, and we went through all that together last month, I realized it was all still there. I love you. I don't ever want to be apart from you again. I'll understand if you don't feel the same way."

"Michael?"

"Yes?"

"Shut up and kiss me."

Later, I propped myself up on his chest, where I could look into his eyes. He had a small, contented smile. His eyes were half-open. He saw me looking at him and sighed softly.

"I love you, too," I said.

"Yeah, I got that." He pulled me up and kissed me. "I quit my job," he said suddenly.

"What?" I sat up and stared at him. He immediately got distracted, and I had to playfully slap his hands away. "What happened?" He loved being a marshal.

"You happened," he said, smiling up at me. "They wanted to send me off to Puerto Rico, permanent relocation. Henderson may have been behind it. I told them to go to hell." He shrugged.

"That sounds like something he would do. What are *you* going to do?" I realized that I didn't even know where he lived.

"I don't know. I have plenty of money saved up; I've never had many expenses. I'm always on the road. I was hoping that you might want to settle down, raise a cat or two, maybe a dog. Work together, that sort of thing. We'd make a hell of a team."

I kissed him again.

I'd been hoping he'd say something like.

We got up and took a shower together. I needed to get dressed and get moving that morning, but he was so damn distracting. I finally managed to get dressed. Michael and I sat and talked about what had happened with my case. I had a lot to cover. I wasn't going to tell him about getting injured, but he'd seen the body armor and immediately noticed the two marks from the bullets.

"Please tell me that those marks were there when you got it," he said.

I sighed, and told him the rest of the story. He shook his head at parts, growled at others. It was almost noon before I'd told it all. I was wondering where Taylor was. She usually called me early in the morning. Maybe she was giving me time to recover from the funeral.

Someone knocked on the door.

It was Taylor.

She walked in, bitching about the local cops. "Turn to channel three and look at these fucking idiots," she said as she walked. She suddenly stopped when she saw Michael. "I'm sorry, I didn't realize..." She trailed off.

He stood up and held out his hand. "You must be Special Agent Taylor. We spoke on the phone." When she looked blank, he added, "Michael Delling."

"Oh! Oh, right. I thought you sounded familiar." She shook his hand. "Nice to meet you."

I flipped on the television and tuned to channel three; it was on a commercial. "So what are we watching?" I asked.

"You'll see."

The local news came on with a special bulletin about a gunfight in downtown Pikeville that had left two officers dead and another five wounded. The suspect, identified by anonymous sources in the police department, was Reginald Sharp, also known as Reggie the Snake. He was shot and killed at the scene of the crime. They even had film.

I flipped off the TV and sat on the bed. There went our lead.

Taylor moved one of Michael's bags and sat at the desk. "You're not here in an official capacity, are you?" she asked him.

"No, I'm no longer with the Marshal Service," he said.

"Oh."

"I quit. I'll be in town for as long as Michelle is, however, so if you would like me to pitch in, I'd be happy to."

"Hmm, I'm not sure I could get the FBI to foot the bill for another consultant."

"I'll work pro bono on this one," he said.

"That, I could afford."

"I'll call Tony at CRI and get you tacked onto the case. He'll agree in a heartbeat," I said.

"I'm not sure I want to work for them permanently," he said.

"Not a problem."

"Okay, that's settled. Back to the Reggie problem. I'll make a wild guess here and say that this Reggie the Snake was someone that you wanted to talk to, and the local police just botched the job."

"Reggie is the guy that Matt told me about," I said.

"Well, even in death, he should be able to tell us something," said Michael. "You should secure the crime scene."

"Being taken care of," Taylor said. "Special Agent Mullins is down there now. He's the one who called me. We can check it out whenever."

I nodded.

"I'm also curious about this Sam guy. It seems that he might have useful information," said Michael.

"I've been in contact with him; he can't remember anything about the men who abducted his aunt. They were in dark robes," I said.

Taylor frowned. "I don't remember him saying that."

I smiled. "He didn't, but he remembered it while talking. I gleaned that out of his memories. He didn't have a word for how they were dressed."

"I'd like to see if he could put us in touch with the other hill witches," Michael said.

"Oh, I hadn't thought of that."

"Hmm. Not a bad idea, if you think he'll do it," said Taylor. "I feel for him. He still might lose his leg. They won't know for a while."

"It seems like we should notify his next of kin as to his whereabouts anyway," I said.

"And hope they don't think we're cultists and take an axe to us," Taylor said.

"We'll just make sure not to wear black robes," said Michael.

We all chuckled at that.

CHAPTER SEVENTY

"Okay," I said. "What do we do first?"

"I'd say we check out Reggie's place and see if we get any leads," said Taylor. "Then, if we don't, we can fall back on the second plan of trying to find a hill witch to talk to."

"Right. Is there any problem with me coming along?" asked Michael.

"I don't see why there would be," Taylor said. "It's an FBI crime scene, no matter what the local boys paid for it. We get dibs, and I'll tell them to take a hike if they say anything. I've taken enough shit from them on this case."

"Michelle told me about some, the harassment and the missing coroner's reports."

"Is there anything you *haven't* told him yet?" Taylor asked me.

I blushed. "Sorry. I should have asked you first. I'm just used to consulting with him."

"Don't worry about it. I'm glad to have another set of eyes on this case. We need all the help we can get. Listen, you call your boss, and I'll call mine, and we'll meet downtown in half an hour. How does that sound?"

"Sounds good," I said.

She left, and I got out my cell phone.

"Still up to working with me?" I teased.

"Of course," Michael said with a grin. "The benefits package is awesome."

Damn, he was making me blush again. I dialed the main number for CRI before I got distracted again.

"Criminological Research Institute, Jamie speaking. How may I help you?"

"Jamie, this is Michelle Fredericks. Let me talk to Tony," I said.

"Just a moment, Ms. Fredericks." She was learning. Jamie was the secretary at CRI and probably hated my guts. I didn't like her much, either, and I'd never even met her.

"Yeah, Michelle, what is it this time? More money, or a vacation?" Tony was direct and gruff. I liked him. A little.

"Actually, Tony, I've got a deal for you."

"Oh, shit. I knew I should have bought catastrophe insurance. What's the deal?"

"A new consultant for you."

"If Mark finally said yes, I'll permanently double your salary. Otherwise, I'm not hiring."

"It's not Mark, as well you know. And you will be hiring the new consultant."

"Oh? I will, huh? Why is that?"

"Two reasons. The first is that it's a condition of me continuing to work for you."

Silence. "That's one good reason. Do I want to know the second?"

"You'll like it," I said.

"I can't wait."

"He'll work pro bono, this case only, and then you're rid of him unless you two work out an agreement later."

"So who is this Good Samaritan?" he asked sarcastically.

"His name is Michael Delling."

"And this means what to me?"

"Ex US Marshal, ex Special Forces."

"You have a way of being persuasive. Let me talk to him."

I handed the phone to Michael and went into the bathroom to change clothes. When I came out, Michael was off the phone and finishing getting dressed in a dark suit. He had a shoulder holster with his Sig P220 .45 semi-auto tucked into it. I was sure that he had other weapons secreted around his person. He put his suit jacket on over the holster, and it disappeared into the line. The jacket was tailored to fit with the gun there. I was a little jealous.

"You look nice. How'd it go?"

"Well, of course," he said. "He didn't say much except, *Welcome to the team.* He said he'd like to meet me sometime and maybe offer me a regular job."

I smiled. I was sure Tony would love to have Michael working full-time for CRI. It would look good for the reputation of the company, if nothing else.

We finished getting ready and went out to the Jeep. It was a cold, damp morning. The weather had warmed slightly overnight, just enough for the snow to turn to slush. Something like a fine mist was falling. We stood in the lobby while the Jeep warmed up.

A different clerk from usual sat behind the desk. She didn't look happy, either. None of the clerks ever looked happy. In this town, you'd think they would be happy just to have a job.

Once we got on the road, I called Taylor and got exact directions to the crime scene. She told me she'd be there shortly. She was waiting for some paperwork to be faxed in. I drove down quiet streets, and Michael and I talked about things, mostly last month's events. I suddenly realized that I might have someone to celebrate Christmas with.

I lost my smile when we reached the crime scene and saw the red-stained snow. The recent death was like a physical blow. I could hear and feel the echoes of that in my head. Michael gripped my hand, and it faded, replaced by a calmness. I met his eyes, and he smiled.

"Ready?" he asked.

"I think so. Thanks." He was really good at shielding psychic emanations. I got out of the car and looked around for Taylor.

I didn't see her, but I saw Mullins and headed toward him. He was talking to a couple of police officers near the entrance to a small brick building. It looked like an old school.

"Special Agent Mullins?" I said.

He raised one finger and finished giving instructions to the police. Then he turned and gave me a small smile.

"Dr. Fredericks, good to see you," he said. "You must be Michael Delling."

Michael flashed him a smile and extended his hand. They shook. "Glad to be able to help out."

"Taylor's bringing your papers over with her. Everything is squared away. She mentioned that it was certainly no difficulty with the security clearance. Are you working with the CRI on a permanent basis," Mullins asked, "or just for this case?"

"Just for this case, for now. I'm not sure where I'll end up yet." He smiled at me.

"Hmm. Well, if you're still interested in law enforcement, the FBI is always looking." He winked to show that he wasn't trying to be pushy.

"So where did we lose Reggie?" I asked.

"Right. To business. He was killed just over here. Took two rounds in the head." He pointed to a spot near the door.

Michael looked around at the surrounding buildings. "Do we know which officer fired the shots?"

"Not yet. Why?" Mullins looked confused. "I'm sure it will come out in the internal review. Is it an issue?"

"I don't know." He looked around again. "Do you have a portable video unit? I'd like to look at the footage of the death again. Something seemed odd when I saw it on the news earlier."

"I'll see what I can do. Some of the news boys are still hanging around. I'll try to get something worked out. Be right back." Mullins walked off.

"What is it, Michael?" I asked.

"I don't know." He smiled apologetically. "I just have a weird feeling, that's all. Reggie didn't have body armor on, so why go for a head shot?"

"I almost always go for a head shot," I said.

"So do I. That's my point."

I thought about it for a moment, and he was right: it didn't add up. Most local police only hit with three out of five shots at ten feet. The blood stains from where Reggie was killed, were twenty to fifty feet from where the police had been. That was an impressive pistol shot for anyone, much less twice. That meant a rifle, but the local police didn't have a SWAT team. So they couldn't have had a sniper on the rooftops, but someone else could have.

I felt a sudden chill.

CHAPTER SEVENTY-ONE

Michael had been watching me. Now he nodded. He knew I'd just worked it all out.

I looked at the ground. The blood spray was off to the right of the door and in a long pattern. If a police officer to the front of him had shot him, the blood should have been up and shorter. I scanned the surrounding buildings; the shooter had been on one of them.

"I think I'll take a look around," Michael said, looking toward a building across the street.

I caught his arm. "Be careful."

He nodded and walked off.

Standing alone there, I once again felt the pressure of recent death and trauma, but not as bad as before. I tried to figure where the bullet would have gone if it passed through the skull.

"Where'd he go?" Mullins asked from behind me.

I looked around and saw him and a squat man with a television station logo on his jacket. The technician was holding a portable display.

"He went across the street to check something out," I said. "Let me see the video."

"This is uncut," the technician said, glancing at Mullins.

"I think I can handle it," I said dryly. I took the display from him and watched the video a couple of times in slow motion. "Thanks. You can go," I said to him.

"Hey, I'll need that back!"

"It'll be returned before the end of the day. Thank you," Mullins said. He waited for the guy to leave. "Okay, what have you got?"

I looked across the street and saw Michael on the rooftop. He gave me a thumbs-up sign. "We've got a shooter on the top of that building," I gestured, and Mullins turned, watching Michael for a moment.

"Let me see that," he said.

I showed him the footage, pointing out the angle of blood spray from the wound. I also mentioned my surmises about the accuracy of the shots.

Michael came back across the street.

"We've got bipod marks and muzzle flash burns on the rooftop," he said.

"No brass?" asked Mullins.

"No, the shooter must have scooped them. I looked. This was very professional."

"Somebody didn't want Reggie to talk to the police," I said.

Mullins sighed and rubbed his temples. "I really don't need this shit," he muttered.

"Did Reggie have an apartment here?" asked Michael.

Mullins nodded. "Second floor, back corner. The door is open. We've evacuated all the tenants for now. I told them there might be a bomb in there." He smiled mirthlessly. "That shut them up and got them out."

"Can we go look around?" I asked.

"Go ahead," he said and walked off.

"Shall we?" I asked Michael.

He gestured for me to proceed.

The building was nicer-looking on the inside that it had appeared from outside. It had been freshly painted, and the woodwork was stained a dark cherry. We went up the staircase and entered Reggie's apartment.

Reggie hadn't been a good housekeeper. At first, I thought the police had trashed the place, but I think Reggie had lived like that. There were old pizza boxes and plates with food on them all over the place. The place stank of rotting food, garbage, cigarette smoke, weed, incense, and something else that I couldn't quite identify.

A feeling of brooding anger hung about the place. I handed the video unit I was still carrying to Michael and moved around the room, lightly touching things, trying to build up a picture of what kind of life Reggie'd had.

It was not a pretty picture.

He had an interesting collection of cheap statues; they looked like the typical pseudo-satanic crap you can buy at any Spencer's Gifts. There must have been the stubs of over a hundred candles melted onto just about any flat surface.

I didn't find much in the living room that had any useful impressions on it.

"Find anything?" asked Michael.

"Not really. There's not a lot of information on any of this stuff. I don't think it was deliberately wiped; I think he just used a lot of sage and frankincense. He also didn't seem to be thinking of much, most of the time," I said. "I think he used drugs."

"Yeah, there's a pile of used syringes in the bedroom and a truly frightening number of used condoms."

"Ugh! I didn't need to hear that." Taylor was standing in the doorway to the apartment. She handed a few papers to Michael. "Welcome to the team. So what's this about a rooftop shooter?"

We told her about our surmises, and she watched the video again.

"So why do you think it was a professional shooter?" she asked.

"Three hundred yards, suppressed fire, medium wind, double tap to the head without a miss." Michael marked off each point on his fingers as he talked.

Taylor sighed. "So we need to know if anyone in town is capable of doing that. Crap. They could be anywhere by now."

Michael and I exchanged glances.

"What?" Taylor hadn't missed that.

"Either of us could have done it. Any military-trained rifle expert could make the shot. I suppose a good hunter could do it, but it doesn't really fit."

She nodded. "Well, you two have ironclad alibis; I was right next door. We'll need to get a list from the Veterans office, I suppose."

"I doubt you'll find the shooter that way," I said.

"I know, but we've still got to jump through the hoops, or someone will pin me to the wall at an internal review later and ask why I didn't do everything possible to get the shooter." She rolled her eyes.

"We've got nothing here, so far," I said. "Are you getting a phone log?"

"Working on it. The phone company is based out of Atlanta, so it's going to take a while. The office down there has to get them a court order. This would be a lot easier if he was suspected of being a terrorist," Taylor said.

I saw Michael nodding. I guess he was used to all the legal crap people have to do to get information. I'm so used to gaining illicit information with my abilities that I tend to forget that it's not just as easy for law enforcement agencies.

"Michelle," said Michael. Something in his voice made the hair on my neck raise up.

I walked over to him. He was holding some pictures. He handed them to me.

"What?" Taylor asked. She didn't like being left out of the loop.

I looked through the pictures. Most of them showed Reggie and various goth-looking girls. There were few with other people. The last two made me gasp as I held them, for I had known the man next to Reggie in the pictures. It was Victor Owens.

I showed the pictures to Taylor and explained about who the man was. She wasn't as interested in them as Michael and I were. For us, it made Reggie's death a lot more personal.

CHAPTER SEVENTY-TWO

Snow was falling again as I crossed the street.

The old brownstone building was smudged in places with coal dust. I entered the building and walked upstairs. Michael had left the ladder to the roof down when he came back. I climbed up it and stood outside. The wind was fiercer, two stories above ground. I walked toward the front of the building. Most of the marks had been obliterated by the wind. I could still see the scorch marks from the muzzle flash, though.

I felt odd up here, looking out at where Reggie had been shot. I squatted down and lined myself up. I felt my hands rise of their own accord and felt the rifle in my hands. There had been strong emotions here. I started getting flashes of vision, something that usually only happened when touching someone.

Then I knew.

I recognized the particular flavor of those emotions. I'd been quite close to the person they belonged to. She *had* almost killed me, after all.

I stood up and wiped the snow off my pants.

My eyes wandered around the city. She was here. She was alive. I couldn't tell anyone, not even Michael. He would want to go after her. He might get hurt. She might get killed. I knew what his reaction would be.

I sighed.

I'd always known Julia was still alive. I think Michael did, too. He'd probably already guessed who the shooter was.

I started back across the roof. Down in the street below, a shadow darted from building to building, watching me. I could feel it down there, but I didn't have the energy to worry about it.

I met Michael back by my Jeep.

"Did you find anything?" he asked.

"No. Whoever took out Reggie was cool about it. I got a faint impression of the actual act and the satisfaction of making a good shot, but not why it was done or who did it." I started up the engine and started back to the hotel.

"Well, it was a long shot. I'd say the shooter probably didn't even know why someone wanted Reggie dead."

"Yeah, probably not."

"I'd like to look over the information on the other deaths. Being told about it isn't the same as seeing the pictures and forensics reports." He leaned back, lost in thought.

I was happy to have the topic change. I hadn't wanted to keep lying to him. Especially since I was certain he knew I was lying.

I stopped at a drive-through and picked up some food. We went back to the hotel and ate, and then we sat and talked about the case for most of the night. It felt good to just sit and talk with someone. We'd gotten close during the stuff with Julia; there's nothing like a bit of danger to draw people together.

It felt odd, sleeping in the same bed with him. I'm used to having the whole thing for myself. I'm a bed hog. It also felt good knowing he was here. We kissed, said goodnight, and he rolled over and went to sleep. I lay awake and listened to him breathe, and thought about the project and what it had done to us.

I'm not sure when I fell asleep, but it was early in the morning.

CHAPTER SEVENTY-THREE

After breakfast, we headed over to the hospital to talk to Sam.

Taylor was waiting for us in the main lobby.

"How's he doing?" I asked as I walked up.

She shrugged. "He's not happy to be here, but he understands that his leg is hurt. I think he'll answer our questions."

"Have the state police decided what they're going to do with him yet?" asked Michael.

"No, not yet," Taylor said. "They have a psychiatrist coming from Frankfort to judge his competence."

I sighed. I wished he could just be let go, but I understood their point of view, as well. We took the elevator up to the third floor and followed Taylor to the nurse's station, and then down to Sam's room. The state police officer at the door let us through without asking any questions. Taylor had already been up and cleared us.

Sam was sitting up in bed, eating. He looked a lot better. He'd been shaved and cleaned up. Someone had cut his hair. He looked like a normal guy lying in the bed. He looked curiously at us as we came in. I couldn't tell if he recognized me or not.

"Sam," Taylor said gently, "this is Michelle. You might remember her from the other day. And this is Michael. They would like to ask you a couple of questions, if that's okay with you."

He stared at each of us for a moment. I got the uncomfortable feeling that there was more looking through his eyes than just him. "Sure, what 'cha wanna know?"

"Sam," I said, "do you know anything about those men you saw in the woods?"

"The ones what took ma aunts?" he asked.

"Yes."

"Them dark'ens."

Michael and I exchanged glances. He shrugged.

"Darkens?" I asked.

"Dark ones," Sam said slowly. "Them is touched by the dark place."

I felt a cold chill that had nothing to do with temperature.

"Where is the dark place, Sam?" Michael asked.

"You know where it is," Sam replied. "It inside and outside. Down there."

"Do you mean like hell?" I asked.

He shook his head. "Nah. Well, maybe a bit."

"Is it the place demons come from?" Michael asked.

"That's it. That's the place. I knew you knew it." Sam grinned childishly.

"Sam," I asked. "Were these men…?" I hesitated. "Possessed?"

"Nah, just them as likes the dark."

Good, I thought. *I didn't need any more of that.* "Do you know where they are?"

"Ma mamma might. I don't reckon I do."

"Would we be able to talk to her?" I asked.

"I don't know. She don't ever come down, and they say I ain't gonna be walking for a piece. B'sides, others might just think you was like them others. Why you want to be talkin' to her fer?"

"We want to stop those men who worship the dark," said Michael.

"*Hmph*. I reckon that's a good reason."

"We also thought she might be worried about you. We want to tell her where you are. You'll tell us where to go?"

"I don't rightly know if I should. I don't want none of them up there hurt."

"We don't want to hurt them, either. We just want to talk to them," said Taylor. "If they can help us catch the bad guys, then we *need* to talk to them."

Sam sighed. "All right, but don't do nothing to 'em."

He told us how to get there from his aunts' home. It was a long walk through the mountains. He said he could normally walk it in less than half a day. We hoped we could do it in less. We needed to get in and get out today.

He told us who to look for. He couldn't give us any names, but he gave very accurate descriptions of what they looked like. I didn't feel really confident about going up there asking for "Sam's ma," but that's what he told us to do.

It was getting close to noon by the time we made it back to the hotel. Taylor had gotten a phone call from Mullins and decided that she wasn't going with us, if that was okay. I was frankly relieved. I was sure Michael and I could cover more ground, faster, without her along.

Mullins had been looking over the list of phone calls from Reggie's place and found some interesting correlations. Most of the calls had been to a trailer just outside Pikeville. Two of the calls had been to the hotel room where we had found the two skinned bodies. The calls had been around the estimated time of death. Mullins and Taylor were going to check out the trailer while we were up in the mountains.

I changed into jeans and combat boots. Michael changed into jeans and a pair of black hiking boots that would serve as well. I hadn't seen him in jeans before. He looked good, and we almost got distracted again.

We picked up a quick lunch on the way out to Majestic. We were starting from the old ladies' hut and going from there. I wished we'd had more time to prepare. I would've liked to have gotten a geologic survey map of the area. At least we were well armed. I took my pistols and the MP5. Michael was armed with whatever he was carrying, and my G3 rifle.

We'd pulled off to the side of the road around one o'clock. Taylor was supposed to notify the state police that we were up in the woods here. That way, they wouldn't ticket or tow my Jeep. Cell phone reception was problematic.

It was cold, but walking helped keep us warm. We started out briskly and made it to the hut in just over twenty minutes. I was glad to see that I had remembered how to get here. I would have loved to have listened to music as I walked, but it would have been rude. It also would have been tactically unwise. We didn't know who or what we were going to encounter.

"I'm curious about what's inside," said Michael.

"There's not much. I checked it out when we came up here before. Nothing really stood out." I shrugged.

"Pretty place to live."

I stared at him for a moment, and then I looked around. It really was pretty up here. I hadn't noticed before. I'd been a bit distracted, though. Strange, how sometimes you just have to stop and look around to realize just how precious life is.

CHAPTER SEVENTY-FOUR

"You know," Michael began, "if people have been disappearing around here for years, then they've probably written Sam off as dead. They should be glad to know he's still alive."

"You're right. I guess we need to get moving."

The woods seemed oddly quiet, but then, it *was* December. We walked on, taking breaks occasionally to get our bearings. Sam had given very accurate directions that were full of landmarks. I guess in the mountains, it makes more sense to navigate by the terrain rather than by the sky, since much of the sky is visible at any one time.

"Michael," I said suddenly.

"Yes?"

"What are we doing?"

"Uh, walking?" he said with a grin.

"I mean *us*. Where is our relationship headed?"

He sighed. "Hell, Michelle, I don't know. I love you, and you love me. Do we need to know anything other than that? It's kind of new for me, too."

"I know. I'm sorry. Things have just been so confusing. I lost all my stability last month. The ground dropped out from under me. Where am I going to land?"

He gently grabbed my arm and pulled me to him. "In my arms," he said gruffly.

I clung to him.

"Seriously, though, what would you like? I think it's a little early to talk about moving in together. Besides, your parents might not approve."

I laughed. "You know damn well my parents have been dead for years."

"I actually meant Mark and Jen. We had an interesting talk on the way down here."

"What did they say?" I asked curiously.

He gestured for me to start walking again. He held my hand as we walked, though.

"Actually, it was mostly Mark. He threatened to cast me into the nether realms, or some such, if I hurt you."

I laughed. That sounded like Mark.

"I asked him if that was the fate of all of your previous lovers, and he said no, that it was a fate reserved for me. I said thanks, I felt special now. He said I should. And I do." He squeezed my hand.

I didn't know what to say. I was a bit teary-eyed.

We walked on in silence for a while after that.

Later in the afternoon, he suddenly stopped and gestured for me to be quiet. We'd been walking along a creek. I looked around and listened, but I didn't hear anything.

"What is it?" I asked quietly.

"Someone is watching us," he answered. He had his pistol out.

"Someone or something?" I asked. I'd been used to having something following me.

He shook his head.

"Someone," he said. "That direction." He nodded toward my right, then made a finger split gesture at me and tilted his head.

I nodded and drew my pistol. Then I ducked low and moved behind a tree. He moved off down the stream and then sharply to the right. I moved around the tree and moved to get ahead of the person we were stalking. It was odd, how natural it felt.

I saw motion and froze. A person crouched behind a tree with a rifle. He had it tilted down, but he was definitely trying to track Michael. I moved toward him quietly, acutely conscious of hidden twigs under the snow.

Our quarry moved forward to a tree closer to the stream. I couldn't see Michael, but I found that I could just barely sense him. I moved to the tree the man had just left. Then everything happened at once.

Michael stepped around the tree in front of the man and rushed forward. The man cried out and tried to raise the rifle, but Michael knocked it out of his hands and moved toward him. I noticed that Michael had put his pistol away.

The man drew a wicked-looking hunting knife and lunged at Michael. Michael avoided the cut easily. Then I stepped up and placed the cold barrel of my pistol against the back of the man's skull. He froze.

"Might be a good time for you to drop the knife," Michael said. I noticed that he had slightly altered where he was standing so that if I had to shoot, he wouldn't get hit by the bullet passing through the man's skull.

The man dropped the knife.

"Up against the tree," I said.

He stood against the tree, trembling. He was dressed in an old, ragged-looking coat and slacks. I could see a faded flannel shirt and red long underwear showing past his collar. Michael frisked him quickly. He was unarmed.

"Okay, turn around." I stepped back but kept the gun pointed at his head.

"Who are you?" asked Michael.

"*Who are you?*" The man spat. "This here is *my land.*"

"Fair enough. My name is Michael Delling, and this is Michelle Fredericks. We are currently working with the FBI. Now, who are you?"

"You don't look like FBI," the man said suspiciously.

Michael gestured for me to put away my gun and pulled out his papers. The man just stared at them.

"What's that chicken scratch? Where's your badge, city man?"

"These are my papers that show I work for the FBI. I'm not an agent. I'm a civilian who's working with them. I used to be a US marshal."

"So what?"

"You know, I'd show a little more respect, if I were you," I said.

"I imagine you would, girly."

I was suddenly flushed with anger. I could read the intent behind that thought. I started forward, but Michael stopped me.

"You had more respect for her when she had a gun to your head," said Michael.

The man spat to the side. "So what do want here?"

"Do you know a Sam?" Michael asked.

"Maybe I do, maybe I don't. What's it to you?"

"He got hurt when his aunts were taken by some bad men," I said. "He's in the hospital in Pikeville."

"What? He's still alive? How bad is he hurt?"

CHAPTER SEVENTY-FIVE

Michael raised his hand. "Answer our questions, and we'll tell you. What's your name?"

The man sighed and sagged a little. "My name's John Rogers. I live down close to Argo, but I been coming up here since I was boy in '76. I've known Sam since he was a little'n. He's a good boy."

"We're looking for his mother," I said.

He squinted his eyes at me. "And why be you looking for her?"

"Well, for one, to tell her that her boy is still alive," Michael said. "We would also like to ask her if she knows anything about all the killings up here."

John scratched his head absently. "If anyone would know anything, it would be her. She knows lots of things."

"Sam told us how to get up here. He's doing okay, but his leg is hurt pretty bad," I said.

"How'd that happen? Them men do it?"

"Not exactly," Michael said, looking at me.

"He saw those men take his aunts. When a state policeman came around later, he attacked him," I said.

"What? Sam attacked a cop? What happened?"

"He hit the officer in the leg with an axe and then ran off. The officer shot him in the leg, but he got away. He didn't get picked up till a week ago. The wound had gone bad."

"Oh, no. Poor Sam." John sagged against the tree. "Is he gonna be able to keep the leg?"

"The doctors aren't sure yet. It was bad, but I think he'll be okay. He looked healthy this morning."

"You talked to him today?" asked John.

I nodded. "Will you lead us to his mother's place?"

John slowly nodded his head. "I suppose I should. You was going the long way."

I picked up his rifle and knife, and handed them to him. "Let's get walking, then."

He led us far to the left of the stream and up close to the cliffs. Eventually, we turned and had to climb over a ridge. I could see for miles from the top. I could see a river in the distance. That would be Tug Fork, I remembered from the maps.

"You can see three states from up here," John said.

He was breathing hard, so we took a short break.

I was happy just to stand and look around. It was beautiful. Michael stood next to me, equally absorbed by the scenery.

"You two are a lot tougher than I would've thought," John said suddenly.

I looked at him. He was red-faced. Michael and I had barely broken out in a sweet from the climb.

"Not all city folk are soft," Michael said without turning.

"I guess not. Look at me, not too old to learn something new. I'm as ready to get going again as I'll ever be."

We began the long climb down the other side of the ridge.

The light was beginning to fade when as John led us up a steep hollow to a shack.

He called out something I couldn't make out as we approached. The door opened, and a large woman came out. Her age was indeterminable in the poor light, but she was old.

"What you doing up here, John?" She eyed us with suspicion, but I guess the fact that John was carrying his rifle made her think things were okay.

"Helping these two get here faster. They gotta talk to you."

"'Bout what?" she asked.

"Are you Sam's mother?" I asked.

She stiffened. "I born him. What's it to you?"

"Then you should know that you're *still* his mother. He's alive and doing okay," I said. "He hurt his leg and got taken to the hospital."

She wobbled for a minute. "Come in, and we'll talk."

She held the door for the three of us. It was cramped in there with four people, but definitely warmer.

I told her about the murder of Sam's aunts, her sisters, and what had happened afterward.

"So you come up just to tell me about my Sam?" she asked.

I sighed. She was perceptive. "No, not just that."

"What, then?"

"We're trying to catch the people who are doing this," I said.

"They're your people, *city people*. Thar' idiots that don't know what forces they be messing with. They come up here and kill sometimes, but we get them back. We been at war with them for years. Why the sudden interest?"

"We didn't know about it until just now." I held up my hand when she started to speak. "I don't know about the other people around here, or the police down in Pikeville, but we just found out."

She nodded slowly. "I can see that you speak the truth, and you both are touched by the powers. I can feel that. At least neither of you is with *them*."

Michael cleared his throat. "You're a..." He hesitated. "Witch?"

She shrugged. "You can call it whatever you want."

"Do you know where we can find them? The people that are bad?" I asked.

"They're down there, near that city. They're probably all holed up together, I sent them a couple of horrors to trouble them. They better not go outside alone at night." She cackled.

I felt the hair on my arms rise. This woman had been waging a mystical battle against these people for years. I could feel the power in her.

"Can you help us find them?" I asked.

Her eyes got a glazed look. She spoke slowly. "I don't have to. Your people have already found them." She snapped back to us, suddenly intense. "You better get back down there. Bad things are going to happen before morning."

I looked at Michael; he nodded. We'd learned everything we could. I would have loved to talk to the woman and learn from her, but we did need to get moving. We had a long way to go tonight.

She stopped me as we were leaving. "You get me my Sam back. Okay?"

I nodded. "I'll do everything I can. I promise."

She nodded and shut the door on us.

CHAPTER SEVENTY-SIX

We walked slowly away from the hut.

"John, I hate to ask you, but do you think you could help us get back to our car?" said Michael.

"You're walking the whole way back tonight?"

"I think we need to," Michael replied. "You heard what she said."

John sighed. "All right. We should take the long way, though. It's a lot safer'n the way we came."

"We'd be okay with the other," I said, "if it's faster."

"I don't think I'm up to it, honestly. I'm old, and it's cold out here. I was hoping to be home long before this."

"We can drive you home," I said. "Or at least as close as we can get."

I could feel his eyes on me. "A lift would be appreciated. I'd never make it back tonight otherwise."

We walked along through the woods for hours. It was darker than I had thought possible. There were dense clouds overhead, and what light they didn't block, the trees and mountains did. It was also numbingly cold. I found myself slowing and thinking about other times I'd been out at night in a forest with snow on the ground.

"Michelle?"

I looked toward him but could only see a silhouette of Michael. "I'm okay," I said softly.

"You stopped walking," he said.

"Oh, I was just thinking," I said.

"That was a long time ago, Michelle. It's cold out here. We need to get back."

He took my arm and led me through the darkness.

We dropped John off along the road near Argo. He said that was as close as we could get, but not to worry. He'd be home within half an hour. We then turned around and headed for Pikeville. It was almost midnight, and we were both worn out.

"How far do you think we walked today?" I asked Michael.

"I don't know. Probably not as far as it feels like, as the crow flies." He was leaning back in his seat with his eyes shut.

I was just happy to be sitting and warm.

"It feels as if it was more than twenty miles," I said.

"That's probably about right."

I knew I'd be aching in the morning, and I didn't even want to know what shape my feet were in. It had been a long time since I'd walked like that.

My cell phone rang as we got closer to Pikeville.

"Hello," I said.

"Michelle! Thank God," said Taylor. "I was beginning to worry about you. Did everything go okay? Are you both all right?"

"We're okay, just worn out. That was a long hike. We found Sam's mother. Things went well."

"Good. Listen, that trailer checked out. I don't know if we got everyone or not, but we got a lot of them all in one place. Right now."

I sat upright. "What?"

"I think we found them. We've got two in custody. The others are holed up in a trailer. The police have it surrounded. I've called in an FBI SWAT team from Charleston. They'll be here in the morning. Then we're going in."

"When? What time?" I asked.

Michael was looking at me curiously.

"First light, say about six o'clock. I'd like you here in the morning with us."

"Okay, but we need to get a little sleep first. How about I call you at five AM? We'll meet you there then."

"Sounds good. Get some rest. Sleep fast." She disconnected.

I told Michael what had happened.

He nodded. "Looks like we'll have some more people to question soon."

"I hope so." I drove us back to the hotel.

We needed showers and sleep. I ignored the shadow lurking in the darkness at the edge of the parking lot. I'd gotten used to it being around. It was probably happy I was back. I don't think it had wanted to follow me up into those mountains.

I was just happy that this case seemed to coming to a close.

We took a shower together and got distracted, but that was a good way to recover, too. I certainly slept well afterward.

CHAPTER SEVENTY-SEVEN

I did not want to drag myself out of bed at four o'clock.

Four in the morning is not a good time. There's a reason it's called the soul's midnight. More people die at four AM than at any other time -- relative to their location, of course. It's the point when the body's natural rhythm swings the lowest. The life force ebbs, and people close to death pass on.

It's hard to get your body to wake up. I know mine felt asleep.

Cold water helped. I washed my face and brushed my teeth. I didn't worry about my hair. I just pulled it back. Michael wouldn't care; he's seen me look a lot worse. He was sitting on the edge of the bed, rubbing his right shoulder. He had a lot more scars than I did. I wondered about the story behind each one.

"Get up, sleepy head," I said.

He stood up and stretched with much cracking and popping of joints. Then he grinned mischievously. "Okay, I'm up," he said.

I threw my towel at him and started getting dressed. I didn't need any more reasons to get back into the bed. Sleep was too much of a temptation. My whole body ached, but not as badly as I'd thought it would. I had some bad blisters on my feet though. Those would be a bitch.

I dressed in a dark suit while Michael was getting ready. I was vaguely disappointed to see him dressed when he came out of the bathroom.

"Have you called Taylor yet?" he asked.

"No, not yet. My brain isn't awake yet."

I dug my phone out of coat pocket and called her. It was almost five o'clock.

"Taylor," she answered.

"It's Michelle. We're ready."

"Good. Get on over here. We could use advice from both of you on this."

"We're on our way," I said.

Michael had gotten his coat on while I was talking. "I'll go start your Jeep," he said, picking up my keys and walking out the door.

I was suddenly alone.

It felt odd. I'd been around him now for a couple of days and I was already so used to him being with me that I missed him when he left the room. *Gods*, I thought to myself. *Sometimes I hate being in love.* I feel like my IQ drops or something. I'm suddenly all blushing and giggly. *Ugh.*

Enough! I had work to do. It still felt odd.

I got my coat on and left the room.

Michael was waiting by the doors downstairs. He handed me the keys and absently put his arm around me. I hugged him fiercely, surprising him. Then I let go, walked out, and got in the Jeep. He climbed into the passenger's seat and gave me an inscrutable look.

The Jeep wasn't warm inside yet, but it was warmer than the outside air. I pulled out of the hotel and drove out of town, following Taylor's directions. It was starting to get light in the east. There were still a lot of clouds. It wouldn't get light until late in the morning. I hoped it would snow. I've always thought that if the weather is going to be cold, it should be snowing.

I didn't have any trouble finding the location. The whole area was lit up, and there were police cars, ambulances, fire trucks, and news vans all over. I parked, and we had to thread our way through reporters standing around in front of cameras. State police officers were trying to keep people back behind wooden sawhorse-type barricades. Reporters and gawkers shouted and pushed.

It was a zoo.

After we showed our papers, we were let through, and we eventually found Taylor. She was talking earnestly with Mullins and a tall woman in black fatigues with *FBI* stenciled on the back of her body armor. Taylor introduced us to her. Her name was Thomson; she was the head of the FBI counter-terrorist unit that had been called in.

"What's going on around here?" I asked, gesturing to the many reporters.

"The *fucking* Pikeville police department leaked news of the raid," said Taylor. "We caught some of the officers giving interviews, for Christ's sake!"

She didn't look as if she'd slept at all since I had seen her last. Mullins didn't look much better. He had bags under his eyes and was quietly sipping coffee at regular intervals.

"So the people inside know exactly what we're doing out here?" I asked. That couldn't be good. They would know about the raid.

Mullins shook his head. "No, we managed to get the news crews to agree to tape delay."

"That's something, anyway," Michael muttered. "So what's the situation?"

Thomson answered him, crisply military. "We've got fifteen to twenty adult cultists in the trailer. There are an unknown number of children, but at least five. The cultists have guns. Some, anyway. They shot a police officer who tried to talk them into surrendering."

I shook my head. Someone had bungled that.

"I've got my team positioned and ready to enter. We're loaded with frangibles, so chances of collateral damage are low."

Collateral damage is what they called it when a child took a bullet to the head. I knew that in any raid, there were going to be injuries, maybe even deaths. No matter how they did it, people were going to die today.

"This seems awfully messy," said Michael. "How sure are you that these are the right people?"

"Well," Taylor said, "we were hoping that you two occult specialists could tell us that once we're inside. Either way, though, they go down now. They shot a police officer and refused a search warrant. Our path is set in stone."

"Damn," Michael said. "There should be some way to negotiate with these people."

"I didn't think federal marshals ever negotiated," Taylor said sarcastically.

"I'm not a marshal anymore, remember. Besides, I got tired of shooting people in the head when they wouldn't listen to me."

Taylor just glared at him. I noticed Thomson had shifted slightly to his rear. This could get ugly really fast.

"Well, I guess that's one way to get some sense in there," I said with a lightheartedness I didn't feel.

CHAPTER SEVENTY-EIGHT

That broke the tension.

"Look, if we go in there now," Thomson said, "we have a chance of stopping this from getting even uglier than it already is."

Michael nodded and looked away.

"Thomson, take your team in," said Mullins.

Michael walked away, toward the Jeep. I followed after giving Taylor a quick squeeze on the arm. She didn't want to anyone to die, but what choice did she have? Tempers were short this morning. No one had gotten enough sleep. We didn't need to be fighting each other.

I went to go find Michael.

"Michael?"

He stood with his back to me. "I'm sorry. I'm okay. I just hate not having a say in how things are done. I'm used to working on my own and doing whatever needs to be done. This brute force, frontal assault thing is so typically FBI, and it never, ever, goes right. This operation has Ruby Ridge and Waco written all over it."

He turned around, and I gave him a hug.

"We'll need to be up there once the area is secure. We need to know if this is the right place," I said, looking up into his eyes.

"Oh, it's the right place," he said.

"How can you tell?" I asked, letting go and stepping back.

"I can feel them in there. They've done many bad things. They keep trying to do more, but the sheer numbers of skeptics gathered around here is keeping them at bay."

"Never thought I'd be happy for those vultures," I said, looking at the reporters milling around. They knew something was up.

"I guess I need to go apologize," he said suddenly.

"Probably couldn't hurt," I said. I smiled up at him.

He took my hand and walked back to where Taylor and Mullins were directing the team. Maybe we could minimize the damage. Maybe we could make a difference.

I let him walk ahead so he could make his peace with them. I stood back and watched the trailer. I *could* feel the cultists inside. They were scared and angry. I could also feel the gathering of energies. They had been caught unprepared, but they kept trying to summon aid. Like most amateurs, they didn't realize that magic doesn't work on short notice. Besides, no entity would want the attention that showing up here would provoke.

I walked over to Michael and Taylor when I sensed they were done talking. I took Michael's hand again, and we waited. The sky slowly grew lighter.

The time came, and the SWAT team ran forward from two positions. They entered the trailer from both doors at once. Police officers waited around the edges to catch anyone trying to come out a window. Gunshots rang out immediately, the low barking cough of the FBI sub-machine guns and the occasional roar of a shotgun. A sudden staccato burst of machine gun fire rang out; that had to be from the cultists. That was silenced when another couple of shots rang out. Then all the gunfire ceased.

The silence held for a moment before the crying and screaming could be heard coming from inside the trailer. Taylor's radio barked *all clear* and *officer down* at the same time. We ran forward with Taylor and Mullins. The SWAT team brought the few uninjured people out in twos and threes. We would need to talk to each and every one of them, I suddenly realized.

I had just gotten a lot more tired.

It was almost eight in the morning before we were allowed inside. The FBI had to clear out the wounded and the dead first. One member of the SWAT team was dead, two wounded. Altogether, five of the cultists were dead; most of the others had been wounded. The inside of the trailer looked like a charnel house. Blood was everywhere.

We entered and began to search for clues.

"Taylor," I asked suddenly, "just what the hell are we supposed to find in this mess?"

"We need to find something solid that links these people to the second set of murders," Taylor said tiredly. "The DA is going is going to have our asses in a sling for this, as it is. What a royal cluster-fuck." She kicked a chair that had been shredded by a shotgun blast.

"I'll do my best, but I'm having trouble in here," I said. I had to wade through bloody clothes, children's toys, and pop bottles just to move around. It looked to me as if many of the people the FBI pulled out of here had actually lived in the trailer. That was too many people for one little space.

"Please, just find me something," Taylor said. "The media got film of us bringing blood-covered children out of here after we stormed in. People are going to want scapegoats to pin this on. I want the blame to go where it *should* go, rather than on me."

I nodded. My head was throbbing. I hadn't gotten enough sleep, and the psychic atmosphere of this place was oppressive. I would've had problems with the inside of that trailer even if six people hadn't gotten killed in here just a few hours before.

I could also sense the entities that the cultists had dealt with, seething in rage on the other side of the veil. They couldn't come into our world without assistance, but they were there. I could feel their hunger.

Michael was in the kitchen, which appeared to be the least affected area of the whole trailer. He was looking through the cabinets and in the drawers, trying to find anything interesting. So far, there was nothing.

I moved out of the living room, the area with the strongest association of death, pain, and despair. Holes in the walls were from the shotgun blasts and stray bullets. I walked back through the trailer, touching things at random. I was getting many nasty impressions, but nothing that would do Taylor any good.

At least I knew these were the right people.

I walked into the main bedroom. I tried to ignore the blood and brains on the wall by a bookcase. The shelf held a selection of grimoires on a wide range of occult subjects, notably Satanism and Crowley, and even a Vampire bible. I'd heard of that book but never seen one. I was tempted to flip through it, but this was definitely not the place for that. Besides, I was sure I didn't want to touch that copy.

It was under the bed that I found what we were looking for.

"Taylor! Michael!" I yelled. "You guys will want to see this."

I felt the floor shaking as they ran in.

"What?" and, "What did you find?" they asked at the same time.

I pulled a large square of carpet out from under the bed. Under the carpet was a hole in the floor. I pushed the bed back. In the hole was a selection of long, wicked-looking knives. I recognized at least two of them as skinning knives. Two boxes were in the hole under the bed, too. I pulled them out. A foul odor made me retch.

My hands were shaking as I opened the first box.

Inside the box was a severed head. I immediately recognized it as belonging to Dave, the young hunter who had gone missing when we found the last bodies. I guess the cultists had been active in the woods that day, after all.

I closed my eyes and leaned back. "Well, Taylor, this alone is enough to get them on murder."

"Oh, Jesus," she whispered.

"Are you okay, Michelle?" asked Michael.

"I'm coping, but I wouldn't say that I'm okay."

Once I regained my composure, I opened the second box.

Thin sheets of leather had been carefully placed inside the box. Each sheet had been covered with fine writing and diagrams, what looked to be demon summoning rituals and other assorted nastiness. I knew without touching them that the sheets were made of human skin.

CHAPTER SEVENTY-NINE

I took a long hot bath at the hotel to restore my mental balance.

Michael came in with a cold Coke for me, and we talked while I soaked. I was feeling easier at being naked in his presence. It was comforting to have him nearby.

"I guess it's wrapped up, then," Michael said.

"I guess." I lay back and closed my eyes, letting the water do its work.

"You think some of them got away?" he asked.

"I'm sure of it. Aren't you?"

He sighed, and I heard him shift around.

"I suppose you're right. I hate to think of those sick *things* -- I can't call them people -- still being out there."

"I doubt the ones who are left will start things again. Besides, the hill witches will still be watching and waiting. We helped take down the majority of the cultists. The witches can take care of the rest."

"True." He sounded distracted.

I looked over at him. "What's wrong?"

"It seems too easy and neat. I'm used to being there on the sharp end. I'm used to being the one to take down the bad guy, you know? All I did this time was pace around and curse as people died."

"Are you reconsidering being a marshal?" I asked softly. It was hard to even articulate how much I had worried about that.

He met my eyes. "No," he said. "I'm not. I'm just having trouble adjusting."

I nodded, relieved. "I was thinking about taking a vacation. Maybe out West," I said.

He grinned. "I was wondering when you'd bring that back up. I'm not opposed to going and looking for my sister, Michelle. Believe me, I'd like to know that she's okay. It's been a long time."

"Then why don't we?" I felt a sudden need to be anywhere but Pikeville.

"Not right now. No." He held up his hand to forestall my arguments. "Maybe in a month or two. I'd like to get to know you better. We need to spend some time together doing normal things. We could see some movies, go out to dinner, that sort of thing. We need some time together."

"That's sounds nice," I said, smiling.

I called and talked to Taylor that afternoon before I collapsed. I was ready to fall into bed and sleep for twelve hours, but I needed to make sure everything was okay first. We'd filled out statements before we left the site. We'd done all we could there.

"I don't think there's any reason for you two to have to come down here and deal with these people," Taylor said. "With what you found under the bed, we shouldn't need much else to put them all away, anyway."

"I mostly just feel sorry for the children. That must have been what that psycho Heather had gone through," I said. "I hope none of the kids grow up to be like her."

"You and me, both," said Taylor. "I don't want to have to come back and hunt through the hills for anyone ever again."

I shuddered at the thought. "Me, either."

"I suppose you're heading back home tomorrow," she said.

"We're planning on it. I miss my cat and my own bed."

"I can understand that. I don't even remember what my own house looks like," Taylor said with a sour laugh.

"I'm planning to stop by the hospital and visit with Sam before we go. Will you need anything else?" The bed was calling me. Michael was already asleep.

"Not really," she said. "I wouldn't mind saying goodbye."

I smiled. "I'll call you when we get done at the hospital."

"Sounds good. Get some sleep."

"You, too," I said.

Despite how tired I was, I had trouble sleeping.

The wind, or something else, rattled at the window long into the night. I finally fell into a trouble sleep with bad dreams, where cultists held children in cages and empty skins flapped around like birds.

CHAPTER EIGHTY

I woke up early and couldn't go back to sleep.

My mind was racing. I'd had bad dreams again. Nothing like the dreams I'd had before; these were just normal nightmares, but still frightening. I lay there listening to Michael breathe and wondered if I had ever lain beside him like this before.

I still couldn't remember most of what had happened to us in the project. I knew that Michael and I had known each other very well. We had even tried to escape together several times; I'm not sure how many. I remembered leaving him behind one time, the last time we tried to escape, but I couldn't remember the rest of what happened.

I had fallen into a creek or a river or something. I could still feel the icy chill of its grip, but I couldn't remember what happened after that. My head started pounding the way it did every time I tried to force the memories. I gave up and quietly got out of bed. I set out a change of clothes and packed the rest in my bags.

"You're not leaving without me, are you?" asked Michael quietly.

I turned and looked at him. He was sitting up in bed. I wondered how long he'd been awake. "I'm sorry; I didn't mean to wake you. I just couldn't sleep anymore and wanted to go ahead and get packed. I really want to go home today," I replied.

He rubbed his eyes. "I can understand that. I'm ready to get out of here, myself. What do we need to do?"

"I'd like to visit Sam and tell him that his mother knows he's okay," I said. "Then I'd like to say goodbye to Taylor. Other than that, I'm open. We should probably eat today; I don't think we did yesterday."

He made a silly face as he thought about it. "I guess you're right. Something good to eat, then. No crepes."

I shuddered. "You had bad dreams, too?"

He nodded and got out of bed.

He messed up my hair on his way to the bathroom.

I growled playfully and slapped at his hand. It was good to be loved.

After breakfast, we visited Sam in the hospital.

I stopped by the gift shop and got him a plant and some candy. I didn't bother with a card. He couldn't read, so what would be the point?

The officer on duty looked at our IDs and then passed us. I recognized him from the woods. We walked on down to Sam's room.

I was surprised to see that he already had a visitor. John Rogers, the hunter who had guided us to Sam's mother, was sitting on the edge of the bed.

"Hello," I said as we came in.

Sam smiled at us. "Howdy," he said.

John turned and looked at us. "Well, it's my city folk. You two don't look the worse for your little walk in the woods." He smiled.

"It's good to see you again, John," I said. "Sam, these are for you. I thought you might miss growing things." I placed the plant on the table.

Michael quietly shut the door to the room.

"Did you tell Sam about our visit?" asked Michael.

"I did. 'Twas a good thing you two did. I heard about the commotion yesterday, too. You get them all?"

I shrugged. "We think we got most of them. The FBI arrested over fifteen people. We found enough evidence to put them all away."

John nodded. "Good."

Sam was already working his way through the candy.

I smiled at him. He knew how to enjoy the simple things in life.

"John," Michael began, "I wanted to talk to you anyway, so I'm glad you're here."

"*Hmph.* What about?" John sounded suspicious.

"Sam, actually. He's in a lot of trouble, as you know."

John sighed. "I don't see how they can hold it against him, what he did. But I guess they will."

"Maybe, but maybe not," Michael said.

I glanced at him. I wasn't sure where this was going.

"The FBI has a psychiatrist coming in tomorrow to assess Sam's mental competence."

"There ain't a thing wrong with the boy," John said indignantly.

"I didn't say there is, but the psychiatrist may have a different opinion. It would be in Sam's best interest if he did."

"What do you mean?"

"He's going to think that Sam is a bright lad who is uneducated. His ignorance is his best defense right now. He didn't know that the man he attacked was a police officer. He was scared for his aunts and attacked when chased. They can't prove intent to kill, either," Michael said. "He hit the officer in the leg instead of the chest or head."

"Okay, how does this help him?"

"They won't release him on his own, under the circumstances. But they would probably release him to a relative if they promise to take care of him and make sure he gets to court if they decide to press charges."

"Do you think they will?" I asked.

"No, they'd be idiots to even try. All they'd be doing is wasting the taxpayers' money on a case they know they can't win," Michael said.

"You mean they aren't going to put him away?" John asked. He looked like he didn't quite dare to hope it was true.

"There is no way they could make anything stick. He has too many defenses. They'll make a deal and release him to the care of his relatives."

"Gonna be hard to get his momma down here out of the hills," said

John. "She ain't so young anymore. He ain't got any more kin."

Michael rubbed the side of his nose and grinned. "Seems to me that he might have a kindly uncle who could vouch for him."

John just stared at him. "You mean *me*? But I ain't blood kin to him!"

"Does anyone outside this room know that?" Michael asked.

"I suppose not." John grinned. "I suppose you wouldn't mind calling me uncle, would you, boy?" he asked Sam.

"Always have, 'least to myself," Sam replied.

I gave Michael a big hug. "Thank you," I whispered.

"Glad to help out," he said.

CHAPTER EIGHTY-ONE

We left the hospital when the nurse came in with Sam's lunch. I was glad that Michael had found a way to help the young man. Sam's mother had made me promise to help, but I hadn't had a clue as to how I could.

Michael suggested I call Taylor and see if she wanted to meet us for lunch.

"I didn't think you liked her," I said.

He shrugged. "We certainly butted heads a few times, but I fully acknowledge that most of that was me. I'm too used to being in charge. Besides, I thought you said you like small brunettes."

I punched him in the arm. A lesser man might have been broken by it. Michael just grinned.

"Seriously, you like her and want to see her before we leave."

"Thanks." I got my cell phone out.

"Special Agent Taylor," she answered.

"Hey, Jessica, it's Michelle."

"Yeah, I know. No one else calls me Jessica. You getting ready to head out of town?" She sounded much better today. She must have gotten some sleep.

"Yes, but Michael suggested that you might want to meet us for lunch," I said, winking at him.

He scowled back. I think he likes the hard-nosed image that he sometimes portrays.

"Really? Well, who am I to reject the olive branch? Where do you want to meet?" she asked.

"I was thinking we could meet at the Mexican place."

"Sounds great. Give me about twenty minutes."

"Okay, we'll be inside snacking on cheese and chips," I said teasingly. She had really liked the cheese dip the last time we were there. She'd eaten most of it.

"*Hmm*, I may have to hurry to make sure I get some. See you soon."

"'Bye." I disconnected.

I grinned at Michael.

"So, how does Mexican sound?" I asked.

"Do I have a choice?" he said.

"Not really."

"Sounds great. Race you to the car."

He won.

Lunch went well.

They both apologized for being asses.

The food was just as good as it had always been. Northern Kentucky has some good Mexican restaurants, but none as good as that one. As we finished eating, I thought about everything that happened. I was lucky to be here. In some strange sort of way, I was sad it was all over. I'd enjoyed working on the case, and I liked Taylor. I'd miss her.

She insisted on paying.

We walked together out to our vehicles. Michael gave us some personal space and waited by the passenger's door of my Jeep.

I suddenly didn't know what to say, now that it was time to leave.

"Michelle, thank you," Taylor said. "I couldn't have done it without you."

"We made a good team," I said.

She smiled. "Maybe we'll work together again someday. If you ever need anything, don't hesitate to call me, and keep in touch. You have my number." She held out her hand.

"I will, Jessica. I will." I took her hand and then gave her a quick hug before she could get away. I think I surprised her, but she hugged me back. Hell, I surprised myself. "I don't have many friends, but I count you as one. Come visit me in Cincinnati some time. You've got my number, too."

"I will." She turned to Michael. "You take good care of her. I expect to see you when I stop by in the future."

He put his arm around me. "I'll not be going anywhere," he said. "Unless she gets tired of me, that is."

I punched him lightly in the stomach and walked around to the other side.

"Goodbye, Taylor!" I called.

She waved and got in her car.

CHAPTER EIGHTY-TWO

I drove for a while in silence.

Michael leaned back and closed his eyes. I don't think he was asleep, just resting his eyes and thinking. He had offered to drive, but I didn't mind. I like to drive, and I knew he didn't. The sun came out at some point, and I could see the countryside in a better light.

I was still glad to be going home.

We passed the Mountain Arts Center in Prestonsburg.

"I still can't believe that sign says *Kentucky Opry*," I said suddenly.

Michael opened his eyes and craned his neck to look. "Why not?" he asked.

I stared at him. "Why not? It's..." I was at a loss for words.

"We should go there sometime and check it out. You might like it," he said, smiling.

"Okay, that's it. Out of the car," I mock ordered.

He just laughed and gripped my leg for a moment, and then he folded his hands back in his lap.

"Hey! Put that back!" I said.

He laughed again and returned his hand to my leg.

I reached down and gripped his hand in my right. It felt good. I held his hand most of the way back home.

"If you don't mind," Michael said, "you can drop me off at my apartment."

"Okay," I said, confused. I'd been thinking about being home and having him with me, in my own bed.

"I'd like to take a shower, check my mail, and get clean clothes, that sort of thing. I'd like to come over later, if that's okay with you," he said. "I have a car; you wouldn't have to get back out. I'll even bring groceries and fix dinner."

I felt relieved. I'd wondered if I had missed something. "Sounds great. What's for dinner?"

"I'd rather surprise you."

"Okay." I smiled to myself. I might have a few surprises for him, too.

Michael had a nice little townhouse in Erlanger. It was next to the expressway and only a few miles from the airport. It had an attached garage, so I couldn't see what sort of car he had.

I pulled into the parking space out front, and he opened the door.

"Wait here for just a moment," he said. "I'll be right back."

He got his bags out of the back of the Jeep and went inside. After a few minutes, he came back and walked around to the driver's side. I opened the door and got out.

He pulled me against him and kissed me.

My heart was hammering in my ribs by the time he let me go.

"This is for you," he said. He held out a small, round, gray pebble with two bands of white quartz crossing it.

"Okay," I said, confused. I picked it up out of his open palm. I could feel power in it, but nothing else. Damn him and his magic. "What is it?"

"Something to help with that little problem you've been having," he said.

"Which one?" I asked.

He laughed. "The demon that's been stalking you for the last two months, the one that Lucy sent after you."

I'd forgotten we'd talked about that.

"So what am I supposed to do with this?" I asked, holding up the stone.

"I'll tell you."

He spent ten minutes or so going over what was involved. It was simple. He kissed me and promised to see me at home soon, no later than eight o'clock.

I drove home with mixed feelings. I had wanted everything to be over with all of this mess. Soon, it would be. I gripped the little stone and drove home. I was trying to focus my mind for what I had to do there.

I pulled into my driveway.

The house looked good. Mark and Jen had been keeping an eye on it. I didn't have much of a yard, but I paid someone else to do the yard work anyway. It looked as if they'd been here recently; the grass was freshly mown.

The weather was cold, but not as bad as it had been in the mountains. No snow here.

It felt good to be home.

I walked around to the back of the house. It was starting to get dark. I kept the stone in my hand and sat down in the middle of the yard to wait. My stalker entity should be coming soon. I could feel it nearby. I was tired of it skulking about. I knew I didn't have much to worry about. If it wasn't able to hurt me when I was in a weakened state at the hospital, it certainly couldn't do anything now, but it was annoying.

I dropped my carefully prepared layers of shields. That was an open invitation to be attacked, an invitation that it was unable to resist.

The stone was strangely warm and heavy as I walked back around to check my mail. The mailbox was stuffed. I hadn't thought to have the post office hold my mail. I sorted through it as I made my way inside. Most of the mail was the usual assortment of credit card offers and mail order book clubs. I tossed those without looking at them.

The one that interested me the most was from my lawyer, dated last week. I opened it with shaking hands. The trucking company had decided it was in their best interests to settle out of court. If I would agree to forgo any future suits against them for my current injuries, they were willing to settle for a nice amount. A nice, *large* amount.

I sat and stared at the letter for a while. I could live a long time at my current level on that. I could even get a new house in Cincinnati, like I'd been thinking about. I wouldn't have to work unless I wanted to for a least a year.

Eventually, I got up and took a quick shower. I changed the sheets on the bed and cleaned up the house a little. It wasn't dirty, exactly, but it was cluttered. I went out and pulled my Jeep into the garage.

It was dark outside, but I didn't have anything to worry about now. I flipped on the porch light and waited for Michael to arrive. Samson was still staying with Mark and Jen; I'd have to go get him tomorrow. I missed the little furball, but I was glad I didn't have to watch him tonight. I wanted to spend tonight with Michael.

Michael showed up almost exactly at eight. I helped him carry in groceries, and then I went over to the table and got my letter. I waved it at him. "Looks like we have our vacation paid for," I said, "when we decide to go."

He walked over and looked at it, then raised an eyebrow. "Are you planning on spending a year in Europe? Or just go bingeing for a weekend in Vegas?"

I laughed and hugged him.

It was so *good* to be home.

About the Author

Paul B. Spence is a practicing archaeologist who hopes to one day get it right. He currently lives in New Mexico, where all the cool kids hang out, with too many cats.

Like most authors, he had an eclectic career path. He's worked as a retail gofer, a food service monkey, brute laborer, a rennie, a writer for the RPG industry, and many other rewarding jobs that didn't pay enough to feed him or his cats.